Dark Obsession

A Dark Student Teacher Romance

Blackmore University
Book 2

Cora Kent

Copyright © 2024 Cora Kent

All rights reserved. No part of this book may be reproduced or used in any manner without the prior written permission of the copyright owner, except for the use of brief quotations in a book review.

To request permissions, contact the publisher at cora@corakent.com.

Second paperback edition November 2024

Cora Kent
www.corakent.com

To the girlies that like a little plot with their smut.

Content Warning

Dark Obsession is a dark romance novel containing morally ambiguous characters and plot lines that include sexual content, violence, and questionable behavior. This book contains subject matter with the following themes:

Sexual Content: dubious breeding consent, daddy talk, spanking

Behavior: graphic violence, torture of a side character, criminal activities, PTSD

This list may not be a complete picture of triggering content. Please remember that even though this book contains a happily ever after, you can put it down any time the storyline, characters, themes, or sexual content exceeds your expectations.

Contents

Dark Devotion	1
1. Christine	3
2. Niccolo	9
3. Christine	15
4. Niccolo	19
5. Christine	25
6. Niccolo	29
Dark Obsession	35
7. Christine	37
8. Niccolo	45
9. Christine	53
10. Niccolo	59
11. Christine	65
12. Niccolo	73
13. Christine	79
14. Niccolo	85
15. Christine	91
16. Christine	99
17. Niccolo	107
18. Christine	113
19. Niccolo	119
20. Christine	123
21. Christine	129
22. Niccolo	137
23. Christine	145
24. Christine	151
25. Niccolo	159
26. Niccolo	165
27. Christine	173
28. Niccolo	179
29. Christine	185
30. Christine	193

31. Niccolo	199
32. Christine	205
33. Christine	213
34. Niccolo	219
35. Niccolo	227
36. Christine	235
37. Christine	241
38. Niccolo	251
39. Christine	259
40. Niccolo	269
41. Christine	277
42. Christine	285
43. Niccolo	291
44. Niccolo	301
45. Christine	307
46. Niccolo	315
47. Christine	321
48. Christine	329
49. Niccolo	337
50. Christine	345
51. Niccolo	351
52. Niccolo	355
53. Christine	361
54. Niccolo	367
55. Christine	373
56. Niccolo	381
57. Christine	389
58. Niccolo	395
59. Niccolo	401
60. Christine	409
Epilogue	417
About the Author	423

Dark Devotion

Chapter 1
Christine
6 months before the start of Dark Obsession

Niccolo Terlizzi married my mother five years ago. He was a vibrant twenty-five-year-old, and I had just turned thirteen.

One day, my mother was entertaining men on casual dates here and there. The next, she had a diamond ring on her finger and wanted me to be the flower girl at her wedding.

I liked Niccolo well enough. He was handsome with dark features that stirred something unexpected inside me. Whenever Kaye and I saw him walking around the house shirtless, we dissipated into a fit of giggles. His physique was unmatched, and I swore to my best friend that I'd find a man like him someday—a man who looked like a Greek God and treated me like a queen. I envied my mother for finding someone that loved her.

When Caterina first got sick, she tried to hide it from Niccolo. At fifteen years his senior, she didn't want him to see her as weak. I remember her confiding in me about her stomach pains and swearing me to secrecy. "Niccolo must not know," she whispered behind closed doors.

I carried the burden of my mother's secrets for far too long; I wasn't old enough to make her see that she needed to get help. She was afraid to go to the doctor, fearful that if the doctor found something, she would have to explain it to Nic. "It's bad enough that I'm forty," she stressed, "I can't be forty and infirm."

When she finally got to the doctor, it was too late; all her fears had come alive. She was diagnosed with stage four esophageal adenocarcinoma. Her survival rate was 10%, but mother had always been a fighter. She got every surgery and every treatment the doctor recommended. Including chemotherapy, which decimated her confidence and made her too weak to get out of bed.

Niccolo was by her side night and day. He was finishing his Ph.D. in Philosophy, and I'd find him sitting at her bedside with books scattered on the floor around him. He'd type a few sentences, get my mother some water, type a few more, get her some food, and on and on it went. For a man in his twenties, he was remarkably attentive.

I admired his ability to smile through the hard parts of my mother's illness. He didn't shy away from carrying her soiled body to the shower. He didn't complain when they couldn't go on dates because her hair had fallen out, and she refused to wear a wig. He said nothing; he was a dutiful husband.

Unfortunately, all the hospital care and nursing couldn't save her. My mother died a few months later, and Niccolo spent weeks in mourning. He wasn't married to Caterina for long, but he treated her with dignity, even after her death. His loyalty shaped the vision I had for my future husband.

After my mother's death, Niccolo wasn't sure what to do with me. Caterina hadn't put together a will in her final days, which made matters more complicated. I don't know if he spoke to my uncles or grandfather or if he just took on the burden of parenting me without being asked. Either way, I'd get up every morning to a hot breakfast, and he made sure I got to school. If I needed a permission slip signed, he was there for me. If I needed new clothes or something for school, he took me to the store. He was to me as he'd always been to my mother: the perfect partner.

It wasn't until my uncles came around asking about my future that he snapped out of his depression.

Giovanni and Marco meant well. They allowed us time to mourn Caterina's loss before telling Niccolo *thanks*, but they would be taking custody of me.

"Over my dead body." He put his foot down without a second thought. He had no claim to me legally. Niccolo was my mother's husband, and with her body growing cold in a grave, he was nothing more than a caretaker of her final possessions. He hadn't adopted me when they were married. There were no last wishes to say that he would care for me. Niccolo was doing it out of the goodness of his heart.

"Christine's best friend is here. Her entire life is *here* in Manhattan. This is where her support system is, and I will not let you uproot that."

Giovanni laughed and said that *he* was my support system. "I'm her family, *cafone*. You're a little fuck boy that my father bought and paid for. You're nothing to her."

I wasn't supposed to be listening, but their yelling was hard to ignore. I stood in a hallway as close as I dared, clinging to the hope that somehow Niccolo would sway my uncles into letting me stay.

"I'm her *stepfather* whether you like it or not. Where were you when your sister was dying? Because I was at her bedside every. fucking. night. You know who wasn't?" Niccolo didn't give either of the men a chance to respond. "Her brothers. Do you know who made breakfast for Christine when Caterina was too sick to get up? Me. Who was there for Christine at the funeral? Me. Who's been there for her every day since? Me. If you're her support system, you fucking suck."

Both of my uncles were in their forties with families of their own. They came down from Kansas City for my mother's last few days and were pallbearers at her funeral. But Niccolo was right. The only person who'd been by my side since my mother's death was him.

I wasn't sure how I felt about Niccolo when he married my mom, but I knew now. He was a good man. He loved my mother, and he loved me, too. If anyone could shuffle me through the hard teenage years, it was him.

I came around the corner and made an announcement. "I want to stay with Nic. It's what mom would have wanted."

Chapter 2
Niccolo

I never wanted to marry, but my father said I had no choice. As the consigliere of the Castiglione family, his sons had a duty to expand the reach of the family. We were bargaining chips to make connections; we were chattels to be traded for safety and capital.

When I turned twenty-four, my father sat me down and said, "If you won't join us, you can at least strengthen us." A few months later, I walked down the aisle with Caterina Lucatello, a beautiful older woman with a vast fortune inherited from her shitty first husband, who had left her a few years before.

I loved her as much as a man arranged to wed a woman fifteen years older than him could love a woman. We didn't have much in common, but she was pleasant to be around. She moved heaven and earth for her daughter, and that kind of love was admirable.

My father expected us to pop out kids as soon as possible. He told me repeatedly that the only way to strengthen the alliance between the Terlizzis and Lucatellos was to have a baby.

Christine didn't count because she wasn't mine, which made it easier for my father to make disgusting comments about her. I tried to ignore him, but he knew what he was doing. He knew that he got under my skin.

On the day Caterina and I had been wed for three months, he called me home to ask if she was pregnant. "She's forty, father," I told him. "It isn't as easy to get pregnant the older you get."

He kindly suggested I go home, fuck my wife's brains out, and stop fooling around with the psychology shit. He wanted me to be her loyal stay-at-home husband, not an unemployed college student.

Less than two years later, she was dead. It was a pity because I was coming around to love her in the way that a married man and woman should love one another. But before I got to explore all the romance and intimacy we could have had, she passed away, leaving me with an inheritance I never expected: her daughter.

I didn't want to parent a teenager at first. Christine was moody and sullen. She had her best friend over a lot, and when Kaye was around, Christine's mood improved considerably. I did what I could, but I was lost. I never expected to be married at twenty-five and widowed by twenty-seven.

I had no idea what I was doing. I didn't know how to care for a teenage girl. All I knew was I had to keep her fed and ensure she got to school on time. When her uncles showed up to take her away, it finally hit me that I loved her more than they did.

Giovanni wanted to take her back to Kansas City. He brought Marco as a buffer in case things got ugly. Giovanni said he had three sons and two daughters; Christine would fit in perfectly. I'd grown up in a house with a similar genetic makeup, and I couldn't bear the thought of forcing an only child to suddenly become kid number six in a large household.

"Over my dead body." Caterina didn't plan for what would happen after her death. By law, everything she owned reverted to me, including her daughter. "Christine's best friend is here. Her entire life is *here* in Manhattan." She was in high school, for Christ's sake. Now wasn't the time to uproot her and make her start all over again, and I made sure he was aware of that. "This is where her support system is, and I will not let you uproot that."

"I'm her family, *cafone*. You're a little fuck boy that my father bought and paid for. You're nothing to her," Giovanni laughed. Marco stood behind him and offered a nervous laugh in agreement.

Though Giovanni's words hurt, he wasn't wrong. Leonardo Lucatello paid my father a fortune for me to wed Caterina. She was older, and everyone knew what happened with her first husband. But despite the tradition of taking a mistress, I never fucked around on Caterina. The day I found out I was arranged to be wed, I ended all my relationships. I never looked at or touched another woman until the day my wife died.

"I'm her *stepfather* whether you like it or not." Bought and paid for, just like Giovanni said. "Where were you when your sister was dying? Because I was at her bedside every. fucking. night. You know who wasn't? Her brothers." I was there when her hair started to fall out. I was there when she couldn't stop vomiting. I was there when she spiked a fever that led to her final hospital stay. "Do you know who made breakfast for Christine when Caterina was too sick to get up? Me. Who was there for Christine at the funeral? Me. Who's been there for her every day since? Me. If you're her support system, you fucking suck."

I was too heated to say more, but it didn't matter. Christine came out of nowhere and announced that she wanted to stay with me because it was what her mom would have wanted.

I still didn't know how to take care of a teenager, but I was willing to learn. I would do whatever it took to keep Christine safe and happy because she was right: it's what Caterina Lucatello would have wanted.

Chapter 3
Christine

"You're a dick."

Niccolo crosses his arms over his chest and tilts his head to the side. Caution blazes in his eyes, resignation stalking every line of his posture. "Because I don't want you to risk your life to go to your little friend's house?"

"No," I respond with a petulant tone. "Because you think you can control me even though I'm eighteen."

His upper lip curls into a smirk as he shifts his weight from the balls of his feet to his heels. "You live in *my* home, *dolcezza*."

"The home that you inherited from *my* mother." I match his body language movement for movement. "Because your poor *famiglia* was so disappointed that their son wanted to become a professor, they had to marry him off to the first woman that would take him." A roar of thunder booms outside, the rumble punctuated by the crack of lightning.

Niccolo's arms slacken to his sides. His voice rings out with ferocious intensity as a stream of curses and insults pour from his mouth in a torrent of Italian.

It's been a few years since I actively studied the language, but I make out phrases like *'little brat'* and *'you'll learn to respect me'*. I bide my time in silence until he stops to breathe, his face red hot with anger. "Are you done?"

His eyes narrow, the pupils expanding like pools of blackness until they consume his gaze in a feral glint. His steps echo menacingly as he moves closer, the air thickening with an ominous energy.

My throat tightens as if a clawed hand grips it from the inside, and I step backward from him. The back of my knees collide with the edge of the couch, making me lose balance. I tumble, arms flailing in all directions. My elbow catches on the forgotten bowl of popcorn, upending it dramatically. As I fall onto the sofa, kernels fly everywhere, coating the floor and furniture in butter and salt.

"You are not going to Kaye's house. I don't care if it's on fire and you're the only one that can put it out," he deadpans. "The streets are flooding, and the storm is getting worse. You'll stay where you are, and you'll like it."

I crush popcorn into the couch cushions as I scramble to my feet. Niccolo turns his back on me, but I follow him. He strides down the hallway toward the kitchen with his shoulders straight and head held high. "She's my best friend, Nic. She said Xavier was outside her house, and then her phone died. What if—"

Niccolo turns around so quickly that I slam right into him. The impact knocks the breath out of my lungs and nearly topples me. If it weren't for his strong arms reaching out to grab me, I'd crash to the floor. "What if you call an Uber and get into a wreck on the way there?" He roars over my arguments. "What if you take my car and wrap it around a tree?" The emotion in his voice is palpable, reflecting his passion as he speaks. "You aren't leaving, Christine. Go to bed."

I am suddenly aware of the thin cotton shirt stretching across my breasts. I'm not wearing a bra, and my nipples peak through the fabric. Goosebumps swell on my forearms from cold and nerves, but mainly desire. "It's not even 10:00 p.m.," I challenge.

He releases me, and his breath comes in deep, even pulls. He closes his eyes as if to pause time while he regains his calm. "Don't whine, Christine. It's childish behavior for a young woman. And you know how I get when you act childish."

My breath catches in my throat as I remember the last time we were in a position like this. The smell of his warm skin and the sound of his breathing force the memory to play out again right before my eyes.

Chapter 4
Niccolo
4 months before the start of Dark Obsession

God did not allow Caterina Lucatello and me to have children before she passed. Every day, I thank Him for that. My stepdaughter is more than enough for me to handle.

Christine is having a panic attack. "I can't fit into my dress. Nic! Nic!" She yells as she steps out of her bedroom and into the hallway. "Niccolo!" Her voice echoes through the house, and I consider getting up and locking my bedroom door. "I need you to zip me up!"

My head rings with pain as a migraine forms behind my right eye. A gnawing sensation spreads from the back of my skull and down through my neck. I get up from my bed to search for meds. As soon as I stand, the room starts spinning, and I find myself leaning against the wall for support.

My stepdaughter bursts into the room a few moments later. Her face is flushed as she rushes in, the billowing skirt of her bright pink prom dress held up by one hand.

"Niccolo. I can't fit into my dress. I need you to squeeze me into it and probably cut me out of it later." It's a demand, and I can't handle demands right now.

I walk past her to my bathroom. Behind the mirror is a medicine cabinet with four containers: allergy pills, Tylenol, Rizatriptan, and Nurtec. The last two are for my migraines, and I dry swallow one before letting the other melt under my tongue.

"Hello?" Christine storms into the bathroom behind me. "Did you hear me?"

Pain casts a shadow on my mood. Usually, I would love to see my stepdaughter traipsing around in a half opened dress, an invitation for me to chase and pin her to the ground for its removal. But right now, her voice sounds shrill, and every fiber of my being is screaming at me to put in earplugs. "Please, keep it down, Chris."

She turns, holding onto the door frame to steady herself as she presents her back to me. Christine leans forward, and I can almost feel the curve of her hips resting in my hands. "Zip. Me. Up."

On days like today, I don't remember why I accepted responsibility for Christine after her mother's death. *It's the pain talking,* the little voice in my head reminds me, *you love her.*

I fumble with Christine's zipper, but she's right; the dress no longer fits her. The fabric puckers and bunches to let her breathe. "I don't know if this is going to work."

"Make it work," she responds between clenched teeth. "I don't have any other options, and Kaye is going to be here in an hour!"

I like her best friend; they keep each other grounded. I wish Kaye were here right now to deal with Christine's outburst. "If

I get this zipped up, you aren't going to be comfortable. Why don't you—"

Christine snaps her head in my direction with a look of indignation. "I don't care if I can't breathe once you get it zipped up. I'm fitting into this dress, Nic."

The little voice in my head says to remember that she's still a selfish teenage girl. Yes, she turned eighteen a couple of weeks ago. Yes, technically, she's an adult. But she is still, at her core, a selfish child. "Mind your tone, Christine," I warn her.

She taunts me instead. "Or what? What are you going to do?"

My palm twitches in an inappropriate way. "If you're going to be a brat, you can wait for Kaye to get here and help you. I have a headache and—"

"All I'm asking is that you zip up the dress. It isn't that big of a deal. Just do it, and I'll leave you alone." Perhaps she has a point, though her tone is grating on my nerves.

I work the zipper while she clings to the door frame. Every inch of progress draws the fabric tighter around her chest. It takes a minute, but the zipper gets halfway up before finally gliding the rest of the way to the top.

When she turns around to face me, I get an eyeful of cleavage. The corset-style top cinches her breasts together into a delicious view.

"Thank you," she says with faux sweetness in her tone. "Even though you acted like a real ass about it."

"Hey!" I call after Christine as she turns to leave the bathroom. "*You* needed *my* help, not the other way around. You could try being thankful *without* the attitude."

She snorts in derision and sweeps away from me. "And you could try being a nicer stepfather. But until then, neither of us will get what we want."

I'm driven by anger, frustration, and pain—a myriad of emotions and sensations that power me forward before common sense can kick in to stop me. I grab Christine's wrist and pull her back before she leaves. "Apologize," I hold her tightly, "now."

Instead of apologizing, a small smile plays on her lips as she says, "Make me."

I don't always take my fatherly responsibilities seriously, but my actions are a reflex to the disrespect. My patience snaps like a twig, and I drag Christine across the room, pressing her face-first into the bed. With one hand on the small of her back, I bring the other down on her ass. The blow is cushioned by the prom dress' thick material, but it's a jarring action that catches Christine off guard.

With a small shriek, she glares over her shoulder. "What are you doing?" She demands.

I apply another stroke to her other cheek, feeling my pants tighten and my head throb in disagreement. "If you're going to act like a child, you'll be punished like a child."

Christine's jaw drops, but before she can respond, I spank her again. I feel the curve of her bottom with each slap, and I struggle internally with how to proceed. Part of me wants to keep going until she apologizes. Another part of me knows that if I do this much longer, I'll flip up her skirt and forget that I was once married to her mother.

I only give her another couple of swats, enough to warm her

backside and fuel fantasies that will never happen. Then I pull away from her, letting her get to her feet.

"How dare you!" She roars as she stands up, hands immediately reaching behind her to rub her ass. "I'm going to tell," but Christine stops mid-sentence because who is she going to tell? I'm her legal guardian. She has two uncles who might be interested in hearing what I did to her, but it wasn't illegal.

"Enjoy your sore ass at prom, *dolcezza*." I point toward the door. "Now get out."

Christine flounders over what to say next. Her mouth opens and shuts like she's gasping for air. When she can't find the right words to say, she stomps out of my bedroom, slamming the door shut behind her.

I might have fucked up by spanking her, but it improved my mood. My head feels a little lighter, but maybe that's the meds talking.

Chapter 5
Christine
1 day before the start of Dark Obsession

"Don't you *dare* threaten me." My voice quivers in stark contrast to my confidence. "I can do whatever I want, whenever I want. I don't have to ask for your permission. I'm an adult."

Niccolo snorts in amusement. "If you have to tell people you're an adult, are you *really* an adult?" He asks with a teasing lilt before growing serious again. "If you take my car without permission, I'll call the cops. I don't care if you're my stepdaughter; I'll turn you in so fast you won't even make it out of the neighborhood."

I hate him. He makes me so angry that I burn from the inside out. My rage controls my thoughts, forcing me to act out. "I can't wait until I'm out of this house," I roar at him. "You can't tell me what to do when I'm at Blackmore."

"Newsflash, *dolcezza*, you're going to be my student. I'm going to be your professor. I can still tell you what to do."

He's so infuriating. How is it that he and my mother ever got along? "You're my professor for *one* semester," I remind him. "After that, I never have to see you again."

He raises an eyebrow, his eyes twinkling with mischief before his handsome face wrinkles into a grin. "If that's what you want, then by all means. Never see me again." Niccolo turns and leaves, each footstep swallowing up sound as he walks away from me. Finally, only the hollow thud silence echoes off the walls.

I should feel victorious, but instead, I feel defeated. I deflate with disappointment and return to my place on the couch. While I clean up the mess of popcorn left in my wake, I try to make sense of it all.

Niccolo pushes my buttons more than anyone ever has. He has a tendency of getting under my skin. I can never seem to win against him, no matter how hard I try. And I can't shake the feeling that he enjoys putting me in my place.

A few months ago, when he turned me over the foot of the bed and spanked me, I left his room wishing I'd gone to Kansas City with Giovanni after my mother's death. But as the minutes passed to hours and hours became days, I found myself conflicted by the discipline.

I couldn't quite put my finger on it, but something about being under his control made my body tingle with excitement. Maybe it was because he was the first person to ever truly hold me accountable for my actions. He saw through my facade of bravado and called me out on my bullshit. It was both terrifying and thrilling, and it made me wish he wasn't my stepfather.

It's one thing to enjoy being spanked by a lover; it's something else entirely to enjoy being spanked by someone who was once married to your mother.

Chapter 6
Niccolo

My relationship with Christine changed about a year ago. I can't remember exactly what happened or when, but one day, I walked into the kitchen and saw her standing by the sink, filling a glass with water from the tap. Our eyes met, and in that instant, my heart yearned for her.

Christine had grown up to be a rare beauty, as smart as a whip and just as funny. She looked at me for a moment, and something passed between us—perhaps it was desire or affection, or maybe even love. But whatever it was, it made me realize that we were more than just former family members living together under the same roof.

I tried to ignore my feelings after that. At seventeen years old, Christine was off limits in more ways than one. I felt like the world's biggest creep even though I didn't act on my feelings. I went as far as to go to a therapist to discuss what was wrong with me. He said that there was nothing wrong, per se.

"The wires in your brain have gotten crossed. You've been caring for this girl for years now, and it's normal that the intimate feelings you have for her have changed as she's matured. But you are her stepparent. Therefore, you need to put those feelings away."

I tried to lock them up like he suggested, but it's been difficult. Christine is more than just my stepdaughter; she's my favorite person to be around, even when she's being a pain in my ass.

When we aren't at odds with one another, it's like being with my best friend. She's insightful and intelligent in a way I've never encountered before. She makes me look at things differently and second-guess my preconceived notions.

Last year, she told me she wanted to become a therapist, and when I asked her why, she got shy. It took some coaxing, but she told me in the end.

"I guess I sort of knew when Kaye and her mom were going through everything with Owen. She used to pour out her heart to me like I was the only person in the world who could understand what she was going through. And I didn't, not really," Christine added with a frown. Her home life growing up had been radically different from Kaye's.

"But it seemed like she had some form of PTSD, and she still has a lot of anxiety about what happened. I keep thinking that if she talks to a professional, she can get the help she needs. But how do you tell someone you think they're depressed without hurting their feelings? Anyway," she waved me off. "I don't know. I either want to be a therapist or a psychologist. One or the other. I think there's a lot of kids like Kaye that could use someone to listen to them."

Psychology is a complex study. I worked my ass off to get my doctorate, and I still don't feel like I know everything. But I knew that day that I'd never been prouder.

Then, the day came when Christine turned eighteen, and I went out for drinks with my brothers. I got ass over elbow wasted until I was falling down in the streets. My brothers had to carry me home when I threw myself on the hood of a police car. Thank God it was empty, or else the fuckers would have let me get arrested.

"What the hell, Nic?" Dante and Luciano had to haul me into my own home. My older brother was unimpressed. "This is why nobody wants to marry you."

The world spun on its axis, and I was sure I would throw up. Then I caught sight of Christine's red hair disappearing around a corner with Kaye in tow. "Chris," I mumbled.

"No," Dante grunted as he forced me into my bedroom, "you leave that girl alone. You're going to get your ass beat by the Lucatello brothers if you don't cut this shit out." He had a minute understanding of what was going on between Christine and me. Though he didn't offer his opinion on my infatuation with my stepdaughter, I knew how he felt about it.

"You're right," I slurred, the words coming out in a soupy mess of unintelligence. "She couldn't love me anyway. I'm old."

Luciano snickered as he came back into the room with a cup of water for my bedside. "You're about to be thirty, dumb ass. You're not old."

"You only say that because you're old, too!" I accused.

Dante tossed me on the bed without any concern for my landing. "Sober up, Nic. Figure your shit out. And leave the Lucatello girl alone."

I've been a mess ever since.

I love Christine. I've watched her grow up from pain in the ass teenage girl to pain in the ass young woman. I didn't have feelings for her before, but now they're unavoidable. And when she stands in front of me in a thin shirt with her nipples poking through the fabric, it's hard to resist her.

One more day, the little voice in my head says. In less than twenty-four hours, we'll be at Blackmore University. We'll be away from my family and hers.

Maybe we can make some magic happen.

Dark Obsession

Chapter 7
Christine

Psychology 101 is taught by the one and only Niccolo Terlizzi. The university website has a handsome, smiling picture of my stepfather right above his biography. He might be new to the campus, but the reviews from his past year of students sound promising.

"He has a stupid, ugly face," I grumble as I scroll to the top of the page to get away from him.

Someone plops down beside me and hovers over my phone. "Looks pretty hot to me," she announces.

I toss my phone three feet in front of me and almost pee myself. "Jesus Christ," I swear at her.

"Sienna Richler, actually," she says with a grin, "but you can call me Jesus if you want."

I dislike her immediately. She's bold, beautiful, and blunt—not to mention sticking her nose in my business. What a bitch. "Didn't your parents teach you it's rude to eavesdrop?"

Sienna pulls a laptop from her backpack, dropping it unceremoniously on her thighs. "You're, like, the only person here; I didn't realize you were talking to someone. You got multiple personalities or something?"

My jaw hinges open, and I'm not sure how to respond. "Wh-what?" I stutter, taking a minute to regain my faculties. "I don't think you can go around asking people that."

With a shrug, she places her backpack by her feet and prepares for the hour. "My mama always told me that if I don't know something, I should ask. I don't know if you've got a personality disorder or something, so I'm asking."

I trip over my words trying to figure out how to respond. My brain can't formulate a proper response because I'm so surprised by her extroverted personality.

"This is Psychology 101," she reminds me after a moment. "I'm sure it's normal for people with psychological disorders to take the class in hopes of better understanding themselves."

"Who are you?" I finally ask when my mouth starts working again.

She turns to look at me and offers a patient smile. "Sienna Richler," she reiterates, "I'm from Minnesota. You know y'all don't even get two feet of snow here in Kansas?"

I'm not sure I know my name anymore, let alone how much snow we get in winter. I feel like a slow computer struggling to reboot. My brain takes a solid five seconds to comprehend what she said before it kicks into gear.

I clear my throat and reach out to shake her hand. "Maybe we should start over. I'm Christine."

"I'm Sienna."

"And you're from Minnesota?"

She enthusiastically nods her head yes. "Duluth. We get seven feet of snow every winter. Not all at once," Sienna clarifies. "Though if you ask my mama, she'll tell you about that time I was five when we got two feet dumped on us overnight. She likes to show people pictures of me bundled up like a parcel, sinking to my neck in the drifts."

I feel like I'm in an episode of Punk'd because I have no idea what's going on. This girl came up to me, sat down, and started talking like we were friends. Thank God a rush of students come through the door and fill in the chairs around us because I don't know what to say.

"You were looking up the professor?" Sienna asks after a minute, gesturing toward the door.

I follow the line of her gaze and see Niccolo walk into the classroom. He carries a briefcase and wears a suit atypical of the other professors I've seen this morning.

"I think he's hotter in person," she whispers. "What do you think?"

I think he's my stepfather and potentially deranged. When he locks eyes with me, the corner of his lip curls into a smirk that makes my stomach flip-flop. "He's okay."

Sienna snorts in derision. "You're trying to tell me he doesn't sizzle your bacon?"

Once again, Sienna leaves me speechless. Thankfully, Niccolo tells everyone to quiet down, and I don't have to come up with a response.

"I'm Professor Terlizzi, and this is Psychology 101. If you want a syllabus, it's on the campus website," he announces. "I didn't print out copies because it's a waste of paper, a waste of ink, and a waste of my time and yours. If you care enough to work on the scheduled assignments ahead of time, you'll go to the website. Otherwise, I expect you to do all the required reading, submit your papers on the specified due date, and know you're in college now. You're an adult, and you are the only person responsible for the choices you make. You might have fucked around in high school and gotten an A, but you won't in my class."

Everyone laughs, including Sienna, who leans over to whisper that not only is the professor attractive, but he's funny, too.

"Only if you aren't his stepdaughter," I mumble back to her under my breath. "He's a tyrant at home."

Sienna's eyes widen in shock, her words coming out in a choked gasp. "Shut up," she whispers scandalously.

Niccolo stops mid-speech and directs his gaze at us. With an eyebrow more manicured than my own, he crosses his arms over his chest and asks, "You, dark hair," he gestures toward Sienna, "What's your name?"

I avert my eyes. She got herself into this mess; she can get herself out of it.

"Sienna Richler, sir." She doesn't sound so confident anymore; Niccolo tends to have that effect on people.

"Miss Richler, can you tell the class what the biological basis of behavior is in the study of psychology?"

Her cheeks flush bright red, and uncertainty clouds her voice as she answers. "To, um, explore biological factors and how they, um, impact behavior?"

Out of the corner of my eye, I can see Niccolo's jaw twitch. "This isn't Jeopardy, Miss Richler. Don't answer in the form of a question."

Sienna clears her throat before repeating herself with more surety. "To explore biological factors and how they impact behavior."

Niccolo's stern gaze softens slightly as he nods in affirmation. "Correct." His voice remains firm yet measured. A few silent seconds pass as he sizes Sienna up again before continuing. "Don't talk when I'm talking, Miss Richler. This is a place of learning, not idle chatter. Shall we continue, or do you have some *riveting information* you'd like to share with the class?"

She shakes her head quickly, then proceeds to face forward for the rest of the hour. It's her first day of class, and she's already pissed off the professor. Better her than me, in my opinion.

But I can't escape my stepfather's watchful eye for long. He spends the rest of the hour informing us of the year to come, breaking down the schedule for midterms and finals from now until spring. When he finally dismisses everyone, he shoots me a look that almost glues me to my chair. "Not you, Miss Lucatello," he says when I stand up. "I'd like to speak to you privately."

There are a few *'oooh, she's in trouble's* from the back of the lecture hall, all from boys who haven't matured past high school yet, but the jeers subside as everyone files out of the room.

Niccolo turns to scribble on the whiteboard, his muscular form silhouetted against the pristine surface. Although his back is turned, I can feel his presence commanding the room. As the last few students pack up their things and eagerly flee from the palpable tension, I remain in my seat until the door closes behind the last person.

"What do you want, Nic?" I'm ready to go back to my dorm room and take a nap.

He turns on his heel and scowls. "That's *professor* to you, Christine."

Chapter 8
Niccolo

My stepdaughter shows up to class looking like she wants me to bend her over the hood of my car and make her scream my name.

Dressed casually in shorts and a tank top, her bare legs are just begging me to get on my knees and worship. I'm so turned on that I have to think about bugs splattering on a windshield to keep my dick from getting hard at the sight of her tanned, delicious thighs. I fight tooth and nail with my lust through the hour because my brain is conjuring up images of grabbing her by the hips, ripping off her tiny little shorts, and grinding my cock deep into her center.

I drone on about the syllabus and my expectations for the semester, checking off points on an imaginary list in a monotone voice. It's almost enough to keep my mind off Christine. *Almost.*

At the end of the class, I ask her to stay after even though I have no reason to. I need to see her alone, eye her up and down without fifty other students seeing me do it. It's the first time we've been away from home together, and I need a moment to collect my thoughts.

"What do you want, Nic?" Christine asks from her seat when everyone is gone.

I want everything I've been holding myself back from for the last few months; I want her. "That's *professor* to you, Christine." My voice tightens as I turn to take her in. She is arousing from head to toe, a walking wet dream demanding to be debased, and I'm just the man to give in to do the job.

My stepdaughter rolls her eyes as she gets up, yawning to show her complete lack of concern as she saunters toward me. "Oh, you want me to call you professor now?" She asks with a teasing lilt. When she reaches my desk, she leans forward and spreads her hands wide across the mahogany. The neckline of her shirt dips into an inviting V-shape, so low that her breasts look like they might pop out of her dark red velvet bra at any moment. "Then why did you keep me after class, *professor*?"

I drag my eyes away from her chest before I lose control of my senses and give in to my cravings. "You need to conduct yourself properly in the classroom, Christine."

She raises a confused eyebrow and asks, "Excuse me?"

"*That*," I look her up and down, "is not an appropriate outfit for a college classroom." A too-tight tank top cinching her breasts together should not be paired with jean shorts that cup her ass in a way that makes me jealous of a piece of fabric.

Christine snorts in disdain as she pushes off the desk. "It's 102 outside, Nic. I'm not showing up in a parka."

She's deliberately trying to bait me, and it makes my palm twitch. "That's not what I mean, and you know it."

With a wave of her hand, she makes it clear that she isn't interested in what I mean. Christine slowly walks around the edge of the desk until she's only a few inches from me. "Even if I was the only one dressed like this—and believe me, I'm not—you can't tell me what to do anymore," she announces with a smug look on her face.

But that's where she's wrong. I don't tell her what to do because I'm her stepfather or professor. I tell her what to do because she likes it. I see it in the way her nostrils flare when I give her a command. I see it when I threaten to spank her for being a brat, and her eyes darken with lust. I can, and will, tell her what to do as often as I like.

"That's where you're wrong, *dolcezza*." I close the gap between us, bringing my hand to her throat and wrapping my fingers around her soft, delicate neck.

Christine reaches up to grab my wrist. I am only a couple of inches taller than her, but she is all curves and femininity, while I am fueled by rage and desire; my strength easily overpowers hers. "Nic," she pleads, her confident defiance dissipating in the face of my dominance.

"That's right, say my name." If I tightened my grip, she wouldn't be able to say anything at all. It's a fantasy right now, but one day I'll do it. One day, I'll steal the breath from her lungs while I'm thrusting deep inside of her, and she'll pop off like a rocket.

"We can't do this." Her words are beautifully desperate, but they fall on deaf ears.

I've waited for this day since she turned eighteen. We're finally away from her family, away from everyone back home who knew about our prior relationship. It is just her and I at

Blackmore; this is our fresh start. I don't have to pretend not to want her. I don't have to act like she's *just* my stepdaughter.

"But we *can* do this, sweetheart. We can finally indulge in our desires."

She fights me, struggling against the tight collar my hand makes around her throat. "I don't know what you're talking about."

I'm so close that I can feel her warm breath against my chest. If I lean in a little closer, I could graze her lips with mine and indulge in our first kiss. "Don't lie to me, *dolcezza*. I've seen the way you look at me when you think I'm not looking. You want me as badly as I want you."

Christine shakes her head, swearing the opposite. "That's not true."

I'm tired of fighting her; I'm tired of fighting fate. My father arranged for me to marry Caterina Lucatello five years ago. She died and left me with her daughter. This was our destiny; this was always where I was meant to be. "I have waited a lifetime for you, Christine. You can lie to yourself all you want, but you're mine now."

Christine's bottom lip quivers. "Nic, no. Don't do this; it can't be undone."

"Good." I sew up the chasm between us by pressing my mouth against hers and taste my stepdaughter for the first time. I have waited an eternity for this moment, and I can no longer hold back. I surrender to my desires and savor the sweetness of our first kiss.

As I drag my tongue across her lower lip, exploring its contours, she tilts her head ever so slightly in acceptance. She tastes like sunshine after a thunderstorm, like lying in bed after a long day, like a tall glass of water when it's hot outside. My longing for her is impossible to resist.

Christine's eyes close in anticipation as she parts her lips, our tongues dancing against one another with wild abandon. Desperate for more of her, I delve deeper into the kiss, my tongue tangling with hers as my free hand moves down to cup her ass through her shorts. She gasps into my mouth as she grinds against my hand involuntarily. I groan, lost in the sensation of having her body pressed against mine.

But the kiss is over all too soon, and it leaves us both wanting more. I'm forced to pull away to stop myself from taking more than she's willing to offer. This is just an amuse-bouche; the main course is still to come.

"I know you've been with other boys, Christine." I've listened to her late-night calls with her best friend, detailing every moment of the time she lost her virginity. I've seen her kissing other guys and letting them feel her up in the parking lot at the high school. I know she's no pristine virgin. "You let an inexperienced teenage boy pop your cherry, and maybe you've been with other boys since. I don't know, and I don't care. You're with me now, *dolcezza*, and I'm not some two-pump chump that's going to leave you wanting more. I'm the man that's going to fuck you until your legs are shaking with pleasure."

Her eyes meet mine, and I see defiance melt into desire. "Nic, we can't do this," she repeats. But under her disapproving tone is deep-seated yearning; Christine wants this as much as I do.

I toss her arguments to the wind; I forget she ever gave voice to them. "You called me dad when I was married to your mother. By the end of the year, you'll be calling me Daddy."

Christine's breath catches in her throat as a pink stain of carnality spreads across her cheeks and creeps down her neck. "Nic," she pleads once more, one final petition before she gives in.

"Keep saying my name like that, sweetheart, and I'll fuck you until you're screaming it."

Chapter 9
Christine

Back in the dorm, sitting opposite Kaye, I try to put into perspective what I just went through with Niccolo.

"He's a sick and twisted man. That's what you're thinking, right?"

Kaye has a textbook on her lap and a highlighter in her hand. Even though it's the first day of school, she's studying. Her eyes scan across the page in rapt attention. "Yeah," she mumbles, "terrible."

With a heavy sigh of frustration, I correct her. "*Twisted*, Kaye, he's twisted."

I snatch a second of her attention as she looks up from the textbook. Her eyes are wild, as if I pulled her from another dimension. "What?" She asks with a frown. "What happened?"

I would be surprised if she remembered anything I told her in the last twenty minutes. "Nothing," I grumble. It's probably a good thing she didn't hear me. I don't need her, or anyone else, recalling that I didn't deny my stepfather's accusation that I'm sexually attracted to him. "How are you?"

She shakes her head, frustration burrowing in the lines around her eyes. "Exhausted," Kaye groans. "I don't know what I was thinking when I signed up for 23 hours this semester. Well, that's a lie." She pulls her feet under her, reaching up to push a strand of hair behind her ear. "I was thinking if I could take as many classes each semester as possible, I could graduate early and get out of here sooner."

Kaye has as many problems as I do if not more. Ever since her mother married prominent divorce attorney, Malcolm McCade, she's been dealing with her obsessed stepbrother, Xavier. He stalks her like he has nothing better to do than show up at her house in the middle of the night and torment her. Xavier is the reason she wants to race through her time at Blackmore and doesn't have a moment to spare for her best friend. I hate him.

"How's your wrist feeling today?" I ask.

She gingerly displays the wrap Everton Health Center gave her a few days ago. We had just made it to campus to settle into our new dorm, when one thing led to another. She refuses to admit exactly what happened or what he said to her, but Xavier left her with a sprained wrist and a healthy fear of the future. "It doesn't really hurt unless I take off the splint thing."

The corner of my lips quirks upward. "Then don't take it off, silly."

My best friend groans in frustration, pushing the textbook off her lap and onto the blankets beside her. "I can't deal with him this semester, Chris. I've got five million papers to do, and I need to find a job. He can't follow me around all semester; I'll never get anything done."

I've been telling her for years to do something about Xavier. Tell her mom. Call the cops. Put it in writing in case he tries to kill her one day. But Kaye has been resistant to all of my recommendations. "You want me to beat him up?" I offer. "I could break his leg or something."

It breaks the tension, and she grins at me. "I could run him over with my car," Kaye perks up. "You think I could get away with it?"

I grimace in response. I love my best friend, but she isn't the person I would call if I had a dead body to dispose of. She's more fragile than she cares to admit, and she would crack under the pressure. "I don't know, Kaye. You're not much of a liar."

She wrinkles her nose and sighs. "Yeah, you're right. I'd wind up getting caught trying to get rid of the body, and then I'd go to prison. And I'll never make it in prison," she says with an exaggerated groan. "I'm too gentle."

"Absolutely," I agree. "Someone will make you their bitch on day one."

Kaye flips me off, but there's a smile on her face. "You're supposed to make me feel better about myself, Christine."

I stretch out on my bed, feeling the stress of the last hour with Niccolo disappear from my limbs. "I'm off my game today. Did I tell you about the weird girl in my Psych class?"

"Weirder than you?" Kaye teases me with a mischievous grin and a playful poke of her tongue.

"Yeah. Sierra or Sienna or something. I don't know. I was looking at Nic's bio on the campus website when she sat down next to me and said he was hot. Then she started talking about snow in Minnesota and her mom." I almost forgot to mention that she asked me if I had a personality disorder. "She was so weird."

But Kaye points out that I thought the same thing about her when we met in elementary school. "I was the lonely little five-year-old that brought a Barbie lunchbox to school when Barbie wasn't cool," she reminds me.

The first time we met, it was like comets colliding. I hated her for reasons I can't even remember now. "God, you were chatty, too," I shake my head. "You kept talking about your crush on Arthur." I barely remember the PBS Show from back in the day, but I know she was weirdly in love with the animated Aardvark.

"All I'm saying is don't write her off just yet. You're going to need a new best friend when I go to prison," Kaye reminds me.

Oh, god. If my only option for a new best friend is some crazy girl that thinks my stepfather is hot, I'm screwed. "Maybe I'll pack my bags and flee the country if you go to prison," I offer. "Find a new man, one I'm not related to." One that doesn't make my stomach do backflips every time he looks at me a certain way.

Kaye gives me a pointed look. "Crazy men like Niccolo exist everywhere. You're gonna have to become a lesbian if you want to avoid them all together."

I snap my fingers and point at her. "New plan. You and I become lesbian lovers, and then Xavier and Nic will have to leave us alone." I'm a genius.

"Yeah, no," she responds, immediately shooting down my idea. "I might not have been with a man yet," Kaye's cheeks fill with color upon admission, "but I want to one day."

I bury my face in my pillow and whine, "You're breaking my heart, Kaye Pennington."

She giggles from her bed on the other side of the room. "I'm sure you'll get over it when some tall, dark, handsome college senior sweeps you off your feet. Then you'll forget all about step daddy dearest."

God, I hope so. I just need one hot, experienced college boy to make me forget about the kiss I shared with Niccolo. And maybe a couple more to make me forget everything else. Kaye doesn't know it, but this isn't the first time I've been in a predicament like this with my stepfather.

And if I'm being honest, I don't think it'll be the last.

Chapter 10
Niccolo

My brothers have the audacity to show up at my door on a Friday night and ask me to go partying in the Rosedale bar district—as though I'm not going to run into a single student of mine. "You're fucking crazy. I'm not partying with a bunch of college girls."

My youngest brother, Luciano, breezes past me and heads for the kitchen. He's always hungry, and by the time we reach him, he's got a bag of popcorn in the microwave. Lucky starts looking through my cabinets, searching for a bowl. "Don't be so critical, Nicci," he says as he allows a cabinet door to slam shut. "You hang out with college girls every day, *Doctor*."

My brothers never call me 'doctor' to show recognition for the hard work I had to put in during graduate school. When they call me 'doctor,' it's to make fun of me for choosing a different career path than theirs.

"I *teach* college girls, Luciano. I don't hang out with them." I'm not about to jeopardize my job when one of those girls gets too attached and reports me to Human Resources. It took me too many years to get my Ph.D. to blow it on a one-night stand.

Dante snickers and elbows Salvatore. "What are you *just teaching* Christine then, eh?" He teases.

The corner of my jaw ticks as I clench my teeth, trying to contain the mountain of irritation I feel. Dante is an arrogant bastard whose opinions are like a disease: contagious and easily passed from him to the others. "Christine is," I search for the right word, coming up short, "different." Which still doesn't explain why she's so special and all the other eighteen-year-old girls in my Psychology 101 class aren't.

"You call her what you want, Nic. Father always said if there's grass on the field, play ball," Salvatore grins. "I haven't seen little Lucatello naked, but I bet the carpet matches the drapes. Eh, Nic?" He winks disrespectfully. "She got a ginger bush?"

Rage courses through my veins like hot magma, stirring up a hatred that permeates every thread of my being. I despise them. Every single one of them. From the moment I was born into this family, I've never belonged, and they've never let me forget it. I am an outsider, the son who never lived up to the family name.

"I thought you guys were going out," I change the subject. If I don't control my anger, I'll do something we'll all regret.

Dante, the oldest and the pride of the Terlizzi family, hops up on the kitchen counter and grabs an apple. He pops the red delicious between his lips and takes a bite. "We are. We just thought we'd extend an invitation for you to join us. We miss you when you're away at college."

His teasing gets the better of me, as it's done since we were children, and I snap at him before I can stop myself. "And what's Adalina going to say about you partying with nineteen-year-olds?" I narrow my eyes at him. "What's *your wife* going to say about you taking body shots off a barely legal teenage girl?"

Dante's relationship with Adalina has always differed from what I expect of my future bride; I never understood why he settled for marrying someone he hated. They were in love once, but something changed. We rarely see her, and when we do, she looks at her husband like she might gut him without remorse.

Dante hops off the counter and strolls across the room, stopping once he's in front of me. With more force than necessary, he taps me on the cheek with an open hand. It's a gesture of affection, but it stings. "Worry about yourself, Lolo," he calls me by the disrespectful nickname my brothers came up with when we were kids. "Don't stick your nose in my marriage unless you want me to give your relationship with your *stepdaughter* the same treatment."

My brain rapidly fires off a dozen insults. I have every nasty thing under the sun to say about him. I know Dante's greatest weaknesses and the struggles he holds close to his heart. If I wanted to, I could make him hurt.

"You coming out or not?" Luciano breaks the tension. The microwave dings, and he pulls out the popcorn, ripping into the bag immediately. "You used to love breaking in college virgins."

Before I met Caterina, when I was in my twenties, and didn't feel guilty about sleeping around with girls who put too much stock into a one-night stand, sure. I loved going out, getting drunk, and hitting on every girl I could find. It was a treat to be their first, to teach them what they should expect from a man.

"Yeah," I grumble. "But that was years ago. We're too old for trolling college bars for freshman pussy."

Salvatore snorts, flipping me the bird in the process. "Speak for yourself, Grandpa. There's no such thing as being too old for freshman pussy."

This isn't an argument I'm going to win. The Terlizzi brothers are stubborn, all of them, including myself. But being a Terlizzi is like being popular. While it comes with the perks of strangers knowing your name and everyone wanting to be your friend, you're constantly pressured into doing things you don't want to do by people who will mercilessly bully you if you say no. I hate my brothers, and yet I seek constant validation from them.

"Whatever. I'll come, I guess. I'm not doing anything, anyway." I've been rebuffed by Christine, and I haven't heard from her since she ran from my lecture hall a few days ago.

"You gonna go get ready?" Salvatore asks, raising an eyebrow. "Or are you going out wearing that?" He wrinkles his nose as he looks me up and down, judgment woven into the gesture.

I follow his line of sight, but I don't understand his reaction. "Is there something *wrong* with what I'm wearing?" Black slacks with a white, long-sleeved, button-down shirt. It's what I wore to class today.

"You look like you a runaway groom," Salvatore deadpans.

"And you look like an ape that's escaped the zoo," I fire back. "What of it?"

Dante rolls his eyes and holds his hands up to stop the bickering. "Just put on some shoes, and let's go. I'm tired of hanging around this house. Why don't you sell it?" He asks with a frown as he looks around at the dated style of the kitchen and the paintings hung in the dining room. "You haven't changed anything since Caterina died. You could build a new home from what you'd make selling this one."

But if I sold the Lucatello mansion, I'd lose the Lucatello daughter. She'd have no reason to see me if we didn't call the same house our home. Christine might be avoiding me since our run-in on the first day of school, but losing her is a luxury I can't afford. "I like it here. It's cozy."

"It's a mausoleum," Dante remarks. "It's hardly fit for a Terlizzi."

If his house is the gold standard for Terlizzis, I'll pass. I don't need a dungeon in the basement or an underground crypt for all my dead bodies. "I'll keep that in mind. Can we go now?"

Chapter 11
Christine

Convincing Kaye to come out on Shark Night was not easy. She made plans to spend the weekend doing homework and getting ahead in her classes. She didn't want to embrace the tradition of senior frat boys trying to hook up with freshman girls. Before she caved, I thought I was going to have to go to the bars by myself. Thankfully, persistence paid off; she agreed to come and slipped into a bright red dress I provided for her. It's tight around her torso, accentuating her curves and full breasts, but falls loose around her waist.

"That looks better on you than it did on me," I yell over the music as we stand in line outside of Red Dawg. Even on the street, we can hear the bass drum pounding through the walls.

Kaye tries to pull the hem of the dress down again, but it won't stretch any further. "I wish it weren't so red," she complains. "I feel like everyone is staring at me."

"Kaye, baby girl," I toss my head back, "you're young and gorgeous. *Of course*, they're staring."

The line moves, and suddenly, the bouncer is right in front of us. We've been out for an hour and had a couple of drinks at the last bar, but Kaye and I sober up before the guy gets a whiff of alcohol. I flash him a smile, and he lets us through the door, but not before looking at Kaye's ass as she walks by.

When we get inside, Red Dawg is packed, and the line to the bar stretches to the back wall. Kaye and I decide to secure a place on the dance floor before grabbing drinks.

The sweat from all the surrounding bodies accumulates on my skin, causing my legs to feel sticky and damp. The air conditioning blasts from every direction, but it isn't enough to mask the scent of body odor, cologne, and cheap vodka.

"I'm going to get us another round!" I announce as the song changes. Kaye gives me the thumbs up, staying on the dance floor to guard the small patch of space we've claimed as our own.

As I fight through the crowd to get to the bar, I run into a familiar face. "Dante?" He's my stepfather's older brother and one of the last people I expected to see at the bar tonight. His hair is shot through with streaks of gray, but he's the kind of man who only gets better looking with age, like George Clooney or Idris Elba.

Dante eyes me up and down like he's a single man looking for the right woman to take home. I've met his wife a couple of times at Terlizzi family gatherings; she's a striking young woman. I wonder what she'd think about his lewd behavior. "*Cara Mia*," he grins, "my, oh my. I can see why Lolo is attracted to you."

I came out tonight to get attention, but Dante's eyes trailing across my body feel more lecherous than sexy. I cross my arms over my chest in a vain attempt to hide the cleavage I am eagerly showing. "What are you doing here?" I shift uncomfortably from one foot to the other, wishing I could melt into the floor.

Dante's lips move, but I can't hear him over the fresh wave of music blasting through the speakers. The twist of his lips tells me that whatever he said would have turned my stomach. He looks like a predator stalking his prey, and I'm the only one in sight.

I smile wanly and give him a little wave, pointing toward the bar to indicate why I'm walking away. He doesn't see me because he's already moved on. His eyes are locked on someone in the distance, and he takes off without another word.

Unfortunately, Dante isn't the only Terlizzi at Red Dawg tonight. Salvatore and Luciano stand at a high-top table, throwing back shots.

"Lucatello!" Salvatore yells over the cacophony of music and voices when he sees me. "What are you doing here?"

"Me? It's a college bar. What are *you* doing here?"

His lips curve into a smirk. "Terlizzi night out," Salvatore says with a wink. "Nic is here, too, if you're looking."

My stomach flip-flops. I'm not looking for my stepfather; I don't ever want to see him again. But those aren't the words that come out of my mouth.

"Where is he?" Salvatore nods toward the opposite corner of the room, and when I turn to look, I see some tiny little blonde with her body pressed up against him. My jaw drops open, and I forget the drinks I told Kaye I would get.

I make a path toward Niccolo, pushing my way through the crowd. He sees me when I'm twenty feet away. His posture straightens, and he smiles as he whispers something in the blonde girl's ear. She turns her head to look at me, eyeing me up and down in a catty way that only girls are capable of. Then she rolls her eyes and walks away as if she doesn't think much of me.

"*Dolcezza*," Nic grins as I approach, "I knew you'd be back."

"Shut up," I glare at him, straining to be heard over the music. "Are you stalking me? Is that why you're here?"

He rakes his eyes from my face all the way down my body, sending a ripple of pleasure through me as he gives me the attention I crave. Niccolo doesn't bother responding. Instead, he licks his lips as if dinner's just been served. "Quite the outfit you have on."

Goosebumps pucker the skin across my chest, my nipples tightening into hard little peaks beneath the fabric of my dress. "You need to go, Nic. Kaye is here." I say as if that will persuade him.

Niccolo leans into me, our faces only centimeters apart. His cologne permeates the air, mixing mint and forest with the smell of whiskey and coke. "You looking for some boy to take you home tonight?" He teases, sending my heart into palpitations and causing my breath to quicken.

"It isn't like that," I mumble, even though it's *exactly* like that. How does he know me so well?

Nic reaches forward, his fingers colliding with my hip. His touch sears my skin through the silky fabric of the dress, setting me ablaze. "I should hope not, *dolcezza*. I like to think my offer is more appealing than some frat boy that doesn't know how to fuck you right."

My face burns in recollection of what happened in his classroom a few days ago. I had to flee from Niccolo before I allowed myself to give in to him, and I've been embarrassed ever since.

"Maybe I want a frat boy," I say stubbornly, refusing to let him think he's won.

But it's the wrong thing to say. We're off campus and surrounded by strangers who don't know he was once married to my mother. Niccolo's well-positioned hand on my hip becomes a vice as he twists me in his grasp, trapping me in an unyielding embrace. My back presses against his chest, and I am powerless to pull away.

"Really?" He whispers in my ear. "Tell me why."

I open my mouth to reprimand him, but his fingers find the hem of my dress and dip beneath the fabric. Unable to stop myself, I offer no resistance when his hand caresses my thigh, higher and higher, until his fingers brush against the lace of my panties. "Nic," I groan, torn between desire and disgust.

His touch is gentle but firm, and I can feel myself growing hot and bothered under his ministrations. His fingertips circle the delicate fabric, teasing me with unbearable anticipation. My breathing accelerates as his fingers find their way beneath the lace and start to rub slow circles around my clit.

Niccolo moves his hand in a figure-eight pattern, rotating his fingers ever so slightly as he glides up and down my slit. His movements are maddeningly slow, sending jolts of pleasure through every inch of me. With each stroke, I can feel all the tension melting away until I am nothing but a ball of desire for him.

"Tell me what the frat boys can do that I can't," he growls in my ear.

And I become a puddle of need that can barely make a sound, let alone answer his question.

Chapter 12
Niccolo

Nobody is looking at us; nobody cares who we are. They don't notice my hand moving beneath Christine's dress or her fingers digging into my arm wrapped around her waist. In a crowded college bar, we are all but invisible.

I toy with her clit through the fabric of her panties before dipping my fingers inside, strumming my thumb across her tight bud of pleasure until she bucks against my touch. "Tell me what the frat boys can do that I can't," I growl in her ear.

She moans in reply, her body rolling against mine in response to the stimuli. "They'll last all night," Christine says between gritted teeth, trying to hold back her moans of pleasure. "They're young, and they've got stamina."

As if. I was a college boy once. It takes a lot of fucking to get good at it and learn how to keep yourself from shooting your load in the first two minutes. "You want whiskey dick, little girl?" Her panties dampen as I zero in on her clit. "Because that's all these drunk boys are good for. They'll thrust all night because they can't get hard, and when they finally do, they can't get off."

Christine leans her head back, letting it rest on my shoulder. She tattoos half-moons into my arm with her nails, teeth gripping her bottom lip in sensuality. "Maybe I want to get fucked all night long," she moans, keeping up the charade that she'd rather be with some nineteen-year-old prick than me.

Frustration and jealousy erupt in my chest like a volcano, spewing their ugly emotions through every extremity. Christine's soft mews pull me back to reality, and I delight in her breathy moans. I want her to feel as frustrated as I am. I want her to know what it's like not to get what she wants. It's how I've felt every day since she turned eighteen.

Her body trembles with anticipation, and instead of letting her climax, I hold her on the edge of orgasm, slowing my strokes until her grip tightens with anger. "Niccolo!" Christine begs. "Please!"

"Just say the word, *dolcezza*. I'll fuck you from dusk 'til dawn. I'll fill your pussy with so much cum you'll be a walking, talking Twinkie." If I don't get any satisfaction, neither does she. Funny how that works.

"You're disgusting," she breathes, but her words are that of a woman angry that someone brought her tantalizingly close to finishing and then denied her orgasm.

"And it turns you on," I accuse before starting the slow, cruel movement of my thumb on her clit again, working it back and forth until she's panting with barely concealed desire. As I coax her closer to orgasm, I switch up the rhythm before she comes. "What else can these frat boys give you that you think I can't?"

Christine nearly screams in exasperation, but I begin to caress her once more. Her eyelids flutter shut as the sensations electrify her senses. "They uh," she groans, trying to think through a cloud of arousal, "they'll get me off." If she wants to keep up the façade that she'd rather have an inexperienced college boy than me, I'll play her game all day.

"They won't care about getting you off. They'll leave you on the edge, desperate for a man that knows how to lick your pussy and treat you right." They'll do exactly what I'm doing, but unintentionally. I can get Christine off with just a few flicks of my tongue if I want. Unfortunately for her, she isn't going to find out until she gets down on her knees and begs for it.

Christine tries to angle her hips and get more friction from my fingers, but I won't give her what she's looking for. Call it cruel, call it punishment, call it payback for running out of my classroom the other day. Christine deserves to be held on the edge until she's willing to beg, plead, and apologize for lying about not wanting me. We both know the truth and until she's ready to admit it, I'm going to make her suffer.

"I can do everything those frat boys can do, *dolcezza*." I force myself to strum her clit slower, bringing her down from the third apex she was about to reach. "And I can do it better. Just tell me you want me."

The song seamlessly transitions from one melody to another. Christine tightens her grip on my arm and shoves it away, driving my hand out from under her dress. As she turns to face me, her eyes burn with crazed lust and anger. "I don't want you, Niccolo," she spits vehemently.

The scent of her arousal conveys the opposite is true. I bring my fingers to my mouth and suck on them, licking her excitement off my fingers. "Keep telling yourself that, sweetheart. But eventually, you're going to realize that I'm the only man that can satisfy your desires."

"I'd rather fuck a hundred college boys than you," she hisses, putting another foot of space between us.

If she fucked a hundred college boys, I'd kill every one of them. I'd rip them limb from limb and set them on fire. I have never been my father's son, never wanted to commit a crime against someone to get what I want, but Christine drives me to my darkest self. She makes me embrace the Terlizzi traditions without remorse.

"If you fuck even one of those self-obsessed, douchey assholes, I'll make you regret it, Christine."

"Don't threaten me," she narrows her eyes and huffs.

"It's not a threat, *dolcezza*, it's a promise. I don't care about your past because *I'm* your future. I'm the only man you'll fuck from now on; I promise you that."

Chapter 13
Christine

I run from Niccolo, and when I make it back to Kaye, she's as ready to leave as I am. "The nerve of that man," she yells as she drags me out of the bar.

It takes me a couple of minutes to catch up, but I'm not the only one who received a visit from the ghost of step family past tonight.

"Xavier is a fucking stalker," she swears. "He had the audacity to show up at the same bar I was at and-and-and," Kaye stutters. She stomps her feet and lets out a little scream. "Chris, he fingered me on the dance floor, and I had an orgasm. There were a dozen people around," she exclaims, mortified.

Lucky bitch. The same thing happened to me, except I wasn't allowed to get off. "What a sick and disgusting man," I agree, loyal to a fault.

"That's what I'm saying!" Kaye flings her hands up in the air in exasperation. "To find me at the bars," she huffs. "And then to touch me like *that*. I don't even touch me like that."

For a minute, I forget about Niccolo and raise an eyebrow at my best friend. "You don't masturbate?" I've been in charge of my orgasms since I was fifteen and found out what an orgasm was. The most embarrassing moment of my life happened in a Spencer's gift store when I was trying to buy my first vibrator, and the guy at the counter asked how old I was. A line of people behind me listened to the cashier dress me down for trying to buy a sex toy when I was barely old enough to know what to do with it.

A blush kisses Kaye's cheeks, but it's hidden in the dark hues of twilight. "I, well, it's different," she blusters. "I-I touch myself, but it's never felt like that."

Color me shocked that Xavier McCade has magic hands. At least if he follows through with his threat to take Kaye's virginity, he'll make her feel good while he does it. "What happened to the vibrators we bought a few months ago when you turned eighteen?"

She covers her face with her hands and groans, shielding her embarrassment behind the hollow of her palms. "I feel so awkward when I use it. And I didn't bring it to college," she hisses.

I wrap my arm around her shoulder and pull her close. "It's okay. Some people are more shy about sex than others." I pat her on the back, comforting her.

"I'm sorry I ruined our night out," Kaye moans. "I was having a good time until Xave showed up."

She's not the only one. Until I found out that Niccolo was at Red Dawg, it was shaping up to be a perfect first weekend at college.

As we get back to the dorm, the halls are buzzing with energy despite the hour nearing midnight. The air smells of freshly popped, buttery popcorn and pizza. It's Friday night, and people are playing games, hanging out with their friends, and commiserating over the homework they've already been given. Everywhere I look, students gather in small groups, listening to music and laughing. This was where the party was at all along.

"I'm going to go to bed," Kaye announces when we make it to our room.

I'm still too worked up over what happened with my stepfather to go to sleep. I need to dispel some of this restless energy before I implode, and I know just how to do it. "I feel gross; I think I'll take a shower. I won't bother you when I come back in, right?"

With a yawn, she shakes her head and starts undressing. "I'm so tired that I'd probably sleep through a tornado at this point."

"That's what a good orgasm will do to you," I tease, elbowing her in the side.

Kaye tries and fails to keep from smiling. "I thought you were leaving."

I grab my shower caddy and the fluffy white towel hanging on the back of our dorm room door. "I am. Don't miss me too much." Then, I sneak out and head to the communal bathroom at the end of the hall.

For all the studious kids poring over dense textbooks and pounding energy drinks to stay awake, the bathroom is surprisingly empty. I grab one of the open shower stalls and undress, depositing the evening's clothes over the rail that holds up the shower curtain.

Hot showers usually help me relax, but they aren't doing the trick tonight. Despite the beads of water soothing the tension in my muscles, I still feel on edge. It takes me a few moments to realize why. Niccolo's skillful hands brought me to the brink of orgasm and then coaxed me off the ledge before I had a chance to jump. My body is overcharged, and I need the release my stepfather denied me.

I peek outside the curtain to make sure no one is around. If I do this quickly, no one has to know what happened in the shower stall.

I lean against the cool tile wall and let my fingers glide through my wet, waiting center. I trace a seductive path around my swollen vulva, pausing at each lip to rub the sensitive tissue, caressing it until I gasp with need. My breath quickens as I explore myself, eyes closing to indulge in my fantasies. Niccolo's face is displayed across the back of my eyelids, building up a powerful arousal within me. I remember his strong arms holding me tightly even though his touch was gentle and tender.

My body moves of its own accord, hips undulating in time with my thoughts as I'm brought closer to the edge of pleasure. I skim over my quivering flesh until I find my clit and use my middle finger to massage it gently, stroking harder and faster and then slower again in search of the perfect rhythm to bring me release.

I can still feel the anticipation he built up inside of me. The water from the shower invigorates my senses, working in time with my hands to erode the last of my willpower. My breathing grows heavy and urgent in time with my movements.

His face still swims in my head as an orgasm detonates without warning. A wave of satisfaction washes over me, coursing through my veins. With a small gasp of delight, I bite down on my knuckle to keep from crying out as I arch against the wall and allow the sensations to consume every inch of me.

It takes a few moments to catch my breath, to remember that I'm in a college dormitory bathroom, and at any moment, another student could walk in and catch me. I push off the wall and slip under the shower head, allowing the hot jets of water to cleanse me of my naughty thoughts.

This is it, I tell myself. *This is the last time I'll think of my stepfather when I get off.*

Chapter 14
Niccolo

Christine refuses to look at me during the next class and the half a dozen that follow. She studiously ignores my gaze for two weeks, making conversation with the girl beside her. Sometimes, she looks annoyed by her dark-haired seatmate. Other times, they laugh through discussion questions, and Sienna shoots curious glances my way as if she knows something that colors her judgment of me.

I'm no stranger to my stepdaughter's thriving social life. In high school, she dated football players and brainiacs. I took her to Friday night home games and Saturday afternoon math competitions. When Christine wasn't following a boy around, she was with Kaye or another of her little friends. I rarely saw her at the house because she had so much going on. It made parenting a teenager easier, which I appreciated because I had no idea what I was doing.

When class ends, and Christine finally acknowledges my presence after two weeks of silence, it's after most of the students have filtered out of the room. She lingers near her seat for a few minutes, pretending to tap away on her laptop while the last group of people meanders toward the door.

"Christine." I dip my head in her direction. "Can I help you with something?"

She purses her lips, putting her laptop away in earnest now. "I was wondering if you could take me back to Manhattan after classes are over today."

My heart palpitates with need. *Breathe*, I tell myself. *Don't sound too eager.* "Sure. What for?"

"My car is ready to be picked up," she announces excitedly. "The shop called yesterday to let me know the final part had come in and was being installed."

Her car may be ready, but I'm not. It was only a few weeks ago that I was sitting with her in the hospital after a car accident that never should have happened. "Are you sure it's a good idea for you to drive?" I ask, my face creasing with concern. "If you need to go somewhere, I can always take you."

Christine rolls her eyes in a single dismissive movement. "So if I want to go to McDonald's at 1:00 am, I should call you and wait a half hour for you to drive to Rosedale and pick me up?" Her voice carries a hint of exasperation; her words layered with sarcasm.

Fair point. However, the alternative is that she gets in her car, drives to McDonald's herself, and winds up in another accident. I'm willing to get up in the middle of the night to do her a small favor if it means she won't wind up dead. I remember how I felt when the police called me that night; I never want to feel that way again.

"You can always call me Christine. I'm available to you day or night." For once, I don't mean that sexually. I mean it in every conceivable way she might need me, whether it's a late-night food run or someone to pick her up from the library in the dead of winter because it's too cold for her to walk home.

The muscles around her eyes twitch as she folds her arms at her chest. "Yes, you've made it clear how *available* you are to me," Christine deadpans. "I'd prefer unfettered access to a car, though."

"I can be your personal chauffeur," I offer.

"Nic," she sighs.

"Chris."

Her hands fall to her side in frustration, slapping against her thighs in a loud gesture of annoyance. "I know why you're concerned, but you don't have to be. What happened in July was a freak accident."

She doesn't have to tell me about freak accidents. I was the one that got the call on July 4th. Between one neighbor setting off firecrackers and another throwing a party, I missed my phone ringing in another room three times. When I finally answered, the police officer said he'd been trying to get ahold of me for the last ten minutes. Then he told me what happened, and my heart felt like it imploded from fear.

"Freak accident or not, I'm concerned about your safety." Christine was heading home on an empty stretch of road on Independence Day when someone came out of nowhere and plowed into the passenger side of her car. What if Kaye had been with her? Or, God forbid, the person hit the driver's side instead?

Panic seizes my chest with its long, sinuous claws, wrapping them around my heart and squeezing. I have to stop thinking about the what ifs before I drive myself crazy.

"The more I think about it, the safer I think it'll be if you just let me drive you around," I decide.

Christine gets up and walks across the room, carving out a space for herself on the edge of my desk. She sits atop unread papers and printouts I haven't gotten around to looking at yet. "I get why you'd think that, but I can't rely on you forever," she says gently.

Lie #1. She could rely on me for the rest of our lives if she'd let herself. I would never hurt her; I would never let anyone else hurt her.

"I need my freedom, Nic. Part of that freedom involves getting my car back and being able to go wherever I want whenever I want."

Lie #2. She can still have her freedom while also being my passenger princess. I'm not kidding. If she says the word, I'll be on-call 24/7 for her chauffeuring needs.

"Besides, if I get a job, I'm going to need reliable transportation."

Lie #3. She doesn't need a job, and even if she got one, I'm reliable, and I can provide transportation. I don't see the problem.

"You don't need a job," I remind her. "There's a trust set up in your name. If you need money for classes or textbooks, I'm sure the trustee would sign off on it."

She replies in a monotone voice, "You're the trustee, Niccolo."

I give her a knowing wink. "And I'd sign off on it!"

Christine does not find my charming offer amusing. "Please," she begs, inserting more emotion into her tone, "or else I'll have to ask Kaye to take me to Manhattan, and she's got her own crap going on."

I'm tempted to stall and ask what's going on in her best friend's life, but I decide to save the question for the drive. "If I take you, if," I emphasize, "you have to promise me you'll never get into another accident again."

"Niccolo," she whines, "I can't promise that, and you know it."

It doesn't matter if she can promise or not; we both know I'd take her to the moon if she asked me to. "Fine," I resign, "I'll take you. My last class ends at 2:50. Think you can be here by 3:00?"

Christine hops off my desk with a smile that lights up the room. "I'd be here at 3:00 *am* if that's what it took."

If we're ever together at 3:00 am, it better be because I'm behind her thrusting, not because I'm behind the wheel of a car. Sex is the only good thing that happens after midnight.

Chapter 15
Christine

Six weeks ago, I saw my life flash before my eyes. It was a brief moment, but it felt like it lasted a lifetime. I watched all the forgotten moments of my life like a movie playing in slow motion—the moments that made me who I was.

I saw my mother's smiling face, remembered the way her eyes twinkled when she laughed, and how she hugged me before I went to bed just to make sure I felt safe and sound.

I saw the carnival my father took me to when I was seven. The smell of freshly popped popcorn, the sound of laughter and joyous screams, the sensation of my feet flying high on the Ferris wheel.

I remembered my first kiss, the feeling of pure happiness I felt when I got my first car, the way my heart pounded as I walked across the stage when I graduated high school—and every small moment in between, each one so precious and unique.

In a single moment, I saw it all pass before my eyes, and I felt a deep appreciation for all that I had experienced and for my life itself. When I woke up in the hospital, I felt lucky to be alive.

Kaye and I had gone to the Boomtown USA fireworks display in Wamego. Thousands of people all over Kansas attended the event each year. Getting there and finding a parking place was bad enough, but leaving was a nightmare. It took us an hour and a half to drive fifteen miles back to town; the traffic was unbearable.

After I dropped Kaye off at her place, I drove around town looking for something to do. Almost everyone had gone home, and the streets of Manhattan felt like my own personal playground. I cruised around corners and through back alleys, the wind whistling through the windows cracked for fresh air.

I have broken memories of the accident. I'd made it to the outskirts of town, where turning north would take me back to the hustle and bustle of Manhattan, and turning south would lead me into the countryside. As I tried to decide what to do, I approached a 4-way intersection, and a green light ushered me forward.

I never saw the car that t-boned me barreling down the road. Niccolo told me later that one of its headlights was out, and the driver was drunk. I only remember being in the middle of an intersection when glass started shattering all around me, and my head slammed against the driver's side window.

A witness said the car was going at least fifty miles per hour when it ran the red light. The driver was on his phone texting when he hit me on the passenger side. He emerged with cuts and bruises; they didn't even take him to the hospital before the police carted him off the jail. I, on the other hand, was not as lucky.

The impact of the collision threw me against the driver's side door, my head colliding with the glass and causing cracks to spiral outward. A sharp pain shot through my skull, and I could feel a warm trickle of blood drip down my neck. The twisted metal ridges of the car reached out to grab me while jagged shards of the windshield blanketed my lap. My car radio stopped, and I could hear the muffled screams of onlookers too far away to help.

My injuries weren't severe. I was properly restrained, and my airbags successfully deployed. But I still walked away with a grade 3 concussion, two black eyes, a broken finger, and half a dozen bruised ribs. I was in the hospital for two days—long enough for the doctors to make sure I didn't have brain damage and to bandage my injuries.

When I left the hospital, I was still in shock from the accident. It felt like a dream—the paper-thin stitches on my left temple, the dull ache in my hand from the broken finger, and the sensation of something being off in my brain. I couldn't focus on anything for more than a few seconds before getting distracted by a thought or feeling. I felt like a stranger in my own body.

Though my car wasn't a complete loss, it needed a lot of work. Niccolo recommended selling it for parts and using the money as a down payment for a new car, but I didn't like that idea. My Toyota Camry kept me alive on the scariest night of my life; it deserved the same loyalty from me.

But I'll admit, looking at it now, I'm scared to get back behind the wheel.

"You okay?" Niccolo asks gently. "If it's too soon—"

"No," I cut him off, staring at the metallic blue vehicle that saved my life. "They color matched well, didn't they?"

My stepfather reaches out to hold my hand. It's an intimate gesture but far from the sensual touches of our night at Red

Dawg. With a firm, reassuring grip, he reminds me why I stayed with him instead of moving to Kansas City with my uncles after my mother passed. "I can call one of my brothers if you want," he offers. "They can drive your car back home, and you can wait until morning to drive it back to campus. Or, if you don't feel ready, I can drive you back to campus tonight or tomorrow. Tell me what you need, Christine, and I'll do it."

I want to take him up on his offer. When we're in Manhattan, surrounded by people who know our history, Niccolo is an entirely different person. His warmth and kindness are infectious; they take root in my chest and make a home. But if I let him comfort me now, who knows when I'll summon the courage to get behind the wheel again?

"Thanks, Nic." I squeeze his hand in response, showing my appreciation for his sweet gesture. "But I have to do this for myself."

My fears are quite ordinary—spiders, roller coasters, and a paralyzing dread of failure. But I refuse to accept the idea that getting in an accident should add cars to that list. I am stronger than that.

As I take a step forward, Niccolo reluctantly releases my hand. "Call me when you get back to the dorm," he demands. "Let me know you're safe."

My pulse gallops as I climb inside my newly refurbished Camry. Everything feels the same, but I have to reprogram the radio. It was damaged in the crash and had to be replaced. When I turn it on, I skip through the frequencies until an Ariana Grande song comes on. She calms my nerves as I put the car into drive and inch out of the mechanic's shop.

In my rearview mirror, Niccolo stands watching me. The intensity of his gaze never wavers; he never looks away. He watches me until I'm out of sight, and I know we breathe a sigh of relief at the same time.

We've gone through the same tragedies. We've lost the same people. Our shared grief binds us like a steel chain, and I find solace in knowing that we've been through the same aches and pains.

We may be stepfather and stepdaughter, but our relationship goes deeper than that. Whatever people think we are to one another, it has always been *more*. And maybe I should consider that the next time he holds me tight and says we're meant to be.

Chapter 16
Christine

By the time I make it back to campus, my fear of driving has been forgotten. As it turns out, cars don't come barreling out of nowhere willy-nilly. People will cut you off and change lanes without signaling, but accidents like mine are not an everyday occurrence.

In the parking lot outside of Calvert Hall, I fire off a text to my stepfather to let him know I arrived safely.

> Made it back in one piece. Thanks for everything. 🩶

My phone pings before I'm out of the car.

NICCOLO
> Always, dolcezza.

It's hard to hate Niccolo sometimes. As I've gotten older, he's gotten more protective and possessive, but his actions come from a place of love.

See? You get it. The little voice in my head chirps. *Niccolo only wants to have sex with you because he loves you.*

My throat tightens as I swipe the text chain between Nic and me. I glide my thumb along the phone's screen, deleting our conversation in one gesture. "That's not what I should be thinking about," I mumble to myself.

The only way I'm going to get over how he made me feel the other night is by getting under someone else. I need to find a man who can replace all the delicious, gooey sensations Niccolo made me feel with new, delicious, gooey sensations.

I return to my room to search for Kaye, but she is nowhere to be found. She mentioned that she'd be going to Manhattan to speak with her stepfather about getting a job at his law firm, but I guess she hasn't returned yet.

My stomach growls. I don't know when Kaye will return, but I text her I'm going to the dining hall. I'm too hungry to stay here and wait around. I could make some cup noodles if I want, but real food is calling my name. I haven't been by myself since Kaye and I arrived, but there's a first time for everything. Maybe I'll make a new friend.

The sun has started to set, but the campus is still alive as I make my way to the dining hall. Students mill about in the after-hours, some alone and others in groups. Some sit on benches with headphones in, and textbooks splayed around them. Others lounge on the grass, laughing at inside jokes I'll never be in on. I take a deep breath and remind myself not to be intimidated. Even if I don't have any friends here yet, there's no reason I can't go out and make some.

I take a deep breath and step into the student union. It is bustling with people going in all directions. I try to blend in with the crowd as I push past the double doors leading to the dining hall.

It is a sprawling space full of tables and chairs chaotically arranged. To one side, there's a buffet line hosted by the cafeteria, offering a range of dishes from burgers to salads to pasta. On the other side, there's an array of fast food options for those with a few extra dollars.

I scan the room for familiar faces, but I don't see anyone I recognize from my classes or the dorm, not even Sienna. That isn't surprising, though; everyone has their own activities and friends they hang out with on campus. I feel slightly out of place but remind myself I'm attempting to make new friends.

"Hey, gorgeous," someone nudges me from behind. "I haven't seen you around before."

As I pivot to look at the stranger, I find myself gazing up at a man of towering stature. He is chiseled and muscular, every inch of his body rippling with strength, and he's handsome in the all-American male sort of way with a clean-cut face, well-groomed blonde hair, and blue eyes that make my stomach turn to mush. "H-hey," I stutter, confused by the intrusion, "do I know you?"

"You do now," he says with a grin. "Name's Theo."

"Christine."

He steps closer, and I'm met with the faint scent of freshly cut lawns and warm soil. "I think there's something wrong with my phone." Theo produces a black iPhone out of nowhere, swiping on the screen a few times before handing it to me. "It doesn't have your number in it."

I look down at the phone for a second before bursting into laughter. The audacity of this man to think I'd give my number to a stranger. "Does that line actually work for you?"

Theo snorts and lets the phone drop to his side. "Playing hard to get, I see."

"Playing hard to want, I see," I return, just as quick-witted.

The corners of Theo's eyes crinkle as the curve of his smile deepens. "You got a boyfriend?" Theo asks after a beat.

"No," I admit. "I just don't give my number out to strangers." I'm used to high school boys putting in weeks of effort to get close to me before mustering up the courage to ask me on a date. High school boys are shy and afraid of rejection; Theo is the opposite. He talks to me like he knows I will eventually give in to his charms.

"What do you want to know, Christine? I'm an open book. Ask me anything."

Admittedly, he's attractive. If he weren't, I'd have already walked away. But I don't like his arrogance or the way he assumes he's hot shit. It makes me want to take him down a peg. "How about you tell me something about yourself before I lose interest? You have about ten seconds before I ditch you for some egg rolls from Panda Express."

Theo knits his eyebrows together, and I can tell from the look on his face that he's judging whether I'm worth the trouble. I bet he's used to girls falling over themselves to go on a date with him. He probably isn't used to having to work for someone's attention. But his response takes me by surprise.

"I know you walked into the union from the west entrance. I was in the store across the way looking at shirts. I send one to my mom at the beginning of every year because she likes to wear it to my games. I'm a football player," he says, puffing his chest out with pride. "But I saw you walk by, and I had to follow you. I knew if I didn't, I'd regret it for the rest of my life."

Maybe he sees something in me, maybe not, but he makes me laugh. "The rest of your life?" I question, certain that he's blowing smoke up my ass. Theo is kind of corny, but he might be exactly what I'm looking for to forget Niccolo.

He holds up a hand in defense. "Swear to God. And I'm not the kind of man that lives with regrets, you know," Theo adds with a wink.

"Alright, mama's boy. Let's get dinner, and you can tell me more about your mom and football career." This might be a mistake, but it's one dinner in the student union. What could it hurt?

A lazy, indulgent smile appears on his face; he got exactly what he wanted. "Did I tell you I'm the BU quarterback?" Theo winks. "You're walking with royalty."

That explains the arrogance, but I'm in too deep now. At the very least, I'll have someone pretty to look at while I eat. "Have you considered deflating your head before you come inside? I'm surprised you can make it through the doors."

This could be the start of exactly what I need. I'm not looking for forever; I just want someone to get my mind off my stepfather. And self-obsessed, arrogant quarterback Theo might be precisely what the doctor ordered.

Chapter 17
Niccolo

It's been two weeks since I took Christine to Manhattan to retrieve her car. After our intimate moment at the mechanic's shop, I thought she would have mellowed out a bit and seen that I only want what's best for her. In retrospect, I'm not sure what made me think that. Christine has never been very willing to do what I want her to.

Instead, she's made a complete 180 from the moment we shared. It's as if getting her car back gave her license to be an even bigger brat. I wouldn't say she's deliberately trying to piss me off, but I wouldn't put it past her.

She comes into class three times a week and spends the hour chatting with her little buddy, Sienna. The two of them whisper behind their hands and giggle the hour away. Sometimes, Christine makes direct eye contact with me while she's interrupting the class. It makes me question whether her conduct is accidental or if she's trying to incite me to action.

To Sienna's credit, I don't think any of the interruptions are her fault. I did a little digging into her background and didn't find so much as a detention. She's a nice girl from Duluth, Minnesota, with a penchant for reading and a blue ribbon in quilting from the county fair three years ago. Sienna doesn't strike me as the type of person to make waves, which means all the interruptions are courtesy of my stepdaughter.

Since I can neither confirm nor deny that Christine's trying to piss me off on purpose, I bottle up my frustration until I'm ready to explode. At least once per hour, I have to snap my fingers at the two of them to redirect their attention. My minute outbursts come with snickers from the other students as they giggle and laugh at someone else getting into trouble. It often shuts Sienna up for a few minutes, but Christine is harder to control. Day by day, I get closer to my breaking point until a single whispered phrase takes me over the edge.

"Is he a good kisser?" Sienna asks.

"Yes," I explode in the middle of a sentence, spinning around to face the two of them like a feline ready to pounce on its prey. "Tell us, Ms. Lucatello. Who is he?" I demand loudly enough to wake the sleeping students in the back of the room. "And is he a good kisser? I think this is a more important discussion than the one we're having on brain abnormalities and personality disorders."

Christine's face is a mixture of emotions. Her cheeks are flushed pink with embarrassment, but her expression is one of anger. Her eyebrows furrow together, and her lips purse tight in disapproval, making her look even more stern. "Is there a problem, *Professor*?"

She's an audacious little thing and prone to outbursts the same as me, but I'm sick and tired of listening to her whisper and giggle through my class. "No problem at all. I just figured since your conversation is so fascinating that neither you nor Miss

Richler can pay attention, the rest of the class should weigh in. Believe me when I say we are all waiting on bated breath to find out who your mystery kisser is." I gesture toward the students behind her, which only causes the blush on her cheeks to deepen.

A tense moment passes before Christine gets to her feet, and I pin her with a glare. "Oh, no, Miss Lucatello, don't leave. In fact, please stay while I dismiss the rest of the class early." Nobody stirs. The students stare motionless, their faces blank with shock. There is no scuffling of feet, no shuffling of papers, not even a whisper or murmur. "Did you not hear me?" I look around, turning my anger on the rest of them. "You are all free to leave. Go to lunch early. Take a nap. Work on the paper that's due next week. I don't care. Just get out."

The sound of closing laptops and rustling papers is almost deafening in the quiet room. But slowly, the other students get up from their seats, whispering to each other about my shocking explosion. Christine stays standing by her chair, facing me.

"You're an ass, you know that?" She asks before everyone is gone. A few stragglers wait by the door, eyes wide as they listen in on our conversation. "You didn't have to embarrass me in front of the entire lecture hall. You could have tried to ask me politely to stop talking. Or you could have dismissed me. You didn't have to air my dirty laundry in front of everybody like that." The accusatory tone in her voice makes me homicidal.

I glare at the group of kids by the door, and they take it as a sign to scurry. They're gone within seconds, leaving Christine and me alone. "This is a classroom; it's a place of learning. Listening to you and that girl chatter about boys the entire hour is a waste of your time and mine."

"You're just jealous."

"Jealous of what?" I roll my eyes and curl my upper lip as I fling my arms across my chest. My mouth is contorted with apathy and defiance, my gaze hard and challenging as I watch her for a reaction.

Christine narrows her eyes at me and steps forward, dropping her bag on the ground with an audible thud. "You're jealous that instead of letting *you* fuck me, I'm getting real close and personal with the BU quarterback, and I'm going to let *him* fuck me instead."

I succumb to blind rage. It jolts me forward, and I'm ready to hurt her as badly as she hurt me, but she raises a hand at the last minute, stopping me in my tracks.

"Not so fast, Nic." Christine reaches into her back pocket and pulls out a cell phone. A few quick swipes on the screen, and she's pointing it at me. "You better be careful. Whatever you plan to do, I'm recording. I'm not letting you manhandle me anymore. I'll go to HR," she threatens.

I make a split-second decision to say fuck it. Fuck the stupid camera on her phone taking a video of this interaction. And fuck her threat to go to Human Resources. At the end of the day, she is my stepdaughter, and I can do whatever I want to her.

Chapter 18
Christine

When I threaten to report Niccolo to Human Resources, something inside him snaps like a twig. The air thickens with anticipation as he rolls up his sleeves and gestures toward the phone. The video captures him drawing closer to me, his eyes narrowing in a way that makes my stomach churn. "Give it to me," he orders.

"No," I protest, taking a step back. "If there isn't a camera on you, who knows what you'll do?"

I can think of a dozen filthy things he'd do to me if no one were watching.

His frustration reaches its boiling point, and I see where he crosses over from giving a damn to saying fuck it. Niccolo takes three large, quick strides toward me unexpectedly. When he grabs my wrist, I'm afraid he's going to hurt me. "I'll keep recording," he says sarcastically as he rips the phone out of my hand.

I know I should scream for help. There are people milling about in the hallway. If they heard me, they'd be forced to stop and see what's going on. But sound dies in the back of my throat as Niccolo drags me to his desk. A part of me wants to fight him off, but something else takes over my body, telling me that fighting him will only make things worse.

"You want a video so bad, might as well make it a good one." He shoves me over the front of his desk before struggling with my shorts. The edge digs into my stomach, an irritating sensation that becomes a pleasurable ache as I realize what he's doing. Though Niccolo isn't very dexterous with one hand, he bares my bottom after a few long, exaggerated seconds.

He positions me just so: arched back, bare bottom on display for him like a dessert platter. A cool breeze whips through an open window in the back of the room, causing goosebumps to dimple my exposed skin.

Before I can comprehend what's happening, he lands a stinging slap on my left cheek that echoes in the quiet room like a thunderclap. The pain flares up momentarily before being drowned in a sea of pleasure that leaves me gasping for breath. Niccolo's hand is warm where it lingers on my skin, branding me with his commanding touch.

"I think you get a perverse pleasure out of being a brat." Niccolo senses my arousal, his dark eyes gleaming with implacable intent and unmistakable lust. His fingers trail across the pert fullness of my ass, dipping briefly into the tempting valley between my legs. "I think you *want* me to spank you. I think you *like* it, Christine."

I counsel myself not to respond, knowing that's what he wants from me. He wants me to argue and give him a reason to keep going. His hand lingers on my skin as the heat fades away, replaced by the familiar pleasure of his touch. The brush of his fingers stirs feelings in my chest I have never felt before, and I gasp under their intensity.

"For someone with so much to say during class, you sure are quiet now. Cat got your tongue?" He asks after a few moments. Again, I don't respond, but it only emboldens him.

Niccolo spanks me again. The sound of flesh meeting flesh echoes in the room, a primal crack that strips me down to my base desires. His touch changes, no longer brusque or punishing but sexually teasing. The contrast between the hard spanking and gentle caresses creates exquisite friction that torments and brings me closer to the brink of sweet release. I arch my back in search of more, in search of escape, in search of something I can't quite put my finger on. My moans mingle with the sounds of his skin hitting mine, creating a rhythm that excites us both.

The tension in the room grows palpable, amplified by our heavy breathing and the soft rustling of clothes as Niccolo adjusts his stance. His arousal is visible beneath his pants, straining against the fabric as he takes in the sight of me exposed and vulnerable on his desk.

His rhythmic tempo is a fusion of suffering and sensuality that escalates with each stroke. My body throbs with need as I dance on the tip of my toes, desperate to evade each swat while conversely wanting him to spank me harder. He ignites a heat inside me that makes me moan with barely concealed desire.

I'm deeply aware of the red glow spreading across my bottom under his palm, caught on camera for me to watch later. A million sensations invade my senses as my breath grows ragged.

I reach out to grab the edge of the desk, fingers curling to grip the other side as I ride out a unique blend of aching satisfaction. His firm hand guides me to the height of my desire, leaving me trembling with anticipation. Tension coils tightly around us, a sensual dance that veers on the edge of insanity.

The slaps slowly become playful yet still leave their mark. His movements are measured and precise like he knows just how much of him I need to give in. His roughness is like a drug, and it feels obscene to let him have me like this.

When he finishes, it takes a few moments before I notice. Niccolo strokes my skin, grabbing and squeezing my tender bottom to feel the heat of his discipline radiating back at him. When I look over my shoulder, his eyes are dark with lust and desire, as deep and devious as my own.

"Good girl," he growls.

I'm mortified, ashamed, embarrassed to my core, and still, I know my center is wet. As I move to stand, Niccolo steps back, the camera continuing to record my every movement.

"You want to take this to HR? Go right ahead. But your wet little pussy is damning evidence. When you show them this video, they're going to hear you moaning and see you shoving your ass back at me, wanting more."

He tosses the phone back to me, and I barely catch it as I'm trying to pull my shorts up. "If you want to play hot and cold with me, that's fine. But don't bring that shit into my classroom, Christine. If you walk through my door again, you better respect me when you take your seat. Otherwise, I'll repeat this performance every day until you do. Do you understand?"

I fumble with my shorts and phone until the former are pulled up, and the latter is shoved in my back pocket. My bottom blushes crimson, throbbing from our actions, and I bow my head in subservience. "Yes," I mumble.

Niccolo steps forward to grab my chin, forcing me to look at him. Our eyes meet, and I see something forbidden staring back at me. "Yes, what?"

"Yes, sir."

"That's my good little girl."

Chapter 19
Niccolo

Admittedly, there is something primal about my desire to spank my stepdaughter. I don't know what Christine does when she leaves the classroom, but I lock the door and go to the back corner of the lecture hall where no one can see me.

My heart races with anticipation as I unbuckle my belt and pull out my growing erection. I've been hard since the second I saw my stepdaughter's bare bottom. I've fantasized about a moment like this since I gave her a few swats on prom night for acting like a brat. God, how I've wanted to take her over my knee and watch her squirm on my lap while I turn her ass a beautiful shade of maroon. But today, I finally got to live out my fantasies and capture them in HD. Too bad I don't have a copy of the video.

I spit on my hand, using it to lube up my thick, unyielding eight inches. A droplet of pre-cum trembles on my tip, providing a warm lubricant that allows me to glide effortlessly up and down the hard length of my shaft as I think about what transpired between Christine and me.

Her curvy silhouette splayed invitingly across the expanse of my desk. Her creamy white skin beneath my hands, flushed with arousal and soft as velveteen against my rough palms. Her plump bottom lifting towards me, the sweet pink bud nestled between her cheeks quivering each time my palm made contact with her ass. Her muffled moans each time my hand landed on her skin, leaving a pink mark in its wake.

The memory of her writhing in uninhibited ecstasy and pain, every inch of her exposed and offered up without reservation, acts like fuel to the fire already raging within me. My breath hitches as my thoughts turn to the humiliation she must have felt from the powerless position she was in. Every stroke of my cock electrifies my senses as I commit to memory the sound of her moans when she sucked her lower lip to keep from crying out.

I focus on our forbidden moment, vivid images filling my head as sensation after sensation floods my hippocampus. I recall the shades of fear and desire in her eyes when she looked at me, vulnerable yet aroused, excited by what was happening even though she knew it was wrong. It's our taboo game of house where daddy punishes his little girl for doing something bad before he makes it all feel better by burying his cock inside of her until she screams.

It doesn't take long for pleasure to mount—raw and unabashed. Fast, shallow breaths come quicker than I want them to. In the quiet room, with just my memories and hands to keep me entertained, I feel myself rushing toward climax. I want to hold off, make it last longer, but a clenching sensation radiates from deep within me, and I know I can't hold out any longer.

I grip myself tighter, each downward stroke pulling another groan from my lips until I explode with a wave of ecstasy that obliterates all thought. I shoot my load at the back of the chair in front of me, coating its enamel in my milky white seed.

God, I should have let Christine's uncles take her after Caterina's death. If I had, I wouldn't have spent another three years watching her grow into a beautiful, strong-willed woman. I wouldn't have fallen for her in the quiet moments of our togetherness. I wouldn't have her in my Psychology 101 class, taunting me with knowing looks and teasing winks. And I wouldn't have to clean my jizz off the seat with some wet wipes before the next hour of students arrive.

But who am I kidding? My grip on Christine was as unyielding back then as it is now. She may not understand the depths of my feelings for her, but there is no denying that I will never give her up. There is no escaping me.

Christine Lucatello is mine.

She is my stepdaughter.

She is my sweetest little girl.

She is my future wife.

Chapter 20
Christine

If I had a dollar for every time Niccolo Terlizzi pissed me off, I'd be a millionaire. I could buy him out of the house that he torments me in and put his ass on the street where he couldn't get to me. He'd regret ever agreeing to marry my mother all those years ago. He'd rue the day he told my uncles he was keeping me in Manhattan instead of sending me with them to start my life over in Kansas City.

Niccolo disgusts me with his actions and words. Yet, there is an undeniable pull towards him I can't seem to resist. A constant battle between my repulsion and the intense longing he ignites within me. How can I stay away from someone who simultaneously repels and entices me?

I regret pulling my phone out to film him as if a camera would change his behavior. He took my idea and twisted it into something perverse. I wanted to use the phone as a shield against his actions, but he turned it around and made it into something dirty.

And I rewatch the video we made every day when I'm alone.

It's a poorly shot soft-core porno. The camera shakes, and the quality leaves much to be desired. But it doesn't need to be in 4K for me to see my alabaster skin turn a deep shade of red under his touch. Even with his hands shaking, the arch of my back in pleasure is noticeable. Anyone who watches this video would see a woman enjoying herself instead of a woman under duress. I can't show it to Human Resources; I can't show it to anyone.

The worst part is how much rewatching the video turns me on, and I can only do it when Kaye is gone. When she's in one of her many classes or going to Manhattan to work at her stepfather's law firm, I hole up in my dorm and let the video play.

Shame and humiliation wash over me with every second of the video I consume. I can't see Niccolo's stern gaze, but I can hear the taunting in his tone. I play the forbidden moment we shared on loop until involuntary sighs escape my lips, and I have to bury myself under the blanket to hide my debasement from the world. Then my hand sneaks between my thighs and dips under the hem of my shorts, and my self-degradation continues.

The incriminating video flickers across my phone screen while I drag my fingers through my slit, growing hot with anticipation. My breath quickens, and my legs tremble as I stroke myself faster and faster, desperate for the pleasure that comes from fantasizing that I'm back in Niccolo's office. The rhythm is instinctual—faster, then slow, deep, then shallow—an erotic symphony conducted by my filthy desires. I can't recreate how I felt after my stepfather spanked me, but I repeat this shameful ritual every day.

Then I have to go to class three times a week and see Niccolo's smug face, smiling, begging for me to disrespect him again. He wants me to give him another opportunity to upend me over his desk and do what he wants to me. He walks around the room with a superior air that makes me want to get out of my seat and smack the grin off his face. Niccolo takes great satisfaction from watching me squirm under his gaze. Every movement, every action, is a reminder that he knows how I felt after he released me that day. And I hate him for it.

Sienna, whom I've come around to befriending, waits for me after class one day to ask if everything is okay. "You've been off lately," she says with a shrug. "You pregnant or something? Dealing drugs? Do I need to get you into rehab?" She's just as wild as the first day I met her.

But I can't admit what happened between Niccolo and me. I can't admit the truth for fear of judgment. So, I tell her a version of the truth amenable to an average person's conscience.

"After class the other day, Niccolo chastised me for being disruptive. He said if I did it again, he'd kick me off the roster and make me start over next semester." It's a lie, but it does the trick. She believes me without question, then swears she'll never talk to me again.

"During class hours, of course," she amends with a grin. "I'm sorry I got you in trouble. I didn't realize he was such a hard ass. No offense," Sienna quickly adds, remembering he's my stepfather.

"None taken," I reassure her. I've called Niccolo much worse. "It's not your fault that he's crazy. Kaye and I call him

Professor Asshole for a reason. Ever since he started at Blackmore, he's been acting like a dick."

We have to go our separate ways when we leave Brewer Hall, but Sienna gives me a sympathetic half-hug before she parts. "I'm sorry you have to deal with that."

I give her a half-hearted shrug before pulling away. She might be a hugger, but I'm not.

"It's not a big deal. He's a jerk, but he's bearable. Hey," I change the subject mid-conversation, "I know Halloween is coming up in a few days. Would you be interested in coming out with Kaye and me?"

Sienna and Kaye briefly met in the dining hall a few weeks ago. They had a quick chat, but my best friend was between classes, and Sienna was meeting up with a study group. It was a five-minute conversation before they headed in opposite directions. The two have wildly different personalities but seem to like each other well enough.

"Sure! That'd be great. Are we dressing up or…?" Sienna trails off, leaving it up to me to decide.

I purse my lips in thought. Kaye and I talked about doing a couple's costume, going as salt and pepper, but I wouldn't want Sienna to feel left out. "Can I get back to you? I'll look up trio costumes tonight."

Sienna's eyebrow raises, suddenly self-conscious of what she agreed to. "What did I sign up for?" She jokingly asks.

"Probably the best night of your life. It'll be fun, I swear."

Ideas are already flowing. We could go as the trio from Clueless. Or the Power Puff Girls. Maybe the Hocus Pocus witches. The sky is the limit. This will give me something else to think about than that forsaken video on my phone.

Chapter 21
Christine

For Halloween, our trio costume is a tequila shot. Sienna volunteers to be the lime, and Kaye dresses up as the salt, leaving me to be a bottle of Jose Cuervo.

"I definitely couldn't pull that off," Kaye announces when she sees my shimmery gold dress. "Every eye is going to be on you, and that's too much pressure for me."

Kaye wears a little white dress that's simple but stunning, accentuating her curves in all the right places. Tiny, metallic strands of fabric catch the light and make her shimmer like a star. The neckline is cut into a delicate V-shape that frames her collarbone, and the short hemline adds a playful element. She is the salt to our tequila and lime, and the dress contrasts beautifully with her dark features.

"I don't know why you think no one will notice you, babe. You're a fucking catch." I hate that Kaye doesn't realize how gorgeous she is. She may not have the same bold personality as Sienna or me, but she has a quiet confidence that draws people in.

She blushes prettily under the heavy layer of makeup I applied earlier. "Thanks, but no one is going to be looking at me when you're around."

I'm about to tell her to knock it off when a sharp rap on the dorm room door indicates Sienna's arrival. "Come in!" Kaye yells, eager to change the subject.

Sienna steps through the door, looking just as hot as Kaye. She wears a short skirt and an artfully arranged top in lime green. With her hair pulled back into a sleek ponytail, her jawline and cheekbones make her look like a Greek goddess. "Oh, my god," Sienna shuts the door behind her, "this was such a good idea."

"You're telling me." If I could reach, I would pat myself on the back for a job well done. "Ladies, we are single, we are hot, and we're gonna get laid tonight."

"Not me," Kaye frowns. "I'm just hoping *he* doesn't show up." *'He'* only has one meaning between Kaye and me: her stepbrother, Xavier—Mister Tall, Dark, and Deranged.

Sienna doesn't know the whole situation, but I've warned her that if a really good-looking, muscular, tattooed God starts coming toward us, run the other way. "I think you could still make out with some strangers," she offers, oblivious to what Xavier McCade will do if he finds out that his virginal stepsister is kissing other guys.

"Strangers? Like, multiple people?" Kaye's eyes nearly pop out of her head.

Sienna giggles. "Yes, multiple people. A few make-out sessions won't kill you."

"Xavier might," I mumble under my breath.

My best friend points at me. "Yes, there, that," she agrees. "And if he doesn't kill me, then he'll probably kill whoever I make out with. I'm not ready for someone else's death on my conscience."

If I'd informed Sienna of the whole situation, she might have chosen something else to say. Instead, she shrugs and asks, "Who's going to tell him?"

Kaye and I exchange a look because we both know that no one has to *tell* Xavier anything. He finds out whatever he needs to know, with or without help. It's his superpower.

While Kaye and Sienna discuss the merits of going home with strangers from the bar, I open up Snapchat and take a photo of myself in the mirror hanging on the back of our dorm room door.

I study it briefly before deeming it appropriate to send, but that's where I get hung up. I could send the picture to my story and call it a day. The thirsty boys would roll in with compliments, asking if I'm free tonight and giving me the attention I'm looking for.

But then my finger hovers over Niccolo's name—seven little letters and a skull emoji. The little voice in my head is screaming at me to keep scrolling, but my heart races as I add him to the list. I hit *'send'* before I can chicken out, publishing the snap to my story and sending it to my stepfather simultaneously. Then I pocket my phone before I can deal with the repercussions.

"You guys ready to go?" My voice sounds bright. I'm buzzing with excitement and fear, my pulse skittering with nervous energy. What will Niccolo say? What will he do? Do I even care?

Kaye grabs a cardigan and pulls it around her shoulders before announcing she's ready to go. I give her a frown for covering up the costume I worked so hard to design—a white dress with a painstakingly sewed-on letter 'S'—and she explains. "It's literally freezing outside, Chris. You should get a jacket, too. It snowed last night."

The dreaded Halloween snow; it's all anyone has been talking about for the last week. I had hoped that the forecast was wrong and we'd avoid an early snowfall, but the weather reporters got it right for once. "I'm good," I decide. But the minute we step outside, an autumn breeze chills me to the core. Goosebumps crop up on my skin as I pretend to be unaffected by the cold.

Even Sienna, who swears Kansas weather is nothing compared to growing up in Minnesota, pulls a sweater tight around her chest. "We can stop by my dorm if you need a jacket," she offers as we make our way down Prairie Avenue.

I shake my head no. In a few minutes, we'll be at the bars, and they'll be shedding the extra layer they brought for the walk. "I'll be warm once we get some drinks." We might be underage, but a pretty girl can get whatever she wants if she's willing to flirt for it.

My phone buzzes in my pocket, and I pull it out to distract me from the cold. My fingers slowly swipe over the screen, too numb to work with any haste. A response from the snap I sent to Niccolo is waiting in my inbox, and I pull it up with a frisson of nervous energy developing in my stomach.

NICCOLO

Take it off your story.

A command. I knew I shouldn't have sent the picture to him. I type as fast as I can, but my fingers move like they're weighted down by bricks.

> Don't tell me what to do. I can put whatever I want on my story.

He's much quicker than I am. I barely have time to swipe out of the chat and return to my Home Screen before a notification bubble pops up that he's responded.

> NICCOLO
> Take it down, dolcezza. That picture is begging for trouble.

"I'll beg for whatever the hell I want," I mumble under my breath. This garners Kaye and Sienna's attention.

"What's going on?" Sienna asks after a few awkward moments of silence.

I exit the chat with Niccolo and turn off the screen. "Nic wants me to take down the picture I shared on my Snapchat story," I reply sulkily.

Both Kaye and Sienna pull out their phones and race to the app. They share a low whistle when they see the picture I shared. "You're hot," Kaye says with a grin.

"An absolute smoke show," Sienna concurs.

"That's what I thought." Their responses are exactly what I wanted to elicit from the men I'm friends with. What I didn't need was my overbearing stepfather to tell me I'm too sexy for social media.

"Forget Niccolo," Sienna decides for me. "It's your body. You can show it off all you want. Hell, you can get naked on Snap Story if it tickles your pickle. It's none of his business."

"Yeah!" She isn't wrong. I can do whatever I want whenever I want to. "I'm going to tell him that." I've told him before, but maybe he needs a refresher.

Kaye clears her throat and asks if that's a good idea. It's like she's the angel on my shoulder compared to Sienna's devil. But it's too late. I'm already back in our chat and typing out a message.

> It's my body. I can do whatever I want with it.

NICCOLO
> For now.

A shiver runs down my spine, and I can't tell if it's the cold autumn air or an unsettling sense of foreboding that makes me shake.

> What do you mean?

I wait a few moments for his Bitmoji to appear in the chat, indicating that he's responding.

> NICCOLO
>
> Someday soon, I'm going to claim you, dolcezza, all of you. And after that happens, you better not share your half-naked body with anyone but me. Or else.

Bravery takes many forms, but my response is less courageous and more provocative.

> Or else, what?

> NICCOLO
>
> Or else a dead body is going to show up on your doorstep.

I almost drop my phone.

I never should have asked.

I know who his family is; I know who they're connected to. His threat isn't idle just because he chose a kinder career path than the other Terlizzis.

"I need a drink. Now," I tell the girls, my voice sounding as shaky as I feel. I need to forget what I just read.

Chapter 22
Niccolo

"Why so glum, chum?" Salvatore contorts his lips into an exaggerated pout. "Sad your little *bambina* didn't join us for Thanksgiving?"

"I swear to God, Sal, I'll kill you," I deadpan. This is a man that's been on the other end of my threats before. When we were little, it was an everyday occurrence for one brother to chase another down with a golf club and threaten to bash their skull in. Our father never got involved; he said it built character.

Salvatore reaches out to clap me on the shoulder. "Want me to get you some tea, and we can chat about it over an episode of Dr. Phil?"

An unwelcome smile splits my face in two. "Mark my words. One of these days, you're going to get shot for being an asshole."

"As long as I don't get shot *in* the asshole," he grins.

I want to shake off my bad mood, but even with Salvatore's light-hearted humor, a dark cloud hangs overhead. "Don't ever fall in love, brother. She will spurn your invitations and break your heart."

Salvatore lets out a derisive snort and rolls his eyes. He leans back in his chair, nonchalantly propping his feet up on the table, a clear sign of his cocky attitude. "You're not in love, Nic."

"Come again?" I ask with a frown, taken aback by his statement. "You're telling me how I feel?"

My brother looks at me with a weary expression, his head shaking slowly from side to side. "Now, now, Nic, don't get angry with me," he says, raising his hands in a gesture of peace. His body language is defensive in anticipation of my reaction. "I'm just telling you how I see it. You have feelings born out of forced proximity with this girl. You don't love her. It's like Stockholm Syndrome but with someone you agreed to live with. Does that have a name, Professor Big Brain?"

Salvatore has not been punched in the head for having a smart mouth nearly as much as he deserves it. "Don't be philosophical, Sally. It's unbecoming of your intellectual status."

"You calling me stupid?" He asks with a raised eyebrow. "Because if you wanna fight, just say so. I'll kick your ass, Nicci."

I don't know how we got to this stage, but I'm exhausted. I hold up a hand in cease-fire resignation. Salvatore and I have never been at loggerheads before. I've fought with Dante for being the oldest and raged at Luciano for being the youngest and getting treated the best, but Salvatore and I have always been friends. We were the middle children who got used to not being the family heir or the baby.

"Seriously though," I meet his gaze. "What do you mean that I'm not in love?"

He surrenders his anger as quickly as I do. "Love should be easy," Salvatore shrugs. "You and Caterina were in love. You and Christine just want to hump each other's brains out."

"You're wrong." I look around for the bottle of beer I was nursing earlier, but it's tipped on its side on the end table beside me, bragging in its emptiness. "I didn't love Caterina."

Salvatore clucks his tongue in disapproval. "I disagree." He leans forward, placing his elbows on his knees. "You two met and married without so much as an argument. You had a happy enough marriage. You tried to have kids, you took care of her when she was sick, and you were a faithful man when other men in your situation wouldn't have been."

"I think that's called doing the bare minimum," I correct my brother. "We met and married without argument because she was an agreeable woman. Our fathers had already settled on the price; we just had to do our part." My dad told me that if I didn't go into the family business, the least I could do was strengthen the family by marrying a woman of his choice. I didn't expect the woman to come with a premade family, but what was I going to do? I couldn't say no just because she was an older woman with a child from a previous marriage.

"Yeah, but you could have hated her. Dante hated Adalina. The two of them fought like cats and dogs," Salvatore points out.

Our oldest brother is a case unto his own. "I don't think that's a fair comparison. Dante and Adalina had a complicated history. Caterina and I had seen one another in passing, but besides knowing the other's name, we were complete strangers." If Dante had married a stranger, maybe he'd be a happier man.

"Not to mention father harangued me every month Caterina didn't get pregnant." I don't bother to mention that Dante didn't receive the same treatment. I'm resentful of the way Father handled me because he saw me as an outsider. I didn't grow up wanting to be a cog in the Castiglione family machine, and it burned him inside.

Salvatore offers me a sympathetic look. He witnessed a number of arguments between Fausto Terlizzi and me over my wife's infertility. I'll never forget the day that I told Fausto my wife had stage IV cancer and would most likely die within the year. He looked me dead in the eyes and said, 'Good. Maybe the next one will give you a son.' As if Caterina's life was useless because she couldn't bear my children.

"But you never fucked around on her." Salvatore derails my train of thought. "You were faithful to Cat. Even when she was on her deathbed and looking at her final days, you didn't find a mistress or ask Father to start looking for a second wife. You took care of Caterina until she was in the ground."

My brother's characterization of me is humbling. I don't remember being the man that he says I was. I know that I faithfully waited for my wife to pass, but it wasn't out of any loyalty to her or our union. I took care of Caterina in her final days because it was expected of me.

Christine was in the house, watching her mother die, and she needed someone to be strong for her. She needed someone to take care of her mother while she was in school all day. She needed someone to sign permission slips and listen to her boy drama because she was only a teenager. Christine wasn't old enough to do all the things I did for Caterina, so I did them for her.

"I've loved her for years," I mumble, a frown furrowing my brow.

Salvatore looks around as if searching for the person I'm speaking to. "What are you going on about?"

"Christine."

He throws his hands up in defeat before sinking back into the couch. "This again," he complains.

This again, indeed. "I've loved Christine for years, Sal. You said that love is supposed to be easy, and it was. I wasn't *in* love with her when she was fifteen," I explain, "but everything I did for her and Caterina in those last few months was because I loved her." The kind of love that grew and transformed with time.

"Okay. So maybe you love the girl," Salvatore allows. "But you're not *in* love with her."

I shake my head in disagreement as soon as the words are out of his mouth. "No. You're wrong. I wasn't in love with her back then, but I am now. That's why her spurning my invitation to spend Thanksgiving with the family hurts. Because I *am* in love with her."

Salvatore sighs in disgust. "You're hopeless, you know that? Just give the girl up, Nic."

"I can't," I tell him. "I don't even wish I could."

Maybe my brother is right. Maybe the only reason I fell for

Christine is because we lived together for the last five years. But I don't care how it happened; I'm just thankful it did.

Christine is my soulmate. And it took an arranged marriage to her mother, the passing of my wife, and three more years of forced proximity to realize it.

Chapter 23
Christine

Between an endless stream of invitations to Terlizzi Thanksgiving festivities and my uncles trying to convince me to come to Kansas City, I'm burned out on family gatherings.

I'm also tired of studying for finals, which are approaching so fast that I nearly forget what I spent the first half of the semester learning.

The Psychology book I borrowed from Niccolo's library remains open on my bed with highlighted sections and notes in the margins. Bright yellow tabs crease and mark the pages, reminding me of something I found important earlier in the semester. I squint my eyes to make sense of my hurried scribbles, but my brain is too drained to comprehend them.

"I'm headed out," Kaye announces as she tosses a bag over her shoulder.

I look up from my scattered notes, the corners of my mind still foggy from hours of intense studying. Blinking, I try to reorient myself to the present moment and my surroundings. My confusion only deepens as I take in her appearance—fully dressed and ready to go while I'm still in my pajamas. "You're going somewhere?"

"To my mom's," she says, as if reminding me of something she told me before.

"I thought we were going to the foam party at Red Dawg tonight." It's absurd to think she can't do both, but it's the first thing that pops into my head. I've been having a rough go of things lately, and I need tonight to carry me through the rest of the holiday season.

Kaye gives me a wan smile. "We will," she says hesitantly, "but it's been a few weeks since Mom asked Malcolm to move out." I realize with a pang of guilt that I've been so consumed by my problems that I'd forgotten about hers.

"She said she was feeling lonely and wanted some company," Kaye continues. "I'm sure if I asked, you could come, too!"

Going to Carrie's doesn't sound particularly exciting, but I can't bear another minute of reading these dry textbooks. My vision is blurring, and my brain feels like it's on the verge of shutting down from information overload. "I'm in. You think she'll make those snickerdoodle cookies I like so much?"

My best friend rolls her eyes before offering me a knowing look. I've been complaining about forced family time for the last week, but I conveniently don't mind seeing her family. "Do you want to admit that it isn't *family* you want to avoid?" Kaye asks with a raised eyebrow.

I've been dropping hints here and there about what's been going on between stepfather and me, almost as many hints as she's been dropping about her and Xavier. But when she pulls on her know-it-all tone, I turn away and pretend I have no idea what she means. "I don't know what you're talking about," I respond with an air of superiority.

She snorts in derision before coaxing me to tell her more. "Come on, Chris. Just admit that you're trying to avoid Nic. No one is going to hold it against you."

My breathing is the only thing that echoes off the walls, punctuating the tense silence that envelopes us. I force myself to turn back around, but my face is a twisted mask of frustration and despair. The weight of defeat hangs heavy in the air between us. "It's complicated, Kaye."

The teasing, the spanking, the touching myself when no one's around—I'm a mess of complications of my own making. "It's like all the sex dreams you're having about Xavier," I remind her that her life is just as strange and deranged as my own. "Except it's my reality."

Kaye's face remains passive momentarily before her lips curve into a frown. "Are you having sex with Niccolo?"

There's a hint of judgment in her tone. I don't know if it's intentional or subconscious. Either way, when I tell her no, it's the truth. He might have bared my backside in front of him and let his fingers slip into places they didn't belong, but there has been absolutely zero sex to be had. And to tell the truth, it's making me cranky. "Are you having sex with Xavier?" I shoot back at her, trying to change the subject.

A soft blush creeps up her cheeks, a deep shade of pink that hints at her embarrassment. She lowers her gaze before shyly admitting that she is, at least in her dreams.

I didn't see that coming. My jaw falls open, and it takes me a moment to regain my wits. "I'm not doing *that* with Nic." Just seconds ago, I thought she was judging me for potentially sleeping with my stepfather. Now, here I am doing the same thing to her over her sex dreams about her stepbrother. We're quite the pair.

Kaye interprets my silence as an admission of guilt. "But you're doing *other* things," she insinuates.

And I realize immediately that the frustration I've been feeling is all this bottled-up resentment at not having someone to talk to about everything that's been happening. I've been keeping all these emotions pent up, hiding secrets from Kaye that I should have confided in her weeks ago. We're best friends, and instead, I treated her like an outsider. Of all the people I could have trusted with my indiscretions, Kaye is the only one I know who never would have judged me.

Overwhelmed by my feelings, I instinctively cover my face with my hands and fling myself backward onto the soft mattress. My body shakes as I try to contain the flood of feelings welling up inside me. "You can't tell anyone, Kaye." I am overcome by a surge of emotions as I recount to her all that has happened in the past few weeks.

"This is disrespectful to my mother, not to mention the rest of the family. You have no idea what the Terlizzis are going to do when they find out. Or, God forbid, my uncles." Giovanni will tear Niccolo apart piece by bloody piece. And then, when my stepfather is dead, he'll inflict even worse agony on me.

As if sensing my distress, Kaye diverts the conversation. She hastily retrieves her phone and dials her mother's number. They chat for a few moments about my attendance while I wallow in self-pity until Kaye mentions something about me going through her closet. It perks me right up because I love a good makeover.

Kaye's fashion sense has always been lacking. Her clothing choices are a chaotic mix of floral dresses and high-necked shirts that favor conservatism over comfort. I push aside the thoughts of my stepfather and the illicit events that have occurred between the two of us in favor of thinking about how I'm going to makeover my best friend.

Thank God for Kaye. She always knows exactly what to say to make me feel better. Therapists often have therapists of their own to talk about the things that stress them out; that's what Kaye is for me. But she's better than a trained professional because we can put on some pajamas and face masks and talk until 2 am—free of charge.

Chapter 24
Christine

When we show up at the million-dollar mansion Malcolm bought for Carrie as a wedding present, Kaye and I are caught off guard by a handsome, smiling stranger who looks oddly familiar. I can't put my finger on it, but I swear I've seen him before.

Bright blue eyes twinkle with delight as he greets us by name, knowing who we are before we can even process his presence here. He wears a comforting, warm smile as he introduces himself. I offer him my hand, and when he takes it in his, my stomach twists with desire. His skin is warm and inviting, and I swear I feel a spark of electricity between us. *Maybe he'll be the one to get my mind off Niccolo.*

"I'm Jackson, a friend of Carrie's." And for the first time in my life, I wish I was Carrie Pennington. I have guy friends, but none of them look like Jackson, not even Theo.

Jackson guides us to the kitchen for dinner, where the tantalizing aroma of homemade pasta and freshly baked garlic bread fills the air. Carrie is bent over in front of the oven, checking on the bubbling, golden-brown lasagna inside. My stomach grumbles loudly, a reminder that I neglected to eat today. The hours of studying consumed me to the point that lunch slipped my mind. I sneak over to a crudite tray and surreptitiously grab a carrot while Jackson and Carrie wax poetically about some charity event they met at a couple of months ago.

The way they look at one another makes me wonder what secrets Carrie is keeping from her daughter. I know what it looks like when two people want one another, and I'd be willing to bet that Carrie and Jackson are dating.

She and Malcolm only just split up, but she looks at Jackson like he hung the moon. If the two of them aren't banging yet, it's only a matter of time.

But Kaye doesn't like him. Her eyes narrow as she pelts him with rapid-fire questions, hoping to pierce his façade. The tension between them is palpable, like two cats facing off in a territorial dispute. While she seethes in uncertainty about her mother's new suitor, I'm forced to keep the conversation going through dinner. Carrie sits back and lets her beau do all the talking, and when Kaye runs out of questions to ask, the bulk of the transaction is left to me.

I flirt with him. Frankly, it's hard not to. With his chiseled jawline and sparkling eyes, he exudes a natural charm and charisma that draws me in. He effortlessly turns even the most serious topics into lighthearted banter while knowing when to dive deeper into a subject to share his insightful opinions. If I didn't know any better, I'd say that Jackson is trying to impress me. But I *do* know better, and I have a feeling that he's this way with everyone.

After dinner, Jackson leans toward me to whisper, "I'm sure you've been in the garden outside, but how about you give me a tour?"

Kaye gives me a pleading look, and I read in her eyes that she wants to talk to her mother alone. I get to my feet and hold out a hand for Jackson. "I'd love to. I'll show you all the hiding spots in the maze." The two Penningtons begin chatting in hushed tones before we're even out of the house.

"I bet this wasn't how you thought you'd meet your new girlfriend's daughter, eh?" I ask as we head to the backyard. The elaborate garden maze glimmers in the distance, twinkling beneath the late November moon. As we approach, the rustle of fallen leaves crunch underfoot.

"She isn't my girlfriend, Christine. We're just friends. You know that." Jackson isn't the type to be led into easy confidences, and he smiles while politely correcting me.

A scoff escapes my lips, harsh and unladylike. Carrie and Jackson might have successfully fooled Kaye with their lies, but I am not so easily swayed. "*All* I know is that Carrie is married to a rich and powerful man who won't take too kindly to his wife fooling around with someone younger and more attractive." I peep under my eyelashes at Jackson, but the look on his face never changes. "That's *his* area of expertise, if you catch my drift."

He nods in agreement as we meander across the lawn. Out of the corner of my eye, I can see him taking in the sights of the well-trimmed, perfectly manicured backyard. I wonder if he envies the McCade money as much as I do. My family was never poor, but we've never had the kind of wealth to afford a million-dollar home in the rich part of Manhattan. And Jackson looks like he grew up even poorer than me.

"So, if you're not dating Carrie, are you seeing someone else?" I ask when he doesn't respond after a while.

Jackson, who's been holding my hand since we got up from the table, drops it unceremoniously. His gaze wanders off into the distance, leaving me feeling exposed and vulnerable. "I'm single at the moment."

I'm determined to get him to admit what we both know he's lying about. "Want to go out with me?" I tilt my head and coyly glance up at him from the side, flashing an inviting smile. My lips curve into a mischievous grin as I meet his gaze, the corners of my eyes crinkling with playful intent. But I'm not inviting enough because he cocks his head and has an almost pitying look on his face.

"Christine, I think you're a lovely girl," he begins.

I don't need him to finish the rejection. Even though I know he's rejecting me because he's seeing Carrie, it still stings. Despite trying to maintain composure, I can feel my heart racing and my fists clenching in response. "What? Not old enough for you, Jackie boy? You looking for a more experienced blonde? Perhaps one with a rich husband you can exploit?"

Jackson's easygoing smile slowly fades, replaced with a glare. "Enough," he says quietly. "I know you have a relationship with Kaye, and since Kaye is Carrie's daughter, I will respect you. But make no mistake, my interest in you is purely surface-level. You're not my type. To answer your question, yes, I prefer older women. I prefer my women to be mature. I like women who don't act like they're fresh out of high school and can seduce any man they want. I prefer *women*, Christine, not little girls."

Heat unfurls in my chest and stretches its sinewy fingers through every limb of my body. I feel like a puppet formed from my humiliation and shame, barely able to move my limbs on my own. Turning swiftly on my heel, I head back for the house before Jackson can see the tears welling up in my eyes from embarrassment.

I resolve to keep this interaction to myself because of my pride. Jackson calls my name in exasperation from somewhere behind me, but I keep walking until I'm back in the house and I see Kaye. "It's time to go," I tell her abruptly.

As we leave, she offers Jackson a forced *'good night'*. I thank Carrie for dinner but say nothing to her friend.

"Jackson is definitely interested in your mom," I announce as we climb into the car. "I tried my damnedest to flirt with him, and nothing. I swear he only has eyes for Carrie." Thank God for the darkness because it shields my embarrassment.

Kaye slams her hands down on the steering wheel in anger. "Damn it. I knew it. She kept telling me there was nothing between them, and he's just a good guy."

I shrug, more out of insult than indifference. I know I'm not everyone's type, but Jackson calling me a little girl hurt my feelings. "I don't know. Maybe he *is* a good guy, and she doesn't like him back." I hope Carrie realizes what an ass he is before it's too late.

Thankfully, my best friend is over this conversation, and she says exactly what I'm thinking. "I need a drink."

I wipe away my surly attitude and agree wholeheartedly. "Great. Because the foam party starts at 10:00 and we still need to get ready. It's time to get down with our bad selves!" I cheer, trying to forget what happened.

But my bruised ego leads me into temptation and drags me down the path of sin. As we drive back to Rosedale, I text the only man that makes me feel something. I know that I shouldn't, but the second I press *'send'*, it doesn't matter anymore.

Bad boys, bad decisions, right? Hell hath no fury like a woman scorned.

Chapter 25
Niccolo

Before Christine left for college, I sat her down and told her about the dangers of alcohol. I was desperate to protect my stepdaughter from what awaited her at university. I warned her about the manipulative boys who lurked at parties, waiting to take advantage of young, naive girls. I cautioned her against making rash decisions fueled by cheap tequila. But warning a brick wall would have done more good than talking to Christine.

CHRISTINE
Your kinda cute when youre mad

She's been drunk texting me for an hour. I know she's drunk because her grammar gets sloppier with every text. It's something every drunk person is guilty of, including myself.

> Go back to your dorm, Chris.

CHRISTINE
Youre nt my father. You can't tell me what to do

I don't even know where she's at. I was hanging out with my brothers when she first texted me, and it's been downhill ever since.

> I'm the closest thing you have to a father. Now get your ass back to your dorm.

Her text bubble pops up, indicating that she's typing. I watch the animated gray dots until they disappear, but no text comes through. "Un-fucking-believable." I toss my phone, and it sails across the room toward the other couch. Thank God it smacks into the cushions instead of the marble fireplace behind it.

"What's up?" Luciano's hand shoots out to grab my device, his face contorting in confusion as he surveys the conversation between my stepdaughter and me.

"Christine is drunk texting me," I scowl, my lips pursed in frustration.

Dante's eyes widen and his eyebrows raise skeptically before he rolls them upwards, expressing his annoyance and disbelief. "You need to keep your girl on a shorter leash," he says. "You don't see Adalina getting trashed in bars."

Salvatore's nose is firmly planted in a book, but even with his mind on the historical fiction in his hands, he's as quick as a whip. "We never *see* Adalina, period. Did you kill the girl, Dante?"

"No, but I'll let her know you're missing her," Dante replies sardonically. "Anything else you want to say to *my* wife?"

"I'd love to tell her to leave your grumpy ass," Salvatore mumbles, "but considering she's nowhere to be found *in her own home*, I guess I'll save that for next time."

Luckily, Luciano steps in between. Literally. He gets up to toss my phone back to me. "Your girl texted back. It's a pic. I think she's topless," he says with a wink.

With a glare etched on my face, I catch my phone and impatiently look at what he's referencing. "Don't look at my texts."

"Don't throw your phone at me," he snorts.

Dante fidgets restlessly in his chair, his brows knitted. Salvatore, on the other hand, sits smugly with a smirk playing on his lips as he flips through the pages of his book. It's a typical night when the Terlizzi brothers get together—equal parts tension and amusement always seem to mix.

Unfortunately, Luciano is right. Christine is topless in the photo she sent me, along with half a dozen other girls. I barely recognize my stepdaughter. Her red hair is piled on her head in messy curls, she sticks her tongue out, and pulls her dress down to expose her tits. "Who the fuck took this picture?" I feel dirty just looking at it.

"What picture? Let me see." Salvatore asks, setting down his book.

"You stay the fuck over there," I glare. "I swear to God, this girl is going to give me a heart attack."

Dante mumbles under his breath about the leash thing again, and I ignore him.

> What the fuck are you doing?

CHRISTINE

> Girls gOne wILD!!*

I smash the *'call'* button so fast I nearly crack the screen on my phone. I swear if some frat boy convinced her and a bunch of other girls to do a homemade porno, I'll tear him apart with my bare hands.

Christine answers after three rings, and I'm met by the sound of blaring music. "Helloooo, father," she drags out her words. "Whatcha need?"

"Where the fuck are you?" If she doesn't tell me right this instant, I'm going to explode.

"Foam party," Christine yells into the receiver. "Where are you?"

Jesus Christ. I cover the phone and tell Luciano to find out where a foam party is happening in Rosedale tonight. "I'm on my way to come get you. What were you thinking, flashing a camera? People are going to have your naked tits on their phones." It's me. I'm people. She's naïve if she thinks I won't save that photo and jerk off to it later.

Christine follows my train of thought and drunkenly giggles. "*You* have my naked tits on your phone."

I'd rather have her naked tits on top of me, but that's not the point. "I'm coming to get you," I reiterate. "Stay put. I'll be there in half an hour."

"I'm not a child, Nic," she says with a groan.

"That's funny because you like being *spanked* like a child." The words tumble out of my mouth like marbles scattering across a hardwood floor. I suddenly realize I'm standing in front of my brothers, and three pairs of eyes are now fixed on me with varying degrees of surprise and curiosity.

Christine makes a noncommittal sound on the other end of the line. "That's not true," she pouts.

"Stay where you are," I command. I don't have time to argue whether or not my stepdaughter's sopping wet pussy means she liked what I did to her the other day or not. Once I have her safely in my grasp and away from the predatory college boys, we can debate facts all she wants.

I hang up the phone and ask Luciano for the location of the party. He tells me she's at Red Dawg.

Dante's lips twitch into a grin. "So you're keeping your stepdaughter in line, eh, Lolo? I didn't know you had it in you."

"Shut the fuck up," I point at him. "I gotta go." I'm not hanging out with these buffoons anymore. Stupid fucking idiots that always have to give their opinion about shit they don't understand.

My step-damsel in distress needs savings whether she likes it or not. And once I whisk her away from the danger she so willingly put herself in, I'm going to ravage her until she forgets there was ever anyone else. I'm tired of waiting for the perfect moment. I'm claiming my woman once and for all, and there's nothing she can do to stop me.

Chapter 26
Niccolo

The foam party taking place at Red Dawg is no surprise. The place is a cesspool of college boys trying to take advantage of drunk girls. I swear to God, if I weren't on a mission to find Christine, I'd round up all these underage girls and take them home. Unfortunately, I have to find my drunk stepdaughter first.

How anyone can find anyone in this place is a mystery. The smell of soap assaults my senses as I fight my way through sudsy adolescents groping one another while slipping and sliding every which way. This should be illegal. I feel like I've caught a minimum of three diseases rubbing up on these kids.

I find Christine bellied up at the bar next to some tall, tan, blonde-haired prick who looks like he's trying to secure her number. "Beat it, pretty boy."

He stiffens at the sight of me and narrows his eyes. "Who the fuck are you?"

I grab the front of his pristine white shirt and drag him toward me. He towers over me by six inches, but I could kick his ass with one hand tied behind my back. "I'm this girl's stepfather. If you don't get the hell away from her right now, you'll be picking your teeth off the floor one by one. Do you hear me?"

The color drains from his face as his eyes widen in terror, sweat beading along his forehead. "Yo, whatever you say, man. I don't even know this girl," his voice shaking as he responds.

"Theo," Christine chastises. The two of them lock eyes for a moment before he flees. He doesn't even have the balls to look back and make sure she's okay.

"You can do better than him."

Christine rolls her eyes as she grabs the plastic cup in front of her. "Relax. It's water," she says when I reach to take it away from her. "Don't get your panties in a twist."

"Are you here alone?" I ask, ignoring her jibe.

She waves at the space behind her. "Kaye is here somewhere. I lost her a while ago. She went to the bathroom and then never came back. I think she went home."

There are two drunk girls out here making stupid decisions, then. "Text her."

Christine throws back the last of the water. "*You* text her."

I grab her by the arm and tighten my fingers into a harsh band. The skin creases slightly as she tries to pull away, but my grip on her is tight. "Text her that I'm taking you home. Now, Christine."

"You can't make me leave," Christine glowers at me. "I'll scream."

Someone bumps into me from behind, sending me careening

into my stepdaughter. These slippery floors are going to cause someone to break their neck.

"Scream then," I growl. A second later, I hoist her in the air and toss her over my shoulder.

The crowd around us breaks, backing up to give us room. The blonde asshole that was talking to her earlier stands at the end of the bar, watching with wide eyes. Some guy. He doesn't even race forward to save his woman. If I ever find out who he is, I'm kicking his ass.

Christine beats on my back as I carry her through the club. It's a nice massage that helps get the knots out of my shoulders. The flashing lights and pulsing music of the club create an almost hypnotic atmosphere as I navigate through the crowded dance club. "I hate you!" She yells.

I reach up to smack her on the ass, quieting her outburst. "Shut up."

As disruptive as we are to the party, the second we pass by, the crowd re-forms, and we're all but forgotten.

I reach the bank of bathrooms, pick one, and deposit Christine on the ground before shutting and locking the door behind us. "Text Kaye, now. See if she wants a ride home."

Christine petulantly crosses her arms over her chest. "No," she argues. "I don't want to text Kaye, and I don't want to go home. I'm here to party, Nic."

"I don't care what you're here to do; I'm here to take you home. When you text me pics of you and your friends flashing some stranger on camera, the night is over. You can fight me all you want, but I'm bigger and stronger, and I will carry you out of here kicking and screaming if I have to."

Her gaze sharpens, her pretty brown eyes narrowing into slits. "You wouldn't dare," she challenges with a hint of feistiness in her voice as if daring me to prove her wrong.

I take one menacing step forward and crack my knuckles. "You wanna fucking *bet?*"

Something snaps inside Christine. I see the shift in her eyes just seconds before she closes the gap between us and presses her lips to mine.

I fist her hair, tangling my fingers in her red locks. She is soft and demanding, her mouth tart from the taste of vodka cranberry, and I swirl my tongue around hers hungrily.

I slide my hand down to cup her ass cheek while the other cradles the back of her head possessively. The heat radiating off her body matches mine as we press against one another, each trying to take control.

I push her into the sink, and she groans into my mouth. As I break the kiss, I trail my lips down her throat, hunger igniting every fiber of my being. I reach down to grab her, lifting her onto the edge of the bathroom sink—she parts her thighs to give me access.

"Hold onto the sink," I instruct. For once, she doesn't argue.

I release her and slip between her legs, breathing in the intoxicating scent of her arousal. She gasps loudly, her body tensing as I pull her panties down and expose her soft, pink folds.

Christine tosses her head back when I lean forward to bury my face in her hot, wet pussy. Her moans grow louder as I indulge in every curve of her flesh, dragging my tongue teasingly through her slit.

"Oh, fuck," she gasps as I alternate between slow, circling motions on her swollen clit and sucking gently. Her hips rock against me in response, causing the sink to groan under her weight. Someone bangs on the bathroom door, but it would take a bomb detonating to drag me away from Christine.

As she wraps her legs around my shoulders, I drive her to the height of her ecstasy. I can feel the walls of her cunt clench around my fingers while moans spill from her lips like an erotic anthem. "You're so fucking tight," I growl against her skin.

Her trembling thighs tighten around my head like a vice as she explodes on my tongue. The banging on the bathroom door stops as Christine lets out a scream of pleasure.

"I need you inside me. Now," she groans, panting like she's in heat.

"Don't tease me," I glare. "If I fuck you, that's it, *dolcezza*. Your pussy is signing a contract. You're mine."

She bites her bottom lip, eyes alight with lust and need. I can see her weighing the options, trying to decide if this is worth it. "Fuck it," Christine whispers under her breath. "Fuck me, Nic."

With a quick, desperate movement, I push myself up from the ground, my hand instinctively reaching out to grab her chin and lift her head to meet my gaze. "Don't say it unless you mean it." Her eyes widen in surprise and I see the reflection of my intensity in them.

Christine succumbs to her desires. "I mean it. I want you to fuck me."

If I were a better man, I'd make her wait until morning when the alcohol and heightened emotions from the orgasm have worn off. But I never claimed to be a good man.

I pull out my cock and tease her opening with the tip. "Once I do this, Christine, I own you. If you even *look* at another man, I'll kill him and punish you."

Impatience distorts her hearing. Christine reaches between us and wraps her fingers around me. "I don't care. I don't need anyone else. I need *you*."

She may regret this in the morning, but by then, it'll be too late.

Chapter 27
Christine

I'm not drunk; I never was.

A couple of drinks in, I lost Kaye and switched to water, but my head is still tingling from the alcohol. That's the only explanation I have for doing what I did: liquid courage.

When Niccolo drops to his knees in front of me, every bone in my body feels like it turns to goo. His tongue darts into my entrance, and I grip the edge of the sink to keep from toppling forward.

My pussy drips with need, moans echoing off the walls as he drags his expert tongue through my center. The metal tap presses against my lower back as I undulate my hips into his face.

The smell of my arousal fills the air, turning me on even more than before. My clit is swollen and hard under his attention, throbbing for his touch. And when he alternates between gentle swirls and sucking, I can't hold myself back. I tilt my hips higher, granting his mouth better access to my body, as my stomach tightens momentarily before exploding.

"I need you inside me. Now," I groan, desperate for him.

He looks up at me from the floor, his chin smeared with my wetness. "Don't tease me," Nic glares. "If I fuck you, that's it, *dolcezza*. Your pussy is signing a contract. You're mine."

I'd sign my life away if it meant he'd fuck me good and hard right now. I'd give up everything I have and more if he'd take me in his arms and ravish me with wild abandon. "Fuck it. Fuck *me*, Nic." I can't wait any longer. I'm tipsy and horny and needy, and he can take care of me. I'll deal with the consequences of my actions later.

With a sudden burst of energy, Niccolo rises to his feet and grabs my chin with a commanding grip. His intense gaze locks onto mine, searching for something in the depths of my eyes. "Don't say it unless you mean it."

"I mean it." I'd swear on a stack of Bibles if he wanted me to. "I want you to fuck me."

My stepfather fumbles with the zipper on his jeans, and I look down to see him pulling out his cock. He palms himself before teasing my entrance with his tip. "Once I do this, Christine, I own you. If you even *look* at another man, I'll kill him and punish you."

God, I hope he does. Punish me, I mean. I don't want him to kill anyone. But I'd do anything to be bent over his desk right now, feeling his stinging hand coming down on my ass while he fucks me from behind.

I reach down between us and grab his erect member, directing it inside me. "I don't care." Right now. "I don't need anyone else. I need *you*."

My permission is all he wants to hear. He growls my name under his breath as he guides himself into my hot waiting center. My body eagerly welcomes him, and I groan as he fills me up. "More," I beg.

Niccolo's strong hands seize my hips, anchoring me firmly against the cool porcelain of the sink. With a tantalizing rhythm, he begins to move within me. His movements are frenzied and urgent, an unspoken testament to an insatiable hunger that echoes my own yearning. His body fits with mine as if we are two pieces of a sultry puzzle, forging a bond fueled by carnal desire and raw passion.

I toss my head back as he drives into me harder and deeper. Everything disappears. The people outside demanding to come in. The bass drum echoing through the floorboards. The bare fluorescent bulbs bathing us in an unflattering light. It all fades into oblivion, and all that matters is him, me, and the promise we're making with our bodies.

His thick, pulsing shaft throbs against my most sensitive spots, leading me to wrap my legs around his waist and pull him closer. The sink creaks under the combined force of my weight and his thrusts, and water drizzles from the tap. The air is heavy with the scent of sex and sweat, mingling with the faint smell of alcohol.

Everywhere he touches me is electric. His lips on my collarbone, as he marks me with his teeth, send shockwaves of pleasure through my system. His hands gripping my skin so tightly that fingertip-shaped bruises mar my skin.

The heat of his body burns under my searching hands as I slip them beneath the rough fabric of his shirt, my fingers sinking into the solid warmth of his skin. My nails graze against him, leaving trails of palpable desire that seem to fuel him further as he crashes into me, relentlessly stealing my breath away.

My pants echo in the silent room, punctuated by gasping moans and breathless curses. Every thrust leaves me more entwined in his web of forced intimacy. He's an intoxicating mix of savagery and tenderness, and I can't help but surrender myself to his tantalizing dominance.

I taste the sweet intoxication of my own arousal lingering on his lips as he sweeps a hasty kiss across mine, the briefness only sparking an even stronger wave of longing. The raw taste of us strikes a chord of animalistic need in me, making me yearn for even more.

"Cum for me, baby," he growls in my ear, feral in his need for release. "Cum all over on daddy's cock." Niccolo grunts as he thrusts his hips against me, a primal sound of satisfaction that echoes through the room.

I do as he commands; I couldn't stop myself even if I wanted to. My walls tremble around him as I give in to my pleasure, shuddering from the explosion of my orgasm. "Nic," I utter, my stepfather's name on the tip of my tongue as I reach my peak.

"That's right, baby girl." He tightens his grip on me before he comes, too, filling me with his hot seed. "Milk daddy's cock. Take every ounce of me." He drips down the insides of my thighs, coating the edge of the sink with his jizz. Niccolo kisses along my jawline, nipping at my skin as he gently pulls out of me.

My body clenches around the empty space left by him as if yearning for his return.

He pushes a few strands of hair out of my face as we lock eyes. "Let me take you home, *dolcezza*," he whispers in a husky voice. "Let me take care of you."

I'm sore and weak, and I need him. It's silly, stupid, even, but I need my daddy to take me home and tuck me into bed.

"Okay," I resign, feeling more exhausted than I've ever felt in my life. "Take care of me."

Chapter 28
Niccolo

As I drive Christine home, I hand her a bottle of water and watch as she gulps it down eagerly. She denies being drunk, insisting she was only slightly tipsy, but I can feel my fingers tightening around the steering wheel as I focus hard on keeping control of the car. The familiar streets seem to blur together as my mind races with worry for Christine's well-being. It takes all my concentration to navigate through traffic and safely reach my destination.

The danger of Christine's admission is that she thinks it makes me feel better to know she wasn't drunk. But her confession is provocative and infuriating, inflaming my anger. If she was only tipsy, that means she flashed a stranger with a camera when she was still in a state to make good decisions.

I want to pull the car over right now, march her out on the side of the road, and turn her ass a violent shade of red to make up for her misbehavior.

But instead, I drive home while she tells me about her night. She starts with the story about dinner at Carrie Pennington's house and takes me minute by minute through the rest of her evening. My anger dissipates in the long moments down the dark highway, and by the time we reach home, it's almost all gone.

"Let's shower," I instruct as we walk through the door.

Christine looks over her shoulder, teeth grazing her bottom lip. "If that's what you want."

With a gentle touch against the small of her back, I guide her into the sanctuary of my bathroom. Christine slowly undresses, revealing her soft curves in the dim light. I turn on the hot water and watch as steam fills the room, creating a hazy veil around us. As she slips beneath the jets, water cascades over her body, tracing every curve and dip with liquid sensuality. My eyes cannot help but feast upon her naked form—each inch of her is a breathtaking work of art, flawless and alluring.

I follow her into the warm embrace of the shower. The soothing warmth of the water surrounds me, washing away the last traces of tension coiled in my shoulders.

"Come here," I tell my stepdaughter. And she steps closer to let me soap her up.

I meticulously clean her, eradicating any memory of another man she may have. Then I explore her body like I'm discovering new land, dragging a loofah across her breasts until the mesh hardens her nipples into stiff little peaks. She presses her back to my front as I venture lower. Caressing the loofah over her mound, her legs part instinctively. Feeling bold, I swap out the sudsy sponge for my fingers, which delve deeper into her folds.

She already has one mark on her collarbone, but I suck on her neck until I leave another. I'd give her a collar of hickeys if she let me; I'd mark her so visibly that no other man would dare to touch her. Christine doesn't notice what I'm doing as my fingers manipulate her core, working her clit back and forth until she's gasping.

I push her forward, and she reaches up to grab the wall, holding herself aloft on the slick shower tiles. As I enter her from behind, her groans are amplified by the bathroom acoustics–an echo chamber broadcasting our sex-fueled symphony. I could listen to her sing like this forever, her song the lyrics of our lovemaking.

Every thrust into her pussy is a testament to my ownership, a declaration of my claim over her. I whisper into her ear that she is unequivocally mine, now and forever. Christine only moans, pushing back for more as I touch every inch of her that I can reach.

"One of these days, I'm going to leave a permanent mark on you," I tell her. "In the form of a child growing inside you. When your belly is swollen with my baby, every man will know that you are a kept woman—that you belong to me."

Christine's hands on the wall turn into fists. "Nic," she pleads warily. "I'm on birth control."

I surge into her, filling her once more. The water washes away my seed, but she can feel it inside her. I pump back and forth until every last drop has been spilled into her. "Not for long," I purr into her ear. "I told you what having sex with me meant." The sooner she's carrying my child, the sweeter the victory of having her.

As she pulls away from me and turns around, harsh, angry tears spill down her cheeks. "This isn't fair," Christine whimpers.

"Life isn't fair, sweetheart." I lean forward to lick away the tears, tasting fresh water and salty bitterness. A smile plays on my lips as I close the gap between us. "Cheer up, buttercup. Daddy's going to take care of you from now on. You, your sweet little pussy, and the new family we're going to create. I promise that you have my full attention from here on out."

Chapter 29
Christine

I fell asleep in Niccolo's bed last night. I don't remember why.

His menacing words in the shower sent shivers down my spine, causing my bones to rattle like a warning. I drifted into a fitful slumber, fingers tracing the outline of the Nexplanon rod buried in my arm, desperately trying to recall when it was implanted. The uncertainty gnawed at me as I struggled to remember if it needed to be replaced in three months or fifteen —keenly aware of the vast difference between the two timelines and the consequences that would follow if I remembered incorrectly.

But in truth, I couldn't have pried myself from Niccolo's clutches even if I wanted to.

It's something I could never confess to my stepfather, or anyone else for that matter, but last night was the first time someone else had ever made me experience an orgasm. All these years, I've been taking care of myself and convincing myself that it's fine for high school boys not to know how to please a woman.

But last night, while Niccolo's face was buried between my legs in the Red Dawg bathroom, it dawned on me that there are men out there who want their partners to feel just as much pleasure as they do.

Even if I didn't want to go back home with Niccolo, I would have. It was like being trapped under a spell. I'd had two orgasms in that bathroom, and my pussy was leading me around on a leash, willing to follow the Devil into the dark if it meant getting a third.

But his threat holds a palpable sense of terror. I want to have children one day, maybe even with Niccolo, but I can't consider having them before I finish college. I have years of studying ahead of me, over a decade of schooling if my stepfather's route to get his Ph. D can be replicated. Having a child now would make that exponentially harder.

BANG! BANG! BANG!

The sound of pounding jolts me from my reverie.

Niccolo shoots up, his hair in disarray. "So help me God if that's Dante," he swears.

My eyes bulge in alarm, and my stomach turns over. "Your brother can't find me here." I start scrambling out of the bed, taking the sheet with me to wrap around my naked body.

BANG! BANG! BANG!

Another round of knocks forces a curse from Niccolo's lips as he climbs out of bed. "Pounding on the door like they're the damn police," he mumbles. "I'll call the fucking cops on them. I don't care if they're my brothers."

Oh, god. I can't have the entire Terlizzi clan finding me here. "I have to get dressed." I can already feel Dante's steely, scrutinizing gaze and Salvatore's smug, all-knowing smirk. "I'll hide in my room. I don't have to come out. No one even has to know I'm here."

I look up to catch Niccolo rolling his eyes and mumbling in Italian under his breath. "It's fine, *dolcezza*," he says after a moment. "Eventually, they're going to know about us."

Not if there's nothing to find out. If I leave today, change my name, and move to a different country, I'll never have to see Niccolo again or tell the Terlizzis anything. It may seem a bit extreme, but it's definitely a rational choice.

BANG! BANG! BANG!

"Go get dressed," he recommends in a sharp tone. "I'll come get you whenever my brothers leave."

I hurry to my room down the hall from his. Luckily, it's in the opposite direction of the main staircase. The stained glass front door is pretty to look at but entirely see-through if someone puts their face right up to it.

Niccolo is yelling as he makes his way toward the door. "I'm coming! Jesus. Cut that shit out." But the banging only gets louder.

As I fling the sheet to the floor and search for clothes, I hear voices downstairs. I look out my bedroom window as I pull on a shirt and see a dark blue convertible in the driveway that doesn't belong to one of Niccolo's brothers. Who shows up at someone's door at 8:00 am on a Saturday?

The voices increase in volume as I wiggle into a pair of jeans I left behind when I left for Blackmore. "God, these are snug," I groan. The Freshman Fifteen is real, and I am a victim.

"*Fanculo*, Terlizzi." I'm chilled to the bone by the sudden shout. The Italian *'fuck you'* echoes through the house and sends a shiver through my body. "I'll fucking murder you and bury you in your own backyard. Do you hear me?"

I'd recognize my Uncle Giovanni's voice anywhere. I quickly run my fingers through my hair, trying to smooth out any stray strands before hurrying from the room.

The heated voices grow louder and more intense as I approach the grand staircase. There, in the doorway, stand Giovanni and Marco, their postures tense and confrontational as they face off with my stepfather.

"Gio?" I test the waters as I step out from behind the wall and reveal myself. "Is that you?" I try to sound shocked to see my uncles here, but Gio doesn't look like he's buying it.

"Go back to your room," Niccolo says tersely.

Giovanni glares at him. "No, she needs to hear this, too."

I pause halfway down the stairs, a half-humorous, half-strangled expression on my face. "H-hear what?" I stutter.

Niccolo gives my uncle a hard look. "This is between us. It has nothing to do with her."

Marco, as always, stands a few feet behind Giovanni with his arms crossed tightly over his chest. His towering frame casts a shadow over the room, and his imposing presence radiates a sense of danger. He's never been one for idle chitchat—words are not his weapon of choice. Instead, he makes a living as an enforcer. He's all muscle and menacing facial expressions that would terrify me if I didn't know he was a sweetheart deep down.

Uncle Giovanni feels safe with Marco as his backup, and he snorts in derision at Niccolo. "This has as much to do with her as it does with you." He looks past Nic to make eye contact with me. "Your stepfather is a problem, Chris."

"What kind of problem?" I ask tentatively as I make it to the last step of the staircase.

Giovanni attempts to come inside, but his eager steps are halted as Niccolo raises his hand in a firm gesture to stop him.

A flash of irritation ignites in Marco's eyes at the mere contact between his brother and Niccolo. Marco's hands, usually relaxed at his sides, now curl into bulky, powerful fists. The tension in the room is tangible, with each man silently asserting their dominance over the other.

Niccolo sees Marco's response and looks past Giovanni. "What?" He barks. "You wanna try me, meathead?" My stepfather has a death wish, I think.

"Nic," I gently prod, "let them inside. We can talk. They're my family."

He flares up at that remark, and I know what he's thinking. For family, they never give two shits about me until it suits them. But Niccolo takes one look at my face and softens. "Fine," he growls at Marco and Giovanni, "but if either of you piss me off, I'll kick you in the head."

Giovanni rolls his eyes as he walks through the door. He makes himself comfortable, removing his jacket and putting it in the coat closet next to the entrance.

"I should be the one kicking you in the head." He offers to take his brother's coat, storing it next to his. "I'm in Kansas City. I'm over a hundred miles away," Giovanni explains. "So tell me why the fuck I'm hearing rumors about the two of you."

My jaw drops open in shock. "W-what rumors?"

He slams the closet door shut. "Rumors that the two of you are fooling around," Giovanni explains succinctly. "You're the family's prized virgin. You think any man is going to want you now?"

A sudden, sickening feeling hits me like a punch in the gut. I swear my stomach falls through my ass, and I don't know if it's because my uncles think I'm a virgin or because the rumors imply that my family has plans for me that don't include Niccolo.

"We're tired of the rumors, Christine. We're here to settle them once and for all."

Chapter 30
Christine

Niccolo clenches his fists, the sound of his knuckles cracking through the quiet living room. "Start talking, Lucatello," he orders as he paces back and forth with an air of impatience.

Giovanni and Marco share a look, clearly hiding something from us. Their eyes sparkle with mischief, intensifying my curiosity. Gio's lips curl up into a sly smile as he taunts, "I think I'd like it if you begged, Terlizzi."

Instinctively, I step forward, positioning myself between my stepfather and my uncles to prevent a violent confrontation. "Stop," I hiss at Niccolo. "It's not worth it." I can sense the tension in his muscles, his eyes ablaze with anger.

"Listen to your stepdaughter, Niccolo," Giovanni grins. "I could sic Marco on you and solve all my problems. You want that?"

Niccolo's hands tighten into menacing fists at his sides as he cracks his neck. "Get to the point before you make me do something I'll regret."

Giovanni nonchalantly props his feet up on the coffee table, feigning relaxation. But beneath the facade, his face reveals a snake ready to strike. His stretched-out posture belies a hidden restlessness. "I think I'd be more inclined to talk if I had a drink. I know you've got good taste in bourbon, Niccolo. Why don't you pour me a glass?"

Interrupting the growing tension, I step forward, urging Gio to reveal his purpose for coming here unannounced. "Gio, please, just tell me what you came here to say."

My uncle rolls his eyes. "You're too sweet, Chris. And too kind to that bastard of a man that isn't your stepfather anymore."

Niccolo returns to pacing the floor, never taking his eyes off my uncle.

"Noted." I cross my arms over my chest self-consciously. "Why are you here?" I know they want to squash the rumors they're hearing, but how do they plan to do that?

With an exaggerated stretch, Giovanni's relaxed facade dissipates, replaced by a look of unease. "Your grandfather has arranged for you to marry."

My body grows cold, and the room starts to darken. I reach out for something to stabilize me and find Niccolo's hand. He whispers in my ear, but his words are drowned out by the sound of waves churning in an invisible sea.

Time seems to stand still as I struggle to regain my composure. Someone snaps their fingers in front of my face, drawing my attention. It's Giovanni, standing before me, engaged in a petty argument with Niccolo. They bicker like children, their dispute drowning out my own thoughts.

"No," I mumble, my voice building in strength as I push away from Niccolo and Giovanni. "Stop. No." Determination fills my expression as I stand my ground. "I'm not ready."

My uncle straightens his back, drawing up to his full height. "If you can to fuck around with your stepfather, you can marry a Castiglione."

In a daze, I try to step back, only to find myself colliding with the couch. "I can't. I won't," I assert, forcing a look of defiance onto my face. "You can't make me marry anyone, Uncle."

A mask of rage twists Giovanni's features as he takes a step forward. Before I can react, his arm swiftly rises, delivering a brutal backhand across my face. The force of the blow snaps my head back, sending a searing pain radiating through my skull. "That's where you're wrong, Christine. I am in charge of this family, and you are obligated to listen to your elders when they know what's best for you."

Tears burn the back of my eyes, but I won't give him the satisfaction of seeing me cry. Niccolo's hand finds my lower back, the other gently brushing my swollen cheek. "Are you okay?"

Giovanni snaps his fingers, and a second later, Marco is pulling Niccolo away from me. "Hold him for me, Marc," Gio orders.

He steps forward and grabs me by the chin. His fingers digging into my newly bruised cheek cause me to wince; his icy glare as he looks me in the eye sends chills down my spine. "You made your bed, and now you have to lie in the filthy sheets. You will marry Rocco Castiglione this summer. It will be a joyous occasion for the Lucatellos. It will forge a new alliance between our families. And when Fausto Terlizzi dies," he looks back to smirk at Niccolo, "the Castigliones will look to our family to find a replacement Consigliere."

"You keep my father's name out of your fucking mouth, Lucatello." Niccolo is foaming with rage. If Marco hadn't caught him off guard, Nic would be ripping Giovanni apart.

My uncle shoves me away from him, his fingers momentarily digging into my bruised flesh. "You only have yourself to blame for this, Nic. If you had let Chris come with me after Caterina died, you wouldn't have thought you could get away with fucking someone who doesn't belong to you. Now the Lucatello family has to marry her off to an enforcer with a notorious history of abusing his wives. Yes, *wives*," Giovanni emphasizes with a cruel sneer. "The first two died at his hands when they tried to escape. The third took her own life. So, if you know what's good for you," he glares at me, "you'll be a compliant little wife to Rocco."

Niccolo elbows Marco in the gut, but the larger man merely grunts and tightens his grip. "You would willingly marry off your niece to a known wife killer?"

Giovanni locks eyes with me, ensuring that I understand what he's about to say. "I would kill Christine with my bare hands before I let her continue tarnishing the family name with the likes of *you*, Terlizzi."

My breath catches in my throat, fear seizing my vocal cords. I can't say another word, but I flee from the room. I wrap my hand around the handle of the front door and run until I can't see my home anymore. But even though it's out of sight, I still hide behind a bush as I pull out my phone to call my best friend. "Kaye, I need you to pick me up. Something bad happened."

Throughout the drive to Manhattan, Kaye remains on the line, her voice a steady anchor in the storm of chaos and confusion.

She provides me solace and a sense of safety amidst the turmoil.

In this world of constant change, Kaye is my one unwavering constant. There is no one I trust more than her to guide me through this darkness.

Chapter 31
Niccolo

Christine runs from the room before I can stop her. When we hear the front door open, Giovanni laughs. "She's a sweet girl, but she's like her mother," he says with a roll of his eyes. "She stole that Irish prick from Francesca and then had to be forced down the aisle."

Caterina never told me much about her first marriage, but we've all heard the rumors. Francesca Lucatello was to marry Liam Byrne, the son of a prominent Irish gangster. My father called the Lucatellos foolish for wanting to strengthen their family by marrying outside of Italian tradition. In the end, Caterina seduced Liam the night before his wedding and the two of them ran off together. Their affair ended with a shotgun wedding, and everyone who was there remembers Caterina crying as she made her vows. Ten years later, he disappeared without a trace, never to be heard from again.

"Let him go," Giovanni thrusts his chin in my direction, ordering his brother around. Marco releases me a second later.

I pull my arms back in front of me, mumbling under my breath about their brutish behavior.

"Shut up," Giovanni barks dismissively. He strides over to the bar stationed in the corner of the opulent living room, pouring himself a generous measure of Scotch. The liquid cascades into the glass, its amber hue gleaming under the soft glow of the early morning lighting. "This is all your fault anyway," he asserts, a tinge of bitterness coloring his voice. "Word has it that you were seen with her at some college dance club a few weeks ago."

A jolt of panic grips my chest. Fuck. The night at Red Dawg. I thought we were safe because I didn't recognize anyone. "Are you following her or me?" I ask, suddenly feeling paranoid.

Marco imitates his brother's actions by grabbing himself a drink as well. Giovanni observes him with casual interest. "Wrong question, Nic. I shouldn't have to have *either* of you followed."

One of these days, Giovanni is going to mouth off to the wrong person and wind up getting himself killed. I pray to God I'm in the room when it happens. "So *why* are you having us followed then?"

Giovanni swiftly downs the expensive Scotch, savoring its taste on his lips as he smacks them together. The sound echoes through the hallways of the mansion, carrying with it a sinister air that freezes the blood in my veins. "Because it's odd that you would want to keep your stepdaughter around after she was no longer legally your stepdaughter."

"This all goes back to three years ago?"

"Precisely," Giovanni confirms. "You should have made her come to Kansas City. She had a duty to fulfill. Instead, you kept her here and filled her head with nonsense. She thinks she's free, but she will learn the hard way that she isn't. She is a Lucatello, and her future has been determined for her since the day she was conceived."

A surge of revulsion rises within me at Giovanni's callous disregard for Christine's autonomy. "You may arrange your own daughters' marriages as you see fit," I retort, my voice seeping with indignation. "But you do *not* have my consent to arrange a marriage for Christine. Nor do you have hers."

Giovanni's laughter reverberates through the room, a booming sound that echoes off the ornate walls. It carries a malevolence that makes my skin crawl, a haunting chorus of darkness that will undoubtably haunt my dreams. "I don't require your consent, Niccolo," he jeers, a smirk on full display. "You are well aware of our ways. You know our laws. You know that she is the family's property until she is married off, then she becomes another man's property. She does not own her freedom or her independence."

I grew up under the same tutelage as my brothers. I was taught the weight of familial expectations and the unyielding grip of tradition. I knew that my father was made the Castiglione's Consigliere when I was just a little boy. I didn't reject their teachings; I chose a different path. And though my father never understood why, he let me do it without punishment.

Christine doesn't have the same choice. Her family's darkness runs deeper than mine, their insatiable hunger now threatening to ruin her life. They want everything from Christine, and they're willing to break her to get it.

"She is my daughter and—"

"No," Giovanni cuts me off with a glare as he gets to his feet. "She was only ever your *step*daughter. She does not bear your name. If she did, the two of you carrying on as you have would be even more despicable. She is a Lucatello, and therefore, as the elder of the family, she is mine."

A frown furrows my brow. "Leonardo is the elder," I correct. "Is this what your father wants?"

"Father is… *retiring*…from leading the family." Giovanni's jaw tightens in time with his fists, and the vein in his forehead throbs. "I'm taking over. Whatever he wanted is no longer important. All that matters is what *I* want."

Did Leonardo Lucatello envision a future where Christine would be bound to marry a ruthless killer?

Giovanni continues. "If you know what's good for you, you'll send Christine back to me. If I have to hunt her down myself, there will be consequences. She might not get off lightly with a slap on the face next time."

The primal beast within me claws at the surface, craving release, yearning to dismantle Giovanni piece by piece. "Touch her again, *threaten her again*, and mark my words, Giovanni, you will suffer. I will chop your dick off, burn it to a crisp, and force it down your throat. Are we clear?"

He smirks like my threat is meaningless. Then he looks at me in a way that reminds me of Dante, a look that says he doesn't think much of me. "You finally sound like a real Terlizzi. Too bad it's too late." The smirk fades from his face, replaced by a thin line carved into his lips like granite. "Christine will marry Rocco, whether you accept it or not. If you play your role as expected, perhaps I will even grant you the honor of walking her down the aisle and giving her away."

Chapter 32
Christine

"Jesus Christ," Kaye exclaims in disbelief as I climb into her sleek Model 3 red Tesla. "What the hell happened to you?"

I reach a trembling hand up to touch my throbbing cheek, wincing as my fingers graze the swollen flesh. A sharp, searing pain shoots through my face like a bolt of lightning. "God damn it," I grumble, my voice laced with frustration, "can we please stop somewhere to get some ice? This hurts like a bitch."

Without taking her foot off the brake, Kaye glances at me, her eyes filled with concern. "Seriously, Chris, what the hell happened?"

My impatience gets the better of me as panic sets in. If my uncle leaves the house now, he might see us. "Just drive, Kaye! Before Giovanni finds me here."

"Giovanni?" Her voice quivers with uncertainty as she eases off the brake. "Your uncle? I thought Nic did this to you."

Fumbling with the visor, my hands shaking with anxiety, I open it to reveal a compact mirror. As I catch sight of my reflection, Kaye's concern makes sense. My lip is bleeding, and my cheek is swollen and turning an ugly shade of purple. Panic pulses through my veins. "Nic would never hurt me," I tell her quietly.

Kaye snorts her disapproval and ignores me when I shoot her a glare. "Why did your uncle do this to you then?" She asks.

Ignoring her judgmental gaze, I slam the visor shut with a frustrated thud. How could I have been so blind? How did I let myself get that close to Niccolo? I should have trusted my instincts and listened to the inner voice screaming at me to stay away from my stepfather. But I let pleasure cloud my judgment, and now I'm paying the price.

"Hello? Earth to Chris." Kaye's voice cuts through my racing thoughts like a blade, snapping me back to the present moment. "Tell me what's going on. You can trust me."

Trust her. I repeat the words in my mind, desperately searching for the courage to confide in my best friend. Taking a deep breath, I realize it's now or never. "My family wants to marry me off to a man who's killed his other wives, and Giovanni said he'd rather see me dead than with Niccolo," the words tumble out in a frantic blur, my voice barely above a whisper.

Kaye's jaw drops open, her eyes widening in shock and disbelief. In a moment of distraction, she carelessly runs a stop sign without even realizing it. "What the fuck!" she exclaims, but there's no time to dwell on the revelation I just dropped on her. The sight of red and blue lights fills the rearview mirror, followed quickly by a blaring police siren.

It's a fitting break in the conversation. Kaye pulls over, her jaw still agape in astonishment. As we wait for the police officer to approach her window, she stares at me, trying to process what I just opened up to her about.

"Ma'am," the police officer taps on Kaye's car door. "Do you know that you ran a stop sign back there?"

Kaye, flustered from both the unexpected pull-over and my disturbing confession, stammers out a response. They chat briefly, and then the officer bends down to look at me in the passenger seat. "Here's my insurance card," Kaye offers, extending a thick, plastic card to the police officer.

His eyes barely register the card, his gaze fixated on my bruised face. "Miss, are you okay?" He disregards Kaye completely. He leans in closer, his expression filled with concern. "Do you need to be seen by a doctor?"

Instinctively, I turn away from him, shielding my bruised cheek, and feel a rush of embarrassment flood through me. "I'm fine, officer." The last thing I need is the police getting involved in my family troubles. If I bring a suspicious cop home, Giovanni is likely to kill us all.

The police officer moves around to my side of the car, taps on the window, and waits for me to roll it down. He crouches down until we're at eye level, leaning on the door for support. "Ma'am, would you feel more comfortable getting out of the car to chat?"

I'm barefoot because I didn't think to put on shoes before going downstairs in my own home, and then I ran away without grabbing a pair of flip-flops. The last thing I want is to get out of this car and try to explain to a police officer that everything is alright. "I'm fine, Officer. We went out last night, and I got into a fight with some girl at a bar. It's no big deal." If I'd said I'd gotten in a fight with my boyfriend or a family member, it would have been considered a domestic dispute.

Saying I got hit by a stranger in a bar gives him no reason to investigate further.

But he surprises me. Instead of pressing the matter, he simply reaches into his breast pocket and pulls out a business card. "If something like this ever happens again, you call me," he says, his voice tinged with a note of authority. He hands me the card, and his eyes hold a depth of understanding that catches me off guard. "I know things can escalate when you kids are out partying, but there's no reason to be getting into fights. You should put some ice on that and take some ibuprofen, okay?"

Relief washes over me as a small smile graces my lips. I nod quickly, grateful for his unexpected empathy. "We were just on our way to the store. Thank you, officer."

He glances across the car at Kaye, giving her a weary smile. "Keep an eye out for stop signs in the future, alright? You two have a good day." And just like that, he walks away, allowing us to continue on our way without reprimand.

"That was crazy," I laugh nervously.

Kaye puts the car in drive and merges back onto the road. "Chris, should I be worried about you? Who is this guy that your family wants to marry you off to? And why does your uncle think you're seeing Nic? Are you two together?"

I want to answer her questions honestly. I know I owe her that much after dragging her into this mess. But the weight of my situation presses down on me, leaving me overwhelmed and unsure of what to say. The truth feels convoluted and messy, while a lie seems like too much effort.

"I don't know everything. Gio showed up this morning and said that he heard some rumors about my conduct. He said the best way to squash the rumors was for me to get married."

Half-truths slip from my lips, my gaze fixed on the passing scenery outside the car window.

Kaye wrinkles her nose, her face a picture of disappointment. "An arranged marriage, though, Chris? That can't still be a thing, right?" She does not sound impressed.

"It's complicated," I mumble, wishing I had a simpler explanation to offer. Arranged marriages aren't common in the United States, not even among Italian families anymore. But my mother grew up in a very different culture than I did. Her family's roots in the *cosa nostra* dictated how her life would be led. She hoped that my life would be different, but it's shaping up to be eerily similar.

"I think you should stand up to Giovanni," Kaye suggests as she pulls into a gas station parking lot. "You don't have to marry some stranger if you don't want to. Especially now," she adds, concern etching her features. "You're only eighteen, Chris. You have your whole life ahead of you. What happened to bad boys and bad decisions?"

I wish it were that simple. I wish standing up to Giovanni would solve everything. But there are forces at play that go beyond my will. If the bruise on my cheek is any indication, Giovanni won't stop until he gets what he wants. But my heart sinks, knowing that explaining this to Kaye isn't going to be easy. She won't understand.

"You're right," I lie, forcing a smile on my face. "I'll talk to Giovanni. I'll tell him I don't think this is in my best interest."

Kaye smiles, her warmth radiating through the car. "Good. I'll get some ice for your face. You need anything else while I'm inside?"

Shaking my head, I watch her retreat into the store, a mix of gratitude and uncertainty swirling within me. I'm thankful for her steadying presence, but her plan won't work.

There will be no telling Giovanni that I don't want to do as he says. It was only a tap on the cheek this time, but what if it's more next time?

What if he follows through with killing me?

Chapter 33
Christine

The bruising on my cheek where Giovanni hit me the night before has turned a deep purple and is painful to touch. I alternate between ice packs and hot water bottles in an attempt to reduce the swelling, but my face still feels puffy and heavy. I take Ibuprofen every four hours and pray for a miracle.

The sharp sting of Giovanni's ring slicing the corner of my lip lingers as the only visible wound that hasn't worsened. Though it stopped bleeding and formed a scab by the next day, it remains crusty and sensitive to touch. The skin surrounding the cut is a patchwork of red and pink.

Niccolo calls me, texts me, and even pops up in my Facebook messages uninvited to threaten to show up at my dorm if I don't respond to him. I tell him I'm alright and I just need time to think.

In truth, I can't face him yet; I'm afraid that he'd see the bruise Giovanni left, and he'd try to kill my uncle. Giovanni is a force of nature, and Niccolo, on his best day, wouldn't stand a chance against him.

When Monday rolls around, my face is still too mangled to go to class. It isn't until Niccolo calls me and demands to know where I am that I realize I should have said something to him in advance.

"Where are you?" He barks into the phone.

"I'm sick, Nic."

But he knows that's not true. "Liar. I left you alone yesterday because you asked me to, but it's been two days since you ran out on me. Tell me what's wrong."

Instinctively, I guard the truth of the deepening bruise and lingering swelling. While the latter gradually recedes, it will require a formidable amount of makeup to mask the repulsive shade of purple blossoming across my face. I'm hoping that some of it will have faded by tomorrow so I can return to class without too many questions.

"I just don't feel well, Nic. I'll be back in class on Wednesday, okay?"

The sound of shattering glass breaks the silence like a gunshot, echoing off the walls of Niccolo's classroom and vibrating through the phone. "I need to see you, Christine," he begins with desperation creeping into his tone. "You ran away so quickly the other day. I need to know that you're okay."

Am I okay? My heart pounds in my chest like a drumbeat, the weight of my future now tied to a man responsible for the untimely deaths of three women. And if I were to do a little digging, I have no doubt that I would uncover a trail of bodies left behind by Rocco Castiglione. The thought alone is enough to send fear shivering down my spine and make my skin crawl. "Physically, I'm fine, Nic. It was just a little slap."

An unspoken truth hangs heavily in the silence, its burden shared between us. If I am *physically* fine, then it logically follows that my mental state remains anything but.

My stepfather knows what I mean without me having to say it, and I'm thankful that he doesn't force me to talk. Instead, he clears his throat and says, "We should discuss what happened before you make any decisions. I know it might look like you don't have options, but I told you the other night that I would take care of you. It wasn't just pillow talk, Christine; I was serious."

I know what he's going to say, or at least the gist of it, and I'm not in the mood to hear it yet. He'll wax poetically about how much he loves me and cares for me and how he'll save me from this nightmare of our own making. But I'm wallowing in self-pity, and I feel terrible despite the pain meds and ice packs. I need another day to feel this way before I let Niccolo come up with a solution.

"I'll swing by your classroom tomorrow," I offer. Technically, my class schedule dictates that I see him on Mondays, Wednesdays, and Fridays, but I can carve out some time in my day tomorrow. "I have a free hour around 2:00. Would that work?"

"Of course," he reassures me. "I'll clear my schedule."

When I hang up the phone, a wave of relief washes over me. I expected my stepfather to push back against my suggestion, but he caught me off guard by accepting it instead.

It just gives him more time to plot, the little voice in my head says.

Two days ago, Niccolo thought that my giving myself to him would change everything, but neither of us expected Giovanni to show up and ruin it all.

My stepfather won't take kindly to his plans being changed. In fact, I wouldn't be surprised if he was passively giving me another day to myself because he needs it to plot his revenge.

Chapter 34
Niccolo

Christine shows up at my lecture hall on a gloomy Tuesday afternoon just as my last class for the day is about to begin. Following our call yesterday, I immediately sent out an email to the 2:00 pm students canceling the lecture.

No one is around when she walks in and thank God for that. The mere sight of Christine's face seizes my breath, encasing my lungs in a suffocating grip.

"It looks worse than it feels," she says, her voice tinged with a mix of weariness and defiance as I rise from my chair.

"*Porca puttana. Giuro su Dio che ucciderò quel cazzo di tuo zio.*" I walk over to her and we meet in the middle.

Christine heaves a sigh, her shoulders slumping. "You're not going to kill my uncle," she argues, her voice holding a note of resignation.

Running my thumb across her cheek, a thin layer of powdered makeup appears on my pad. "It's worse than it looks," I glare. "It already looks bad, but you covered it up."

"Of course I did," she retorts, pushing my arm away. "I don't need people asking questions. If they do, I can just say I got in a bar fight this weekend. It worked on the cop."

The lump that forms in my throat feels like it's the size of Texas. "You spoke to the cops?"

Christine dismisses my worries with a wave of her hand. "No, not like that," she groans, frustration evident in her voice. "Kaye got pulled over when she was picking me up, and the cop saw my face. He asked what happened and I told him I got into a fight with some girl at the bar. It's fine, Nic."

Confusion washes over me, leaving me adrift in a sea of untold secrets. There's more to this story, I sense it, but I don't know where to begin probing.

"Anyway, we should talk," Christine shifts gears, her tone tempered with a mix of determination and trepidation. She grabs a seat in the front row and settles down. "I think what happened between us the other night was a mistake."

"No," my response spills forth instinctively, thudding between us with an unwelcome weight. "What happened *afterward* with Giovanni was a mistake, but what happened between us was meant to be. *We* are meant to be, Christine."

She remains resolute, unfazed by my insistence. Our eyes lock, and for the first time in a long while, I don't detect the expected blend of desire and anger in her gaze. Instead, a steadfast confidence shines through. "I'm going to figure out what to do about Giovanni and this forced marriage they're imposing on me," she declares. "But in the meantime, this thing between us has to end."

Enraged, I reach for the nearest item on my desk and hurl it across the room. The stapler explodes upon impact, scattering staples and mechanical fragments into a chaotic display.

This is becoming a bad habit. Yesterday my anger drove me to destroy a glass plaque that had been given to me to celebrate my graduation from the Master's program. If I keep this up, the janitor is going to raise questions about all the broken glass in my trash can.

"Take that back," I demand, my voice laced with a mix of desperation and anger.

"I can't," she replies calmly, her composure unshaken. "If there are rumors getting back to my family, the only way out of this marriage is to squash them."

I slide on my knees in front of her, grabbing the edges of her chair so she can't escape. "That'll get you out of *this* marriage, but not the next. They'll force you to marry someone else, Christine. Eventually, they'll make you marry someone of their choosing. If it isn't Rocco, it'll be someone else."

Christine reaches up and grazes my cheek, her touch a soothing balm after the searing sting of her words. "Not if I leave. If I can stall them until I graduate, I can escape. I can leave Kansas and disappear somewhere they'll never find me."

I don't know what hurts more: the thought of Christine leaving me or the thought of never seeing her again. Both of them make my soul ache. "I know you think this is the only way, but it's not. You could marry me."

She shakes her head, vehemently refusing my suggestion. "They would kill you. If not Giovanni, then Marco. Or, to keep their hands clean, they'd send one of their men to do the job. I can't lose you, my freedom, *and* be married to a murderer. I've considered it, Nic, and I have to choose the least offensive of the two options."

"Losing me isn't offensive?" I counter, grappling with a complex mix of emotions.

Christine sighs heavily as if she regrets beginning this conversation. "Losing you will be hard, but at least you'll still be alive. That's what matters. You'll find someone else one day. You'll move on when I'm gone."

I grab her hand and bring it to my lips, brushing the skin with the gentlest butterfly kiss. "Give me a few weeks. I'm going to take care of this. I talked to Dante already, and we're going to figure something out."

Her bottom lip finds itself caught between her teeth, leaving a faint indentation in her peach-colored flesh. "I don't want your family involved in this, Nic. I don't want your brothers to get hurt."

"They'll be fine," I reassure her, my voice gentle yet determined. "Just give me a few weeks. If we can't find a way out and your only choice is to let me go, I'll understand. But I won't let you go without a fight. If I have to swear allegiance to the Lucatello family and pay a King's ransom for you, I will. I'd do anything for you, Christine."

Her shoulders sag as if a weight has been lifted; I think my words are getting through to her. "I'm scared. I'm terrified that this plan might backfire, and someone will get hurt."

Someone *is* going to get hurt, but it won't be me. "Stop worrying. I promise everything is going to be okay."

My phone starts ringing a second later, interrupting us. I want to ignore it, but Christine tells me to answer.

Retrieving the device from my back pocket, I curse myself for not silencing it when I knew Christine would be here. But on the screen, I see Dante's name. I answer hopefully, thinking that he might have come up with a solution since we spoke on Saturday night. "Hey. I'm with Christine. What's up?" I smile at her as I put the phone on speaker so we can both listen in. "Did you come up with a solution for her problem?"

Dante's reply is slower than usual, laden with an unspoken weight that tugs at my core. "Nic, Dad is dead."

Christine covers her mouth, eyes widening in horror.

I frown at my phone screen even though my brother can't see me. Resentment and relief blend together in a bittersweet cocktail. "I'll have to call you back," I say, abruptly ending the call.

"Nic, we should—" but I cut him off mid-sentence by hanging up.

"My father is dead," I announce aloud, even though Christine could hear my brother as well as me. I've wished for his death a dozen times, all in anger, never in truth. But now he's gone, and I feel a strange mix of emotions.

"Nic," Christine breathes, her voice laden with sympathy, "I'm so sorry for your loss."

For a minute, I forget all about Christine's crisis and become embroiled in my own. They say when it rains, it pours, and right now, it feels like it's storming. "Maybe you should leave. I-I need to-to call…" I trail off.

Who am I going to call? My brothers are my best friends and my worst enemies. They're the only ones I would call; they're the only ones that would understand my complex feelings.

Leaning forward, Christine presses her lips against my cheek. "I'll check on you later, okay? I love you, Nic."

Twenty-four hours ago, hearing those words would have meant the world to me, but now they resonate through my mind like a distant echo bouncing off the walls of the Grand Canyon.

Funny how tragedy can change everything.

Chapter 35
Niccolo

My sister, Lucia, lives in Topeka, but even she shows up to the Grey Goose to mourn our father's loss.

"The doctors aren't sure what happened," Dante explains, his face etched with discontent. The grim line tells us that he isn't impressed by the doctor's explanation. "Fausto woke up a couple of days ago extremely sick. He attributed it to food poisoning from a restaurant he'd gone to the night before. But by the afternoon, his bodyguard was concerned because he was too emaciated from vomiting to stand. The man coaxed Fausto into the car and took him to the hospital."

I take a sip of my whiskey and coke, the comforting burn sliding down my throat as I wait for the bomb to drop. Fausto Terlizzi did not die of food poisoning; it seems impossible that a man who tormented me my entire life and chastised me for picking a different path would be killed by some bad fish.

"When he got to the hospital, it was determined that he was severely dehydrated. This is where the timeline gets a little hazy," Dante sighs. "One nurse said that she gave Fausto an IV for dehydration, while another said that she gave him an IV to help with the nausea and vomiting. However, at some point, he allegedly ripped out the IVs and left. There is no paperwork that denotes what medication Fausto received. I told the hospital that I would be suing for negligence."

"But what happened after father left the hospital?" I frown, my mind grappling to process the chain of events.

Dante shakes his head, weariness filling his gaze. "The bodyguard was nowhere to be found, so Fausto tried to drive himself home. He died en route after hitting a guardrail at 60. Luckily, no one else was involved in the crash, but police officers mentioned charges of reckless endangerment and driving under the influence. Apparently, he had a metric shit ton of drugs in his system."

My otherwise prim and proper sister snorts into her soda, her disbelief resonating through the room. "As if. Father doesn't even take Aspirin when he has a headache. There's no way he was under the influence of anything."

"That's what I thought," Dante concedes with a nod. "We had our own autopsy done, and a toxicology report showed benzodiazepines, methadone, propoxyphene, and PCP in his system."

Salvatore gets to the point before Dante does, his voice dripping with suspicion. "Father was drugged."

My brain feels a little slow. I don't know if it's the alcohol or the shock still setting in, but my thoughts refuse to race at their usual speed. While my brothers start volleying ideas back and forth, it isn't until Lucia asks, "What about Chrissy or whatever your deceased wife's daughter's name is?" that it dawns on me.

"No," I protest, my voice laced with disbelief, feeling like all the sensation has drained from my body. "Christine never would have done something like this."

"What about her family?" Luciano chimes in. "Her uncles are pretty fearsome or something, aren't they?"

Father died on Tuesday, four days after Giovanni showed up. He threatened me, but *only* me. He didn't threaten to hurt my family, only me. Right?

Dante speaks for me. "There has been some controversy between the Lucatello brothers and Nic, but let's not rule out Father's other enemies. The Lucatellos had a problem with *Nic*, not a problem with the Terlizzis."

"What'd you do?" Salvatore asks, a mischievous grin playing on his lips. "You get their little angel pregnant?"

God, I hope so, but I don't think that's it. "No, Sally," I shoot him a glare. "Her uncle wants to arrange a marriage between her and some Castiglione enforcer. He said it'll strengthen their alliance."

Dante's brow furrows as he pieces together an imaginary puzzle. He runs his finger around the rim of the glass in front of him, lost in thought. "Why does he need to strengthen his alliance with the Castigliones? The Lucatellos are a cog in the machine. It would be a step down for the Castigliones to marry off one of their enforcers to Christine." His mind churns, attempting to conceive every possible scenario. This is why he's the prized Terlizzi; Dante can see all sides of a problem at once.

"Unless said enforcer is a known murderer and no one of note wants to marry their daughter to him." Dante knows this; I've told him everything I know about Rocco Castiglione, and I'm sure he's found out even more in his research.

"Which would strengthen the Lucatellos' relationship with the Castigliones by showing their trust and loyalty. Saverio would want to show his appreciation, but the Lucatellos aren't hurting for money," Dante mumbles, lost in his thoughts. His mind works like a detective unraveling a complex case.

"Which means Leonardo Lucatello would ask for a position among the leadership. His counsel and wisdom are widely revered; he would have a lot to offer the Castiglione family. But if no position was open…" he trails off, his voice tinged with realization.

"Giovanni told me that his father was retiring, and he'd be in charge of the Lucatello operations from now on," I remind my older brother.

That's the final piece of the puzzle Dante needs. His head snaps up, his eyes widening with the weight of his realization. "Giovanni killed Father so Leonardo could take up the role of Consigliere. That puts Leonardo in a cushy position that doesn't require him to get his hands dirty and gives Giovanni leadership over the second most important family in the Castiglione machine. They're no longer cogs in the machine; they *are* the machine."

That does not bode well for the Terlizzi family. If Dante is right, after Fausto is laid to rest, Saverio Castiglione will announce his successor. When it comes to Consigliere, a position known for counseling the head of the family, nepotism is forgotten. The Consigliere must be wise but not willing to undermine their boss. They must achieve a delicate balance of wanting to see the family succeed without seeking power for themselves.

"Lucia, we've allowed you to go your own way," Dante begins, "but whatever you hear at this table must never be repeated."

She rolls her eyes at Dante, a lingering hint of her teenage rebellion still present. "Okay, *Dad*," Lucia exaggerates the word, her sarcasm dripping off her tongue. "Tell me something I don't know." Sometimes I envy her for being granted the freedoms that our father detested me for taking without his permission.

Dante gestures at the bartender, and in no time at all, a round of bourbon is brought to the table. Shot glasses are placed in front of each of us, brimming with dark amber liquid, emanating a smoky aroma.

"Things are going to change going forward," he addresses us, his voice authoritative. "If the Lucatellos are making a play for power, we have to be ready. Father thought that marrying Niccolo off to Caterina would create an alliance between our families, but that doesn't seem to be the case."

The moment Caterina died, I became useless to the Lucatellos. If I had been more involved in the family business like Dante, I might have seen this coming.

"I think it's no surprise that I will take over the family now that Father has passed."

Luciano slaps his hand over his mouth, his eyes wide with mock astonishment. "Oh, my God, I did not see this coming."

Dante retaliates by throwing a used napkin at him. "Shut up," he says with a grin. "The Lucatellos are positioning themselves for a war, which means we'll need to adjust our ranks to keep everyone safe."

"Including Christine," I add before he goes on. "She doesn't want to marry Rocco. She's being forced into this. We talked about it, Dante."

He raises a hand to silence me, and the weight of the gesture sends shockwaves through the room. Dante commands all the respect and power that our Father did. "Nic, we'll talk about her later."

I slam my fists down on the table, defying him in the same way I defied our father for the past three decades. "No. We talk about her now. She's being used as a pawn in Leonardo and Giovanni's games. I will not watch her be forced into a marriage that will break and destroy her."

Dante's head tilts ever so slightly, barely noticeable to anyone else at the table who watches the two of us spar. "How far are you willing to go for this girl, Niccolo?" His gaze intensifies as he enforces the question. "What are you willing to lose for her?"

"Everything," I answer, my voice firm with determination. "I'd die for Christine if it meant saving her life."

A menacing grin spreads across my older brother's face, sending a shiver down my spine. "Dying is easy, Lolo. It's living with the consequences of your actions that will haunt you forever." His words drip with malice as he leans in close, lowering his voice so our brothers can't hear him. "If you want to save Christine, you must be prepared to descend into the darkness and confront what lurks within. Are you ready for what that means?"

I grab the shot glass, its smooth surface cool against my fingertips, and bring it to my lips. I never break eye contact as I toss it back, letting the sharp liquid burn its way down my throat. "I'm ready to do whatever it takes to keep Christine safe. Come hell or high water," I nod solemnly, my voice filled with resolve.

"Good," he leans back in his chair. "Because hell is more likely."

Chapter 36
Christine

I would be more worried about Niccolo if Finals weren't right around the corner. The end of Thanksgiving weekend means we are less than three weeks away from the biggest test of the semester—and we have one in every class.

Ever since Niccolo sent me away after finding out about his father's passing, he hasn't answered my texts or calls or even come to class. Suddenly, I find myself empathizing with his previous struggles to get a response from me.

I didn't know Nic's father well, nor was I familiar with their relationship. But losing a parent is never easy.

The first time I met Fausto Terlizzi was when Niccolo married my mother. He grabbed my hand, brought it to his mouth, and told me I was the prettiest little girl he'd ever seen. But he said it in a way that made my stomach ache.

Niccolo advised me to stay away from Fausto after that, but by the time I turned sixteen, it didn't matter anymore. The Terlizzi family events were attended by girls much younger than me, and Fausto had moved on to harassing them. No one ever stopped him, and I thought it was weird. But everyone turned a blind eye to his creepy behavior, and there was nothing I could do.

I think about that in between studying for Finals and spending my days in the library. I wait for Niccolo to text back, and try to figure out what I was doing during Calculus because none of my notes make sense.

Kaye effortlessly progresses through her Finals prep, informing me that if I had dedicated the semester to studying rather than fooling around with Theo from the football team, I would have a stronger grasp of the material.

I playfully respond that if she had spent more time studying instead of fucking her stepbrother, she wouldn't be pregnant. It's a fun little game we like to play where we both wind up angry and frustrated. Finals have a way of driving people crazy.

Studying with Sienna is more my speed. She has flashcards and she bites her nails down to the quick while reviewing them.

"I'm not dumb," she swears, "I just don't test well." But I appreciate the realism of our study sessions because it reflects my own fears: that I spent the entire term learning material but will still somehow bomb the test and fail the class.

I'm almost thankful for Niccolo's absence for the week because it gives me more time to ponder my upcoming nuptials and figure out how to get out of them without hurting anyone. With each passing day that I don't find a solution, I feel a growing sense of dread in the pit of my stomach.

But as I make my way to the library on Saturday night, students filling the seats around me with only one weekend before Finals remaining, my stepfather finally reappears via text message.

NICCOLO

Hi beautiful

As my phone lights up with a new notification, my heart jumps into my throat. I feel a rush of emotions flood through me as I see his name on the screen—excitement, nervousness, and a tinge of sadness. It's been so long since we've spoken, and I didn't realize how much I missed him until now.

Hey. How are you?

NICCOLO

Im gnna need you to pick me up

As my eyes scan the screen, I frown in slight annoyance at the easy misspellings. It's 8 pm on a Saturday, so maybe he's getting drunk with his friends. But then again, why would he want to do that when he could be spending time with me? The thought nags at me, and I can't push it aside. The sound of distant laughter filters across the room, adding to my frustration. A pang of longing hits me, wishing I could be there with him, wherever he may be.

"Don't think like that," I chastise myself. "I don't want to be with Niccolo. Being apart is for our own good."

"Miss," some guy at the other side of the table whisper-yells at me, "can you keep it down? I'm studying."

I shoot him an apologetic wince, my cheeks burning with embarrassment, before hastily typing a response to my stepfather. My fingers fumble over the keys as I write a message and then delete it, my mind racing with excuses and explanations. The bright glow of my phone screen illuminates my face, casting a shadow across my features as I desperately try to salvage our conversation.

> Where are you at? Are you okay?

NICCOLO
biker bar hurry

He's down the street? And he didn't even drop by to say hello?

"Stop," I mumble under my breath as I begin to pack up my things. Just because we had sex and he made some promises that he hasn't followed through with doesn't mean I'm going to fall head over heels for the guy. He's my stepfather, and soon, he'll be nobody to me. Once I convince Giovanni to let me finish college before I get married and I run away to Argentina after graduation, I won't even think about Niccolo anymore.

But right now, he needs me to pick him up. And right now, it's okay that I'm thinking about Nic. Right now, there's nothing wrong with wanting to be with him.

I tug my thick, woolen jacket snugly around my body and sling my heavy backpack over one shoulder, bracing myself for the biting winter weather. I didn't get anything done, but I haven't spoken to Niccolo in almost a week. Maybe it's for the best that I pick him up, get him sober, and make sure he's alright. I remember what it was like when my father walked out on our family and the emptiness that filled me when my mother passed. If Niccolo feels even half as bad as that, I need to be there for him.

"I can be his shoulder to cry on," I tell myself. "He'll appreciate that."

I'm patting myself on the back for being a good friend and stepdaughter right up until the moment I make it to the bar district and walk into Leather & Lager. I've stepped out of my calm and quiet life right into the middle of an action movie. The Terlizzi brothers are fist-fighting with a bunch of dudes in leather, and I don't think they're winning.

What the hell did Niccolo get himself into, and why did he call me to get him out of it?

Chapter 37
Christine

I almost catch a fist trying to break up the fight. It's enough to send me reeling backward, jaw-dropping in shock. "Un-fucking-believable," I mutter to myself, the words escaping through clenched teeth.

My gaze fixes on a security guard standing by the door. With his arms crossed over his chest, he watches the fight unfold with the detached enthusiasm of a spectator at a prime-time show. My frustration boils over, and I confront him. "Are you going to do anything about this?"

Rolling his eyes, the security guard inserts two fingers into his mouth and lets out a harsh whistle, cutting through the chaotic commotion. The fight momentarily freezes, as if someone hit the pause button on a movie. "Hey. Knock it the fuck off."

One of the leather-clad bikers scowls in disappointment. "Bryan, he started it," the man complains while pointing at Niccolo, who stands at the center of the turmoil.

"Well, this little lady wants it to stop," Bryan shrugs, his indifference palpable. "Do whatever. I don't care."

"No!" I yell over the cheer the bikers let out. I force myself through the mess, and men back up, throwing their hands into the air so they can't be accused of touching me. "Nic," I plead, "let's go."

Niccolo looks worse for wear. Blood drips from his nose, a gash above his eyebrow oozes crimson, and a bruise darkens his right eye. But Niccolo is undeterred. "Lemme at'em, Chrissy. I can take any of these fuckers."

The temperature in the room rises, the air crackling with newly formed tension. Fists tighten, the crowd inches closer, and restless voices intensify. "Let's go, baby," I coo, desperately trying to pull Niccolo away from his opponent.

Thank God one of the Terlizzi brothers has common sense. There's a small scuffle a few feet away, and I look over to see Dante shoving someone off him. He adjusts his shirt before walking over and looping an arm around Niccolo's waist. "C'mon, *bambina*, we can take him to my place," he grunts at me.

I don't want to argue, not when the tension in the room threatens to consume us before we get through the door.

Salvatore and Luciano extract themselves from their own fights and follow in our footsteps.

"Is Lucia gone?" Luciano asks when we're blasted with a blast of frigid winter air.

Luciano and Lucia are the twins of the Terlizzi family, the first in a century. Niccolo once told me they were inseparable as children, but they've since grown apart.

"Yeah," Dante grunts as he pushes Niccolo forward, mirroring my lead. "She left an hour ago. Said she had papers to grade or something. On a fucking Saturday night. Stand the fuck up," he changes the subject by yelling at Niccolo. "Christ, who let you have that fourth shot?"

"Four shots?" My cheeks drain of color. "What the hell, Dante?"

We reach my car, and Dante practically tosses his brother into the backseat. Niccolo lands with a groan. "He's a big boy, Christine. He can make his own choices."

"I don't want to be in the car when he throws up," Salvatore declares. "Want to split an Uber?" He asks his little brother.

Luciano simply shrugs. "You guys going to be okay if we head out?"

Dante shuts Niccolo's door and climbs in the front passenger seat. "If we're not, it's because *that one* got us T-boned," he gestures toward me.

"It was one accident," I seethe, glaring at him. "And it wasn't even my fault."

Salvatore snickers and elbows his little brother. "Let's go. They're probably fine."

I mumble under my breath, "Not if I kill them first." I should have stayed in the library and studied instead of responding to Niccolo's 911. What a fucking nightmare.

"Do you know where I live?" Dante asks once I climb inside. "Out by the airport, between—"

"Yeah, yeah, I remember." He resides in a beautiful compound halfway between Rosedale and Manhattan. It's impossible to miss—it's the only structure in the area that breaks up nature with its utilitarian design. "What happened back there? Nic texted me to pick him up. I haven't heard from him since Tuesday."

Dante fiddles with the radio, transitioning from Taylor Swift to Kenny Chesney. The melody of *'No Shoes, No Shirt, No Problems'* fills the car, pulling us back to the early 2000s. "We've been dealing with shit. Shit you're probably responsible for."

My grip tightens around the steering wheel as I speed through a yellow light. "What? I just told you I haven't spoken to Nic since Tuesday. How am I responsible for any of what you're going through?"

"Your uncles," he explains matter-of-factly. "You know they killed our father?"

I open my mouth to respond, but I can't seem to form words. My brain is telling me to apologize and offer whatever I can to make amends for my uncle's mistakes, but I can't wrap my lips around the sentences.

Dante watches me struggle for something to say for a long moment before letting me off the hook. "Relax, little Lucatello." He leans back in the chair to make himself comfortable, reclining the seat until he's stretched out. "I think it's one big orchestrated event that will effectively take the Terlizzis off the map by replacing our family with yours. Nic assures me you aren't part of the family making these decisions."

"I'm not part of the family at all," I swiftly correct him. "My mother never wanted this for me."

Dante extends a hand to pat my lap, a gesture that's meant to be comforting but feels condescending. "That's tough, cookie. You're a part of it now. And luckily for you, you have Nic. He wants to keep you safe."

I shove Dante's hand away and shoot him a glare. Niccolo groans in the backseat and makes a few mumbled remarks, but

I can't understand him. "I have a plan already. I don't need you."

"Sure you don't," he chuckles. "What's your plan? You gonna kill Giovanni?"

My stomach churns. "N-no," I stammer. "I was going to leave after graduation."

"Well, that won't do our family any good. How about you wait until we kill Giovanni, and then you can bask in the benefits?"

I'm going to be sick. I don't like what my uncle is doing, but I don't want him dead. "You can't be serious."

"Serious as a heart attack, little Lucatello." He motions toward the road. "You're about to miss my exit."

As I get off the highway that leads to Dante's house, we finish the rest of the drive in silence. I'm afraid if I say anything else, I'm going to hear more about the Terlizzi plan than I want to know. I've always accepted that my mother and stepfather were part of a sinister organization, but it wasn't what I wanted for myself. I've always maintained a distance from my family's crimes and avoided asking any questions about them. Now, I feel thrust into a scandal that has nothing to do with me.

"He loves you, you know," Dante says as we pull off the road toward his place.

My grip on the steering wheel tightens. "I know," I respond, my voice shaky with emotion. But the realization that he had confided in his brother about it catches me off guard.

Dante yawns as we pull up to the gate surrounding his compound. A bodyguard comes to my window, and when he sees Dante in the front seat and Niccolo in the back, he bows his head and clicks a button that forces the metal barricade to open. "Power has its perks." He tosses me a lazy grin.

"Is he okay?" I look in my rearview mirror to check on Niccolo in the backseat. He's curled up, snoring softly.

Looking over his shoulder, Dante smiles fondly at his sleeping brother. "He'll sleep it off. We made some decisions tonight that I think are weighing heavily on his soul, but he'll be alright."

I'm tempted to inquire about those decisions, but I know it's not my place to ask. "I mean, is he okay after the death of your father?"

The grand courtyard unfolds before us, a dazzling display of lights streaming in every direction. The warm glow casts a mesmerizing spell, beckoning us deeper into the heart of the estate. Rows of sparkling lanterns line the pathways, leading to hidden alcoves and secret gardens. Dante has a beautiful home.

"Nic had a complicated relationship with Fausto. I think he's glad Father's dead but also upset that he's glad about it. He's confused," Dante explains. "I think we all are. Fausto Terlizzi was a hard man to get along with. There were things that he believed in that the rest of us did not. While we went along with him, it was because we had no choice, *not* because we agreed with him."

That only makes me worry about Niccolo even more. He put a great deal of space between himself and his family. What happens now that Fausto is dead? "Do you need help carrying him inside? Will Adalina be upset that he's here?"

With a charming smile, Dante readjusts his seat back to the way he found it. "I'll be fine, so will my wife. If you see your uncles in the next few days, don't mention anything I told you. You understand?"

"I-I didn't have plans to see them," I frown. "Well, sort of. I *did*," I correct myself, "but only to discuss the marriage they're trying to arrange."

With a devil-may-care attitude, Dante offers, "If you're up for it, I can add Rocco to our hit list." His nonchalant tone belies the gravity of his words. "Nic filled me in on what went down last weekend and I've been looking into Rocco Castiglione. He's not someone to be trifled with. He'll probably kill you within the first year." The weightlessness of Dante's voice catches me off guard. I don't know if he's joking or if he's serious. That's the problem with Dante: you never know where you stand because he's sweet and kind until he's not.

"That's what I'm going to talk to Gio and Marco about. I'm going to see if they'll change their minds if I offer to give up —" I stop mid-sentence, realizing that I'm about to admit to Dante that I've been having a relationship with his brother.

A smile, mischievous and alluring, plays on his lips as he indulges himself by leaning forward. The movement is slow and deliberate as if savoring every moment. His eyes sparkle with a hint of mischief, and his lips curl up in a playful grin. "I know about you and Nicci," he whispers. "It's a little scandalous, but I've done shadier things than you fucking your stepfather."

A pink stain spreads across my cheeks. "There's nothing going on between Nic and me." Not anymore. That's what I'm going to promise my uncles in exchange for my freedom.

"Maybe, maybe not," Dante shrugs. "But if you love him the way he loves you, you'll give me a few days to figure something out. The Terlizzi family may have lost their head, but we will come back stronger. And I promise, if you give us a few days, we'll figure out how to protect you from your family's wishes. Nic insists on it, in fact."

I haven't heard from him in five days, but somehow he spent that time juggling his grief and figuring out how to save me from a fate that we inflicted upon ourselves. "I'll, uh, I'll leave it alone for now. Thank you, Dante."

He climbs out of the car and opens the passenger door to haul Niccolo out of the backseat. "Don't thank me. Thank Nicci. He was willing to trade his life for yours if that's what it took to keep you safe. Big heart, this one."

Chapter 38
Niccolo

When I wake up, everything is a disorienting whirl. I'm also not in my room, which is concerning. The only thing I know for sure is the sound of Dante angrily yelling in Italian at someone means I'm in good hands.

As I attempt to sit up, a wave of pain surges through my body, radiating from my skull to the tips of my hair. I groan and quickly lie back down. "I have a hangover." Which seems fitting, since the last thing I can remember is throwing back shots in a bar that smelled like stale beer.

Dante's footsteps echo on the marble floor, gradually growing closer. "Nic?" he calls out, his voice tinged with both worry and amusement. "Oh, shit," he chuckles upon coming into the room. "Your face is messed up."

With aching fingers, I reach up to touch my throbbing forehead, realizing that the excruciating discomfort is not solely due to the effects of alcohol but also the consequence of the gash above my eyebrow. "Did you do this?" I ask, my voice tinged with accusation.

Dante snorts dismissively as he takes a seat on the couch across from me. "I wish I had, little brother. Alas, it was some biker at the bar who did this. Lucky bastard."

I vaguely remember going to Leather & Lager. "Didn't we start drinking in Manhattan?" I frown as more of the night's events come back to me. "How'd we get to Rosedale?"

"Uber," Dante replies nonchalantly, shrugging his shoulders. "Lucky was trying to get lucky, and Sally tagged along. Meanwhile, you rambled on about calling Christine. Which must have been some kind of bat symbol because she showed up at the bar."

Christine. Fragments of her image flit through my mind, accompanied by a flash of red, but that could have been blood. "What'd I say to her?"

Dante busies himself with his phone, his fingers rapidly swiping across the screen. The sight makes me dizzy. "I don't know," he responds, his voice laced with disinterest. "I don't even know when you called her. One moment, we were downing shots, and the next, she walked in just as you were taking a swing at some behemoth of a biker."

That wasn't smart. I don't remember why I wanted to fight the bikers, but I vaguely recall getting punched in the stomach. "Where's Luc and Sal?"

"Home, probably. Unless they went somewhere else after Christine showed up."

Dante makes a sound of amusement before casually discarding his phone next to him on the couch. "Listen, Nicci, are you sure you want to protect this girl?" He probes, a trace of concern creeping into his voice.

"Where is she?" I ask. I'm afraid to sit up again because the pain from the last time I tried is only just now starting to recede.

Dante repeats his previous statement with a shrug. "Home, probably. I don't know, Nic. She dropped us off last night and left. Just answer the question."

The drive home was a blur. Dante threw me into a car, and the rest of the trip was a blur of stoplights. "She saved me."

Dante sits there quietly, staring at me with a rage that I can feel simmering beneath the surface. "Niccolo, listen to me." He takes a no-nonsense stance by leaning forward and placing his elbows on his knees. "She said she was going to give you up. Is that really the kind of girl you want, Nic?"

My stomach churns, an unpleasant reminder that we skipped dinner last night. It explains why I feel utterly miserable. "Christine's uncles want her to get married, and—" I start explaining.

"Yeah, yeah," Dante interrupts dismissively. "I know all about that. You want to fight for her and blah blah blah. But I'm telling you, she was ready to give you up to secure her freedom. Is that the kind of woman you want to fight for?"

He doesn't have the whole story. If the two of them talked last night, that means she didn't tell him everything. "She was doing it to protect me," I interject, stubbornly defending her. "She believes that if she marries me, Giovanni will kill me."

Dante mutters a curse, running a hand through his hair in frustration. "*Gesù Cristo*," he murmurs, pacing across the living room. "You're discussing marriage with the Lucatello girl?"

I shrug my shoulders, watching my brother intently as he paces back and forth. "I love her, Dante. If you're not going to support me—"

He cuts me off again. "I'm going to help you. I already told you last night I was going to help you. We discussed this in great detail. I just wanted to make sure you knew what you were getting yourself into with that girl."

I don't enter into things that I haven't fully vetted. Just because I haven't embraced the family traditions doesn't mean I didn't learn at our father's knee like the rest of my brothers. "Did she seem mad last night when she picked us up?"

Dante dismissively waves off the question. "No, just concerned. If I had allowed her, she would have helped me carry your sorry ass inside, prepared a late-night snack, and stayed with you until you woke up."

"But she didn't do any of that?" I lament, yearning for the sight of Christine's beautiful face instead of Dante's exasperating presence.

"You don't see her around, do you?" Dante retorts irritably. "I sent her on her way. I was perfectly capable of carrying your drunk self to the couch, wasn't I?"

I wish it would have been a bed, then perhaps my back wouldn't hurt so much, but I guess this is better than the floor. "We didn't wake Adalina or anything last night, did we?" I wince. "I can apologize if we did. Where is she?" I make a concerted effort to sit up, and even though my head feels like it's going to explode, I hold myself aloft while I look around for my sister-in-law.

"Don't worry about my wife," Dante replies, his tone indicating irritation. "She's fine. She doesn't even know you're here."

I can't remember the last time I saw Adalina. Was it at Thanksgiving? Or was she visiting family? "I can go. Call an Uber or something," I mumble. "I don't want to interrupt your Sunday."

Dante returns to his seat on the couch, a serious look in his eyes as he speaks to me. "I talked to a guy this morning. He's been keeping his ear to the ground since Father died. There's been some talk of the families turning against us. They see us as weak without Fausto in charge."

I don't have time for this. I have about a million other tasks to focus on, the least of which is worrying about my brother trying to navigate the waters of organized crime now that Dad is dead. "Do you need me to do something?"

"Be careful," he warns. "Everyone thinks you aren't involved in this thing of ours; they'll probably leave you alone. But if some lowly button man gets the bright idea that knocking you off will get to me," Dante shudders just saying the words out loud. "I don't want to have to call your daughter and tell her that her daddy-boyfriend is dead."

"*Step*daughter," I clarify with a glare. "And no one is going to do anything to me or to the family." If they did, they'd be asking for a war, and no one wants that.

Dante remains skeptical, yet he helps me to my feet. "Still, be careful out there. I don't want you getting shot. I love you or whatever."

"Awww," I tease, a faint smile forming on my lips. "Say it again."

He tries to suppress a smile, but I can still make out the corners of his lips twitching. "Never mind. I take it back. I hope they shoot your dick off."

I sling an arm around his shoulder, leaning onto Dante so he can support my weight. "I love you too, brother."

Chapter 39
Christine

Dante told me not to visit with my uncle, but I have to. I already contacted Giovanni to see if he'd be interested in discussing his decision to arrange a marriage between Rocco and me. To change my mind now would be tantamount to slapping my uncle in the face and spitting on his shoes.

I gird my loins and force myself to drive to Manhattan, giving myself a pep talk along the way.

"Gio would never hurt me." When he backhanded me, that was different. It was a show of discipline intended to keep me in line.

"Gio wants what's best for me." Ultimately, he wants me to distance myself from Niccolo because people will think poorly of us if we carry on this way.

"Gio will see my side and change his mind." He isn't so mad at me that he'd force me to marry Rocco Castiglione if I really didn't want to.

I repeat the sentences to myself over and over again, trying to find a flaw in my thinking. But any reasonable person would view this situation through my eyes. I messed up by fooling around with my stepfather, but I can rectify the situation. All I have to do is promise Giovanni the moon, and he'll dissolve the arranged marriage. Then I'll give Dante and Niccolo free rein to figure out everything else.

As I enter Nico's, a charming Italian restaurant in the bustling heart of Manhattan's business district, my eyes immediately fall on Giovanni. He is ensconced at a table with a beautiful waitress, her white shirt crisp and pristine against her olive skin. His hand rests confidently on her waist, his fingers gripping possessively as he dissolves into a peal of laughter. The discomfort on the waitress's face is evident, yet Giovanni either fails to notice or simply doesn't care as he tightens his hold and continues to revel in his amusement.

As soon as I sense the uncomfortable tension between the waitress and my uncle, my body shifts into protective mode. If this were some guy hitting on Kaye and making unwanted advances on her, I'd punch him in the throat. But that kind of behavior would get us kicked out of Nico's, and Giovanni wouldn't listen to my pleas if I embarrassed him like that.

Instead, I approach the pair with a forced smile and interject myself into their conversation with a loud and friendly greeting.

Giovanni releases the trembling girl and stands, offering me a hug. His embrace is surprisingly warm and tight, a rare display of affection from him. But I can sense his eyes on the waitress, trying to impress her with his tender gesture.

"This is my niece," he introduces me to the girl with the

notepad. "Christine, this is Ariel. She's a junior at Blackmore. Have you two met?"

I pull away from my uncle and take a seat, shaking my head at the question. There are 20,000 students on the BU campus. Does Giovanni really think that I know all of them?

"I'm Ariel, your waitress for today. Can I get you something to drink?" Her eyes, glinting with unspoken emotion, remain fixed on mine as if trying to convey a message without words.

I'm not sure what happened before I arrived, but I wish I could assure the girl that she has my support now. The most Gio would have done in front of everyone was make her feel uneasy, but I'll put a stop to that now. "I'll take a water. Thank you."

Ariel nods her head before running from the table. I wouldn't be surprised if she never came back; I wouldn't.

"How have you been?" Giovanni's lips pull back, revealing a wolfish grin. His eyes sparkle mischievously as he leans back in his chair, his posture relaxed and confident. He looks put together with his slicked-back hair and designer suit.

"I'm alright, Uncle."

"And how are your classes? Are you missing any today?" The corners of his lips never falter, forming a flawless smile that conceals his thoughts and emotions.

As another woman approaches our table with a tray of drinks, she quickly sets them down and mentions that Ariel will be back soon to take our order. Before walking away, I catch her giving Giovanni a quick once-over with a disgusted expression on her face.

"No, Uncle. I scheduled lunch around my classes." Not that I have too many classes to schedule around.

Giovanni ordered a draft beer before I arrived. He grabs the glass and downs a quarter of it, smacking his lips together when he's finished. "That's good. I would hate to be responsible for you falling behind in your classes. Speaking of classes," his lips pull tight into a frown, "will you have any classes with Niccolo after the break?"

I hope my face doesn't reflect the fear that tears through my body at the mention of my stepfather. I try to wear a neutral expression, but I'm afraid my emotions are visible. "I believe so. Nic also teaches an Experimental Methods in Psychology course in the spring and a Cognitive Psychology course each semester. Both of them are required for my degree."

"Have you ever entertained the idea of pursuing a different career?" Giovanni proposes, his voice laced with skepticism.

My expression contorts into a scowl, and a surge of irritation courses through me. "No, I haven't because this is what I want to do. I want to work with children."

Giovanni raises a slender finger, attempting to downplay my passion. "Ah, then perhaps you should consider becoming a teacher."

My teeth grind together in exasperation, my frustration manifesting in the clenching of my jaw. The tension builds, causing my cheeks to tighten. "No, Gio, you're missing the point entirely. I aspire to do more than simply *educate* children. I want to make a transformative impact in their lives. I want to help them."

"Teaching, helping," he nonchalantly waves his hand in dismissal, "it's the same thing."

If I scream at him, I'll lose whatever goodwill he's saved up for this encounter. And God, how I want to kick and scream and yell until he gets it through his head that I'm not going to become a teacher. But I have to be the mature one. I have to swallow my anger like a bitter pill and let it sour my stomach instead of releasing it on Giovanni. "Thank you for the suggestion, Uncle, but I don't think that's the right option for me at this time."

A mischievous grin spreads across his face as he lifts his beer to take another swig, but our conversation is suddenly interrupted by Ariel's return.

She takes our order without looking at either of us. Giovanni asks her what she's majoring in while reaching out to grab her again. In a clumsy attempt to avoid his advances, she bumps into our table and hastily excuses herself with an apology. "Sorry. I'm a little busy at the moment. I'll be right back."

She's never coming back.

"Can we talk about the marriage that you and Grandfather are arranging for me?" I ask, changing the subject.

"Of course, we can. We're thinking a June wedding will be pretty. The weather would be warm but not yet burdened with the suffocating heat of the Kansas summer. And yet, far enough into the season that a rainstorm is unlikely. You don't mind having an outdoor wedding, do you?" Giovanni asks after a moment as if remembering I still have a say in the matter.

I have to force a smile on my face. Inside, I'm angry that all the details have already been planned out, but I can't tell my uncle that. "I was actually wondering if you might reconsider the marriage," I offer as cheerfully as I can muster. "I understand why you and Grandfather were upset, but I've ended things with Niccolo and—"

"And, what?" Giovanni raises an eyebrow. His fingers dance along the tabletop, patiently tapping on the dark wood. "What can you offer me that will please the Castigliones more than your marriage to Rocco?"

I gape at him, not knowing what to say. "What can I *offer*?" I echo his words.

"Yes. The Castiglione family is delighted that we've offered a union for one of their prized enforcers. Saverio says that there will be a reward for our loyalty. Can you offer me something better?"

He's gone mad. His actions are beyond rational thought and are evidence of insanity. "Please, Uncle," I desperately plead, my voice barely above a whisper as I glance around the crowded restaurant. "Rocco is a monster. He'll hurt me, maybe even kill me."

Giovanni purses his lips together in a show of mock disappointment. "Maybe you should have thought about that before you snubbed your family to stay with Niccolo after your mother's death. Or perhaps you could have considered it when you were whoring yourself out in high school to any boy that would have you."

"That's not fair!" I argue. "I dated, but no more than your daughters will date when they're in high school."

"My daughters won't date in high school," Giovanni glares. "They know their role. They know that they are to be the pride of the Lucatello family. They are well-trained. They won't throw their virginity away on a sixteen-year-old boy that can't tell the difference between fucking a woman and sticking his dick in an apple pie."

My face burns with humiliation as Giovanni's characterization of me humbles me to the ground. "I'm not a part of the *'family'*, Giovanni. My mother didn't want that for me."

My uncle rolls his eyes. "I don't care what my sister wanted for you when she was alive. It's bad enough that she married an Irish prick who ran out on her because he couldn't handle the family he married into. She won't control your life from beyond the grave. I want you married to someone of *my* choosing, and that's what will happen."

The churning in my stomach intensifies, leaving me feeling nauseous and lightheaded. As if on cue, a tantalizing whiff of freshly baked rolls wafts through the air as a kind soul places a basket brimming with warmth in front of me. However, the mere thought of breaking bread with my uncle is enough to make me want to vomit.

"I will not be coerced into marrying Rocco," I assert, my voice trembling with fear and uncertainty.

He reaches out to open the bread basket, pulling out a fluffy roll. As he bites into it, he savors the flavors on his tongue. Giovanni enjoys every bite, allowing the tension between us to rise until I think I will explode if another second passes.

"Did you know I married my wife right out of high school and was responsible for overseeing her education. I chose not to let her attend university because I didn't want it to fill her head with nonsense."

"I don't know what this—"

He cuts me off before I can finish my sentence. "Your mother should have chosen to do the same with you because now you have it in your head that you have some kind of power here.

But make no mistake, Christine, you are a second-class citizen. You have no rights."

"This is the United States," I protest, "not a third-world country. I have every right—"

"No!" Giovanni slams his fists down on the table, causing the glasses to shake. Every eye in the restaurant turns towards us as he leans across the table and whispers sharply, his voice dripping with disdain, "We are not governed by the same rules as society. The sooner you realize that the better off you'll be."

Are my hands shaking? My hands feel like they're shaking.

"You've had your fun, Christine. You can finish out your second semester of college. You can do whatever you want. Hell, if you continue fucking your stepfather, I'll look the other way. But come June," he menacingly narrows his eyes, "you're done with all that. You'll marry Rocco and move to Kansas City. You'll be *his* to order around as *he* pleases. And if you don't like it, you can argue with him and see what happens. But I guarantee he'll leave your pretty pale skin with fist-sized bruises."

The restaurant has the heat cranked up, but I still shiver with fear. My blood feels like it turns to ice, freezing in my veins.

Giovanni leans back in his chair and smirks at me with satisfaction. "I heard that Fausto Terlizzi died last week. Send my condolences to your boyfriend. It took us a while to figure out the perfect concoction of drugs to give him; then, we had to figure out a delivery method. But in the end, everything worked out. Tell Niccolo he had a chance to deliver what I wanted, and he failed. Now he and his pissant brothers can deal with the fallout."

Sometimes, when traumatic events happen, your brain tries to shield you by blocking them from your memory because they're too painful to handle.

As if in a trance, I rise from my chair without thinking. I walk away from Giovanni, leaving behind the classical music playing overhead and the buzz of people chatting about their Christmas plans. I step into the cold and let the breeze bring me back to reality.

My uncle is a ruthless monster who murdered Niccolo's father and now plans to use me as his next sacrifice. He has no regard for human life, only his own selfish desires. I am nothing but a pawn in his twisted game of power and control.

The thought of being tied to Rocco Castiglione for the rest of my life fills me with dread. But I refuse to go down without a fight.

My uncle thinks he's the king of the castle, but even castles fall when they're under siege.

Chapter 40
Niccolo

Time feels like it's moving at double speed, leaving me disoriented and disconnected from the days and my responsibilities.

As much as I hate to take off time during Finals week to help arrange my father's funeral, the Dean of my college says that this is the best-case scenario. All they need to do is find someone to proctor the test, which is far easier to do than finding someone to teach Psychology to first-year college students.

Christine is just as easy to please. When I ask her to meet up, she tells me that she's studying for Finals and helping Kaye with her pregnancy. The latter catches me off-guard because I didn't know that my stepdaughter's best friend was pregnant. Unfortunately, I'm too busy consoling Mother and discussing hors'd oeuvres options to give it much thought.

Dante promised to assist with Father's funeral arrangements, but I only catch glimpses of him rushing in and out of his office, his bodyguard trailing closely behind. Two men stationed at the entrance of the Terlizzi compound scrutinize IDs and license plates before granting access. I can only assume that ramping up security means the family is in danger.

My saving grace comes in the form of Salvatore, who deals with all the logistics of who should be an usher and what church we should host the funeral at. I can plan a party from a checklist, but Salvatore possesses a deeper understanding of the intricate dynamics within the Terlizzi family organization. When I suggest one of the cousins help as a pallbearer, I'm lectured on the nature of the man's personal activities for ten minutes before being told no.

My sister meticulously organizes floral arrangements for the funeral—a wreath, a spray, and even memorial plants to be taken home by distinguished guests. Initially, I fail to appreciate the significance of her contribution, but I received another lecture when I dare to voice my opinion.

In the end, Salvatore, Lucia, and I emerge as the heroes of the day.

The only person I don't see is Luciano. Dante insists that our youngest brother is working on something important to the family, and I can't help but envy him for finding a way out of the family get-togethers.

After what feels like an eternity, the day of the funeral finally arrives. It's a somber Sunday, the 10th of December, with the ceremony commencing at 11:00 am in the familiar setting of St. Thomas More Catholic Church.

"It's what he would have wanted," Salvatore assures me, reminiscing about our childhood visits. "We came here a lot as kids."

"For Easter and Christmas," I scoff. "I can't remember the last time Father attended Mass."

Salvatore shrugs his shoulders before waving at someone in the distance. An older woman whom I swear I've never seen before is sending us pitying looks and a small wave of acknowledgment. "I think that's our Great Aunt," he explains, interpreting the confusion on my face.

Dante does what we should be doing. He walks right up to our alleged Great Aunt and gives her a hug. We watch as the two of them exchange pleasantries.

"What a suck-up," I roll my eyes.

Salvatore stifles a laugh by pretending to cough into his elbow. "Come on, we should be doing more."

"What more can we do?" I retort, waving off his suggestion. "We've organized the entire funeral while Dante and Lucky managed to wriggle out of their responsibilities with flimsy excuses about helping the family. I'll stand here and look mournful, but I won't engage in small talk with long-lost aunts, uncles, and cousins I haven't seen in a decade. That's Dante's job, anyway. He's the new head of the family."

Salvatore shoves his hands into his pockets and gazes downward. "Speaking of Lucky, have you heard from him lately?"

"Maybe in the group chat?" I frown, trying to recall the last time we spoke. "But not for a couple of days. Where is he, anyway? He shouldn't be allowed to get out of organizing the funeral *and* attending it."

Salvatore anxiously looks in both directions, clocking what everyone around us is doing before responding. "He's uh, he's locked up." I almost ruin the funeral for everyone when I turn to sharply yell *'what'* at my brother. "Hey!" He hisses at me, "Keep your fucking mouth shut. Jesus."

Dante casts us a disapproving look as though we are misbehaving. It feels as if Father is still alive, silently admonishing us.

"Come here." Salvatore grabs my arm and hauls me to the back of the church. "First, keep it the fuck down. I can see why Dante said not to tell you."

"Fuck Dante," I glare. "What the hell happened to Lucky?"

Salvatore punches his fingers to his temples and starts rubbing like I'm the source of his headache. "A few nights ago, a group of guys cornered Luc in an alley. You know Lucky as well as I do. He wouldn't have backed down even if there were a hundred of them." There's a desperation in Salvatore's voice that tugs on the strings of my heart. "He doesn't remember all the details because they beat him up pretty bad. But they broke his hand and branded him."

The room starts spinning. I haven't eaten anything today, but I feel nauseous. "I don't-I can't-I don't understand."

Salvatore reaches out to grab my shoulder, steadying me. "You okay, Nic?"

I manage to nod, but it does little to alleviate my uneasiness. My feet feel numb, and the spinning sensation persists. If it doesn't stop soon, I'm going to vomit. "So, the police locked up Luciano?"

Salvatore guides me to a nearby chair, helping me sit down before I collapse. "No. The Lucatellos left Lucky for dead, but fortunately, he had enough strength left to call Dante. Dante got him to the family doctor in time, but the damage had already been done."

The realization hits me like a ton of bricks. No wonder Luciano hasn't been present to assist with the funeral arrangements.

"It was the Lucatellos?" I ask, confused. "How do we know?"

"Don't lose your shit, okay?" Salvatore prefaces. "The image they burned into Lucky's skin was the Lucatello family crest."

The phrase *'I'm seeing red'* finally makes sense. I think I literally see blood. I know I can taste it because I'm biting the inside of my cheek.

"I think you're on the verge of losing your shit, so I'm going to need you to breathe." He's like a little league coach, telling me to breathe in and breathe out as if I don't know how to control my anger.

"Lucky's okay, Nic. Dr. Stone put him under before burning over the brand. It'll lengthen the healing time, but at least he won't have the Lucatello crest on his chest forever."

The doctor burned over the brand. Jesus Christ. I got a second-degree burn on my hand once, and I wanted to chop it off. I can't imagine what it must feel like to be burned twice in the span of a few hours. "Why did you say Lucky was locked up?"

Salvatore laughs before stretching to his full height. His knees pop as he moves, and he cracks his back from being hunched over. "Oh, he's murderous. Even drugged up at the hospital, the doctor had to restrain him so he wouldn't leave and try to kill any Lucatello he could get his hands on."

"I'd keep your little girlfriend away from him for a while." Dante walks into our secluded area, his face filled with a dark mix of despair and loathing. "I don't know if Luc has the self-restraint to keep from strangling her just for being related to the Lucatellos."

I rise from the chair, the room spinning once more, but I push through the dizziness. "Why didn't you tell me sooner? He's my brother, too." Despite our infrequent conversations, we're still family.

Dante purses his lips for a long moment before deciding that I'm strong enough to handle the truth. "You are not *in* the family, Nic. Everyone knows that. They leave you alone *because* of that fact. And I felt that it would be more beneficial to keep you out of the loop until Luciano regained his wits."

"Where's he locked up?"

"In the dungeon," Dante answers matter-of-factly. "He was a danger to himself and others. The *others* part isn't quite as concerning. If anything, it might work in our favor. But he isn't strong enough to confront the Lucatellos just yet, and neither are we. We're amassing our forces, but it will take weeks before we're ready to reclaim what's rightfully ours."

This is all happening because of me. If I had been a good little boy and followed Leonardo and Giovanni's orders, Luciano would be safe, and Christine wouldn't be forced to marry a murderer. I did this; I have to fix it.

"I'm in." I'm not going to hide anymore; I'm not going to stand on the sidelines and watch as my brothers start a war they can't finish.

Dante and Salvatore share a laugh between themselves. "What do you mean you're *'in'*?" Salvatore questions, feigning confusion. "In what?"

"I'm in the family, asshole," I tell him with a glare. "Add me to your army." Luciano is the last straw. If Giovanni touches someone I care about again, I'll kill him.

"Slow down, Professor," comments Dante, his words dripping with sarcasm and disdain. "Don't go volunteering for wars you're not prepared to fight in. You've always been the softest one in the family. No offense." But it sounds like it was meant to be offensive. "You'll get yourself killed if you're not careful. Mom is already burying her husband. Let's not make her bury a son next."

I clench my fists at my sides, once again feeling like this family doesn't take me seriously. They never have, and perhaps they never will.

"I'm not going to die, Dante. I want to be included in the next family meeting. I'll do whatever it takes to join or sign up, or whatever it is you people do. This is my family, too, and I'm tired of seeing the Lucatello brothers hurt the people I love."

Dante exchanges a glance with Salvatore, and they communicate silently through gestures and raised eyebrows, a conversation I will never fully comprehend. "Why the hell not?" Salvatore finally speaks after a moment. "Give him a shot."

Trusting Salvatore's judgment over mine, Dante nods in my direction. "Revenge and security are good enough reasons," he decides. "And maybe that'll even be enough to keep you safe."

All I need is a baseball bat to protect myself. Point me in the right direction, and I'll come out swinging.

Chapter 41
Christine

I chose not to attend the funeral, not out of disrespect but because both Niccolo and Dante asked me not to.

I expected Niccolo's request. As close as we'd gotten, Giovanni's reappearance and Fausto's death lobbed a grenade at our relationship that was straining the intimacy we shared.

I didn't expect Dante's request. Niccolo's came via text; Dante's came with a personal phone call. He was polite, the nicest to me he'd ever been. I could hear the weight in his tone as he pleaded for me to stay away for Niccolo's sake.

"He loves you, Christine, but this is very complicated. He needs time." And though I wanted to be there for Nic, I respected the Terlizzi family's wishes.

But a few days later, with Finals behind us and the students packing up to go home for the holidays, my stepfather showed up at my door.

It starts with a knock, and Kaye gets up to answer. "I gotta pee anyway," she complains.

She opens the door and I can't see around her at first. "Hey, uh, Chris." She steps aside so I can see. "Your father is here." Her eyes twinkle with amusement, and she double-checks her pockets. "I'll be back in a bit. I should call my mom or something. Nice to see you, Professor," Kaye nods at Nic as she walks past him.

Niccolo wears a bemused look on his face as he steps inside. "I think a few of your dorm mates are students of mine."

"*Former* students," I correct as I sit up in bed. "The semester is over."

Nic gracefully settles onto the bed next to me, his presence both comforting and intimate. I instinctively curl my feet under me, finding a sense of ease in his company. He reaches for a nearby pillow and arranges it behind his back, making himself comfortable as he prepares to settle in for a conversation. "Or maybe they're like you, and they'll be with me next semester."

I shudder to think of another semester in Niccolo's class. These last four months have been difficult for the two of us. We've butted heads and succumbed to desires we wouldn't ordinarily allow ourselves to indulge in. What will happen next semester? Where will we be in another four months?

"Sienna will be back next semester," I announce, changing the subject before I drive myself crazy thinking about the what-ifs and possibilities.

"Oh, god," he groans. "I swear you two are going to drive me into an early grave."

"We aren't that bad," I argue. "We know the material."

Niccolo lets out an exasperated sigh, his eyes rolling in frustration. He reaches over and gently lays his hand on my ankle, a small gesture to comfort and ground me amidst our banter. "That you do," he says with a squeeze. "What's Sienna's plans, anyway? Is she majoring in Psychology or something? Why is she in my class?"

The cadence of our conversation feels natural and almost mundane compared to the last few weeks. And for a few minutes, I forget about all the bad things that have happened to us.

"I don't think she knows, really. She's talked about therapy, law, and becoming a teacher. I think she's exploring her options."

"Nothing wrong with that," Niccolo shrugs. "You'd do well to follow her lead."

I tilt my head at him with a knowing look. "You know I want to be a Child Psychologist one day," I remind him.

"Of course," he replies smoothly, "but that doesn't mean you shouldn't check out other options. Take a creative writing class, or dabble in web design. There could be something out there that fills your well that you haven't even considered yet."

Since I haven't seen him in a couple of weeks, I haven't filled him in on the latest. He doesn't know that Giovanni is taking me away after the spring semester or that I won't be allowed to come back to Blackmore. I'm still hoping that Dante finds a suitable alternative, but in lieu of a reprieve from this marriage, I should lower Niccolo's expectations.

"About next semester," I begin.

"I should tell you about something," Niccolo starts simultaneously.

For a minute, we laugh, and he scoots closer to me. "You go ahead," I usher him forward, wanting to enjoy the comfort of our shared tranquility for another minute before I tear it all down.

But Niccolo's face changes. A dark cloud hovers overhead, shadowing his features. "There was an incident before the funeral. Luciano was caught in an alley by some Lucatello thugs, and they hurt him pretty badly."

Announcing my news first wouldn't have fared any better. Instead of me breaking into a cold sweat, he would have. "He's-he's alive, right?" I stutter, feeling like someone pulled the rug out from under my feet.

"Yes, of course," Niccolo reassures me with a warm smile and another gentle squeeze. "But it's escalating this thing between our families, and I'm afraid this won't have a happy ending."

I'm sure he's right. In what universe does the back and forth between the Lucatellos and the Terlizzis end with a happily ever after?

"I'm sorry about Luc. I don't know what's come over my family. I-I'm not even involved with them. I don't understand."

Niccolo nods solemnly, shifting his weight in my direction. "It's okay. Nobody blames you for what's happening. Family alliances change all the time, and peace is expected but rarely achieved. Even when there aren't full-scale wars, there are skirmishes like ours."

"I wish my mother hadn't died," I groan. "She could have protected me from this. Maybe if she were still alive, the Lucatellos wouldn't be fighting with the Terlizzis."

"Maybe." Niccolo voices with uncertainty. "But if your mother were still alive, we wouldn't have found each other."

My lips part in an attempt to correct him, but the words become trapped in my throat.

Losing my mother meant finding the love of my life; keeping her would have meant spending the rest of my life searching for someone who could only ever make me feel half as alive as Nic has. No matter which course my life would have taken, I would have lost someone important to me.

"But you'd have been safe," Niccolo adds after a moment. "And maybe your safety is more important than what the two of us have."

As he says it, I know that he's wrong. I'm sad I lost my mother, but I needed to. It would have hurt more to spend the rest of my life hoping to find what I have with Nic.

"No," I reach out to lay my hand on top of his. "It's not. What matters is you and me."

At the beginning of the semester, all I wanted was to get away from my stepfather. Now, I would give anything to keep him by my side forever. He is flawed and complicated, and our relationship is messy, but I love him.

Before Nic can respond, the door opens and Kaye returns. "Do you want a Christmas tree or a Santa cookie? Both are sugar." She offers, shoving a plate our way.

Niccolo draws his hand from my leg and places it in his lap. "I think that's my cue to go. Have a good Christmas if I don't see you before then, Kaye," he chirps. "And take care of my girl."

"I always do."

He stretches as he gets off the bed. "These mattresses are trash. You should come home for the holidays, Christine."

He sounds like my father again, but maybe that's okay. With my best friend watching, I'd rather he be fatherly than sensual. "I'll think about it. If Kaye goes back to Manhattan, I will, too."

"She'll be back for Christmas then," Kaye announces as she sits at her desk. "I'll be spending the day with my mother."

Niccolo bows his head respectfully at her on the way out. "Tell Carrie I said hello."

As he leaves the room, Kaye gives it approximately 0.02 seconds after he shuts the door before announcing, "Do you want to set your stepfather up with my mom? I like him better than Jackson. If you're okay with it, I'll give Carrie his number."

"Over my dead body."

Chapter 42
Christine

Niccolo's departure gives us something to talk about. Though Kaye jokes about setting her mother up with my stepfather, she isn't as upset about Jackson as she was when she first met him.

"Xavier's looking into him for me," she announces proudly.

I scrunch my nose in distaste, surprised by the newfound alliance between Xavier and Kaye. "This is all just a ploy to get in your pants," I caution her. "Xavier has never done anything nice for the sake of being nice."

Kaye looks unsure. We've been saying this for years, but for the first time, it looks like she might not believe it. "I mean, he picked me up from the bar the night I met Jackson," she mumbles.

That night preceded my entire world blowing up; I like to pretend that it didn't happen.

"Didn't he make you throw up?"

"No," she argues. "It was probably the hangover and the smell of eggs that did it."

Raising a skeptical eyebrow, I divert my attention back to the Santa-shaped cookie on my plate. "Who's distributing these anyway?" I inquire with a hint of suspicion.

Kaye shrugs her shoulders nonchalantly. "I don't know. There was a bunch of them in the lounge with a sign that said *'take me'*."

"So we're eating cookies from an unknown source?" I tear off Santa's head, narrowing my eyes at his jolly little smile. "How do we know these aren't poisoned?"

She chuckles dismissively while popping the Christmas tree-shaped cookie into her mouth. "This is college, Chris. They're just cookies. Someone's grandma probably sent them."

"Oh, so we're eating someone's stale re-gifted cookies then. These will be delicious," I deadpan.

"You're so dramatic." Kaye rolls her eyes at me before finishing her cookie. "Do you want to talk about why Nic was here?"

The air catches in my lungs, and I have to counsel myself to confide in my best friend because I know how irritable I become when I don't. But how do I tell Kaye about Italian traditions even I'm not familiar with? I barely understand them. How is she supposed to?

"So, how are things with your uncle?" she changes her approach. "You met up with him a few days ago, right?"

I nod my head miserably and recount the horrible experience I had with Giovanni, starting with the moment I arrived. "As if his inappropriate behavior towards the waitress wasn't enough," I begin, my voice heavy with bitterness, "he had the audacity to tell me that I can't—" The words get caught in my throat like glue, refusing to be spoken.

Sensing my distress, Kaye moves closer, sitting beside me on the bed and rubbing my arm up and down in soft, soothing waves. "You can't what?" She asks gently.

I haven't said these words out loud yet. I've thought about them nonstop, but I haven't given a voice to my uncle's orders. I have to force myself to say them, even though my heart hammers in my chest. "He said that I'm getting married in June, and I have to move to Kansas City."

Her brow furrows in surprise. "Wh-what?" Kaye stops stroking my arm, her hand remaining on my bicep. "What about your education? What about me?"

I've been turning this over in my head for days, trying to understand what the ramifications of Giovanni's words will be. And I still have no clue. "I don't know," I slump into the bed, feeling as helpless as I look. "I don't think anyone cares."

"I care!" Kaye glares. "Giovanni can't make you marry a tyrant and move away. Can't Niccolo do something about this? He kept you here when your uncle wanted you to move a few years ago. Can he say something? He has to be able to stop this."

Tears burn the back of my eyes, and I struggle to blink them back. "Unfortunately, Nic is part of the problem. Giovanni is doing this because Nic and I have been sort of seeing each other."

"What!" Her voice raises an octave. "And you didn't tell me?!"

The term *'seeing each other'* is too vague.

"We aren't dating or anything," I explain. "But I guess Giovanni heard that we were together at Red Dawg once. And maybe he has a spy in Nic's class because he knows about Nic asking me to stay after to chat. Gio's been hearing rumors about our behavior, and that's part of the reason this is all happening."

Kaye looks flabbergasted, and I think it's partly because I haven't told her about the extent of my relationship with Niccolo. She doesn't yell at me for keeping secrets, though. Instead, she squeezes my arm and says we're going to take care of this. "We can't let your uncle do this. It has to be illegal. We could go to the cops or—"

But I cut her off before she finishes her train of thought. "We can't go to the cops, Kaye. Gio as good as admitted to me that this thing of his follows its own laws, not the ones made up by our society. If I go to the cops, something bad will happen. I just know it."

"We'll get you into witness protection," Kaye decides. "He can't threaten you, Chris. What aren't you understanding about this?"

What isn't *she* understanding about this? I'm not turning down her notion because I'm being difficult; I'm turning it down because there's no other way. "You know how Malcolm said he'd ruin your career before it ever got started? Why did you believe him?"

Caught off guard by the change in direction, Kaye stammers her response. "He's rich. He's got the money and connections to blackball me in the law industry before I even finish my undergrad."

"That's precisely it," I explain, the weight of the situation evident in my tone. "Giovanni may not have Malcolm's wealth, but he has powerful connections. That's why I can't go to the police. I might find myself in an even worse situation than I am already."

Kaye opens her mouth to argue but quickly closes it. We sit in silence for a few minutes, the echo of laughter from the hallways occasionally breaking the tension.

"I reached out to Dante Terlizzi for help," I confess softly.

"Niccolo's brother?" she asks, her brow furrowing. "What can he do?"

I shrug my shoulders because, truly, I don't know. Maybe he can change Giovanni's mind. Maybe he has more power than Nic does. I don't understand the structure of everything; I just know that if anyone can protect me, it'll be him.

"God, this sucks," Kaye groans. "I thought finally being adults and getting away from Manhattan was going to be fun."

"The grass is always greener or something." For a moment, we laugh, and everything seems like it's going to be alright.

Chapter 43
Niccolo

I haven't decorated for Christmas since Caterina passed away.

I remember the first year I married her. Cat and Christine spent an entire weekend bringing boxes downstairs from the attic. Every time I thought they were finished, a new box appeared. In a matter of hours, the house transformed into a winter wonderland.

Layers of shimmering fake snow covered every surface while the scent of freshly cut pine filled each room. Sparkling lights twinkled from the trees they set up on every floor, casting a warm glow throughout the house. Even the staircase was adorned with elegant tinsel and delicate ornaments, adding to the festive ambiance.

My parents weren't really into the holidays when we were growing up. We put up precisely one tree in the living room the Sunday after Thanksgiving. Each of us kids took turns hanging an ornament on the tree until we ran out of space. And that was it. There was no Christmas music playing through the house or decorations strewn across the cabinets in the kitchen. We got our single Christmas tree and gifts on Christmas Day; then, the holidays were over.

But I tried to recreate the Christmas spirit this year. My heart ached from loss and longing, and I needed something to occupy my mind.

I started by hanging a wreath on the front door. Vibrant red berries and lush greenery instantly added a touch of holiday cheer. Then, I carefully draped fragrant strands of garland along the railing of the porch.

Slowly but surely, I brought down a box of decorations and dispersed them throughout the house. A miniature 3-foot tree adorned with sparkling lights in the kitchen. Lights framing the windows on the outside of the house. A framed photo above the mantle of the one happy Christmas I had with Caterina and Christine before my wife got sick.

It isn't much, but it lightens my mood as I crawl through December. Between hours spent studying the family dynamics to better understand my role within the Terlizzi dynasty and holing up with Dante to figure out a solution to Christine's impending arranged marriage, I feel like I'm suffocating. The weight of it all feels like an anchor on my chest, threatening to drown me before I can get a handle on what's expected of me and what I want to accomplish.

I'm thankful that Christmas is a reprieve from it all. Dante is spending the day with his wife, and my single siblings are taking the week off to go on a booze cruise.

I texted Christine last night, and she said she'd be here bright and early. I wake up at the crack of dawn in anticipation of her arrival. There's nothing for me to do in the early hours of the day except turn on a Christmas movie in the living room and put a ham in the oven. I'm not making a large feast for Christine and me. Though I'm sure my family would be more than happy to eat the leftovers, I don't want to spend the next three days trying to figure out how to repurpose ham into sandwiches and soups.

When 9:00 am rolls around, Christine texts that she's on her way. I pace the living room for a few minutes while waiting for her to arrive, but I feel like I'm going to crawl out of my skin. I'm anxious, and I don't know why.

I move to the parlor where the grand piano Caterina used to play sits in the corner. The ghost of our memories flees from the room as I near the bench.

Once upon a time, the two of us would sit here at the end of a long day and play together. Back when I thought I could grow to love her, back when life was simpler.

I blow a thin layer of dust off the cover and settle onto the bench. As I stretch my fingers, I'm transported back to when I was ten years old, and my parents forced me to learn an instrument. Dante was a musical prodigy, and our piano teacher praised him every chance she got. It took me longer to figure out how to play, and I resented the constant comparison to my older brother.

But I am no longer ten years old. When I press my fingers to the keys, it takes a minute for it all to come rushing back. The first few musical notes sound tentative and unsure, but grow more confident with each passing stroke. I recall the first composition I ever managed to perfect, *Für Elise*, and let muscle memory lead me through it.

I stopped playing the piano when I was fifteen, much to the disappointment of my father, even though he only ever liked it when Dante played for him. At our wedding, Caterina played a flawless rendition of *Can't Help Falling In Love With You*, and it inspired me to take the instrument back up. Only long enough to make a few memories side-by-side before she was too ill to get out of bed.

Somewhere in the middle of the *Moonlight Sonata*, the front door slowly creaks open. My fingers falter on the keys as I glance up to see Christine standing in the doorway, illuminated by the sun's mid-morning rays—the smile on her face tugs at the strings of my heart.

"I'd forgotten you played," she announces when I stop abruptly in the middle of the composition.

I stretch my fingers again, anxious. "It's been a while. The last time was with your mother, I think." Maybe I shouldn't mention Caterina. It brings to light the nature of our relationship: two souls brought together by chance and unlikely circumstance.

Christine closes the door behind her, twisting the deadbolt to lock us away from the outside world. "Mom tried to teach me when I was younger, but I was rubbish. I didn't have the patience to learn and couldn't appreciate my feeble attempts at playing. I only liked the piano when she played it."

Knowing Caterina, she wouldn't have gotten upset if her daughter chose to walk away from learning an instrument. My father beat me once because I said I didn't want to learn how to play *The Nutcracker March* for his Christmas Eve festivities. We grew up very different than one another, which is what makes being together all that more enjoyable.

The family we build together will be a reflection of hers, not mine. Our children will have the privilege of growing up with two devoted parents who will love them unconditionally. We won't impose strict rules or expectations on our kids, except for the annual tradition of taking cringe-worthy family photos at Christmas in matching flannel pajamas. Our home will be filled with warmth and love, a safe haven for our family to grow and thrive in.

"Sit," I pat the bench beside me. "We should talk."

She sets her bag down at the entrance and walks over, nestling beside me on the piano bench. "If you're going to try and teach me piano, you'd have better luck teaching a fish to ride a bike. I can't do anything with my hands."

Caterina could knit and sew; Christine has never been the crafting type. But it isn't fair to compare the two of them. I was forced to marry Caterina to appease my family; I want to be with Christine because she makes me feel like anything is possible.

"I'm not much of a bicyclist myself, so maybe you can just settle for listening," I offer with a teasing grin.

She leans her head on my shoulder in a moment of unexpected tenderness. "I'd love to."

In the last few weeks, Dante and I have talked through a dozen different ways to save her from marrying Rocco Castiglione. I'm still in favor of killing Rocco or Giovanni, but my brother said both ideas would lead to a war that the Terlizzi family isn't ready for.

My fingers gracefully glide over the smooth ebony and ivory keys, each note of the *Moonlight Sonata* filling the room with its melancholy melody as I pick up where I left off. "I think we should get married."

Christine's body stiffens beside mine, but she doesn't outright reject the suggestion. "What if Giovanni sends Marco to kill you?"

I shrug my shoulders, continuing along in the composition. I make a mistake that my father would have screamed at me for making two decades ago, but Christine doesn't even notice.

"We're going to make Giovanni an offer, kind of like a dowry," I explain. "Dante thinks $25,000 isn't enough to sway Gio, and I think he's right. But we're going to make him an offer and if he says no, we will use that money to throw the biggest wedding this side of the Missouri state line."

A small, subtle smile twitches on her lips; I can feel the corners of her mouth tugging upwards against my shoulder. "An extravagant wedding is going to save you from Giovanni trying to kill you?"

"It'll be insurance, yes," I explain. "The larger the wedding, the harder it'll be for your uncles to get away with murder. If we can give the Midwest families a show, killing me will backfire on Giovanni. They'll demand retribution for my death, and it'll be the end of the Lucatellos."

The tension in her body pulls as tight as a garrote around the neck of our enemies. Dante warned me that the hardest part would be convincing Christine to go along with the plan because she values her independence.

"Can I keep going to university?" She asks quietly.

I stop playing mid-key, letting the tune hang in the air. "Of course, you can. Why wouldn't you?"

Christine takes her head off my shoulder but refuses to look at me. Instead, she taps a finger on the keys before her, testing the notes. The piano bench creaks beneath her weight as she shifts slightly, deep in concentration. "Giovanni said when I marry Rocco, I have to move to Kansas City, and I can't go back to college."

"What?" I demand sharply. "When did he say this? When have you been talking to him?"

She doesn't raise her gaze to meet mine. "Just before Finals week. He was going to be in town, so I asked him to meet for lunch."

My knuckles turn white as I ball my hands into tight fists, my nails digging into the flesh of my palms. The urge to slam them down onto the keys in frustration is almost overwhelming, but I force myself to stay still.

"H-he said that we could do whatever we wanted in the meantime. We could be together," she whispers, desperation in her voice. "We could have the next few months. You'll get bored of me, anyway. By the time June rolls around, you'll be glad Rocco is around to take me off your hands. Then," she pauses. Christine clears her throat of the thick emotion building up. "Then I wouldn't have to worry about becoming a widow at 19. I don't want my uncles to hurt you, Nic. I'll trade my freedom for your life if that's what Giovanni wants."

The vulnerability in her voice cracks my heart wide open. I wrap my arms around her waist and pull her closer, forcing her onto my lap, and it still doesn't feel close enough. "Listen to me, *dolcezza*," my voice a raw whisper, "I won't let you do this. I won't let you trade your freedom for mine. You're not a pawn in their twisted game. You are my heart and my soul, and I won't let them take you away from me."

She stiffens in my grasp, and I continue. "I will never get bored of you, Christine. You are everything to me. More than the beats in my heart, more than the blood in my veins. I can't—no, I won't—imagine a life without you."

My hands move to cradle her face, wiping away the tears that have begun to fall down her cheeks. "I will not let you become a sacrifice. Not for me, not for anyone. I'll be damned before I let Giovanni or anyone else dictate our fate. I choose you, and I choose us. No matter the consequences."

In a moment of recklessness, I seize her lips with an urgency that mirrors the intensity of my emotions. The kiss is not a tender promise; it's a fervent affirmation of my love for her. Our mouths meld together, tongues dancing in a fiery embrace that conveys my hunger for her. It's a desperate exchange, a clash of passion that leaves no room for uncertainty. When we part, breathless and entwined, I rest my forehead against hers, and our rapid breaths mingle in the sensually charged air.

"We're in this together. I will find a way to rewrite our destiny and defy the fate your uncle seeks to impose upon us. I promise."

Chapter 44
Niccolo
6.5 Weeks Later • February 10th

"The Saint Valentine's Day Massacre of 1929 is the most infamous of all gangland slayings in the United States." Muffled yells echo through the abandoned building as I pace from one end to the other. "Seven members of a Chicago gang were lined up in a garage and lit up with over 90 bullets from submachine guns, shotguns, and a revolver. The four men who did the job were dressed as police officers."

When I got up this morning, I thought about asking Dante to get me a cop uniform for what was supposed to be tomorrow's event. But Giovanni ruined our plans.

Instead, I had to settle for my wedding suit with a meticulously tied double Windsor knot, lapels, a neatly folded kerchief in my breast pocket, and a pair of expensive cufflinks passed down from my father. Just hours ago, I was wearing this while I pledged to love Christine for the rest of our lives. Now it's covered in blood.

"People think Al Capone ordered the hit. Did you know that?" I turn sharply in my worn dress shoes. There are scuffs along the toes from our fight in the parking lot. "I feel like that's something you would know."

In the center of the room, Giovanni sits tied to a metal chair. His suit from the wedding reception has been stripped and torn. The tie he was wearing now acts as a gag, muffling his arguments. Blood trickles from a cut above his brow. I had intended to bring him here unscathed, but unforeseen complications arose when we were kicked out of the reception.

"Speak up, Giovanni," I shout at him, my voice echoing off the walls of the empty room. "I can't hear you."

Dante snickers in the corner. He leans up against a wall next to a strung-up Marco. With a pair of chains wrapped around his wrists, he remains helpless. Every time Marco displays a flicker of anxiety, Dante lands a measured blow to his gut, exacerbating his torment.

"It's really disappointing that you aren't more attuned to the history of this thing of ours. You," I point at him with the metal baseball bat in my hands, "who have been a part of this longer than I have."

Giovanni looks murderous. If he weren't tied up, he'd have his hands around my throat. Unfortunately for him, Luciano got his cast off last week.

Luciano, the little brother of mine that Giovanni thought he'd teach a lesson by branding him with the Lucatello crest.

Luciano, the literal Boy Scout of the Terlizzi brothers with a badge in knot tying. Giovanni isn't getting out of that chair until we say he can.

I cast a nod in Salvatore's direction. "Remove the gag."

Sal walks up to Giovanni and crouches down to be at his eye level. "If you bite me, I'll knock your teeth out," Salvatore warns, seizing the tie encased within Giovanni's mouth and gradually extracting it.

To his credit, Giovanni doesn't bite my brother. He waits until Salvatore drops the saliva-soaked tie into his lap before he spits on him.

My brother reaches up to wipe the glob of spit off his face, nonchalantly smearing it across Giovanni's once pristine white shirt. "*Animale del cazzo. Pagherai per quello che hai fatto.*" You fucking animal. You will pay for what you've done.

"Go to hell," Giovanni glares at Salvatore before turning his attention to me. "And fuck you, Terlizzi. When I get out of here—"

"*If*," I interject, my voice icy and devoid of mercy. "*If* you get out of here. I haven't decided if you should live or die just yet. So if I were you, I wouldn't be making plans for breakfast with one of your underage mistresses."

A vivid scarlet hue permeates Giovanni's face, his anger morphing into a kaleidoscope of rage. Under his breath, in a barely audible whisper, he utters a string of death threats barely loud enough for me to hear.

"I thought long and hard about what to do with you. Marco is pretty innocent." I toss the enforcer an apologetic smile. "I'm sorry you have to be here for this. I always liked you."

Marco's glare deepens, but he remains stoic, refusing to dignify me with a response.

"You, on the other hand," I turn back to Giovanni, "you've always been a prick."

Giovanni hasn't flinched since we approached him at the reception. I have to give it to him: he isn't a man who backs down from fear. If we were on the same side, I might actually admire him.

"I told my sister you were a lecher when she married you," Giovanni spews, his voice oozing contempt. Despite the chill of the February air, sweat forms rivulets on his brow. He might face fear head-on, but he isn't stupid—he's still afraid.

"I told her if she ever caught you cheating, I'd cut off your balls. When she told me you wanted to become a professor, I thought about doing it anyway."

I tap the baseball bat against my shoe, feeling rage well up inside of me like a hot spring. I force myself to do nothing, but every bone in my body is screaming at me to take the bat to his head.

"I knew the second you went off to college that you'd be fucking around on my sister with barely legal teenage girls. Color me shocked that the barely legal teenage girl you targeted was her own daughter."

Sometimes I swear Dante knows me better than I know myself. Like now, for instance, as he steps toward me with a look on his face that stops me in my tracks. "Don't kill him," is all he quietly implores.

I cock my head, knowing that even though it wasn't a conscious thought, it was in my plans. And Dante somehow knew.

With a curt nod, I agree to his request. Then I raise the bat, bring it down on Giovanni's knee, and watch the bone explode with a shower of blood.

Chapter 45
Christine
6 Weeks Ago • December 30th

Setting up a meeting between the Lucatellos and Terlizzis was not easy.

My grandfather wanted reassurance that nothing would happen to him or his sons if he agreed to come.

Dante offered a hostage, a lesser-known Terlizzi cousin I'd never met. Leonardo required more, demanding that Salvatore stay with the Lucatello family in exchange. He said that it was to ensure if we drew first blood, they could avenge the loss with ease.

Then, there were debates over where the meeting should take place. I foolishly suggested our home, but Grandfather said that wasn't a neutral enough location. In the end, someone rented out the backroom of a restaurant as if this were a celebration instead of a sit down to discuss my future.

Once that was decided, Niccolo didn't want me to attend. "If you're in the room, they might try to take you. Or they'll force you to leave with them."

I had to get all the Terlizzi brothers involved in order to secure a place at the table. Niccolo was willing to fight every one of them to keep me safe, but ultimately, Dante won.

"She has to be there, Nicci. If she isn't, they'll send someone to the university to find her. By the time we leave the meeting, who knows where she'll be."

I never thought about my family kidnapping me to keep me safe, but when Dante brings it up, I fight the static feeling that slithers down my spine and enters my bloodstream. I've learned through all this that my family isn't who I thought they were.

But a week and a half after Christmas, we finally sit down in a private room in the back of Nico's to discuss everything.

"The wine here is shit," Leonardo complains.

Dante looks at the glass in front of him before calmly asking, "Didn't *you* bring the wine?"

Never willing to take the blame, Leonardo squares his shoulders, straightens his back, and meets Dante's gaze head-on. "Yes. And it's shit. What do you want, Terlizzi?" Leonardo shifts his weight in the chair from one hip to the other, causing his weathered leather boots to scuff against the hardwood floors. A subtle wince of discomfort creases his face, a reminder that the battle-hardened veteran has been in the game longer than most of us have been alive.

Dante informed us last week that while Leonardo's presence means he still has some control over his family, Giovanni is the one to whom we are presenting the offer. However, out of respect for the older Lucatello, Dante nods his head deferentially to Leonardo before addressing my uncle. "It has come to my attention that my brother would like to marry your niece. We are aware of her arranged marriage to Rocco Castiglione, and we respect that you are making moves that will benefit your family."

"Then why are we here?" Giovanni sprawls back in his chair, shifting his body until he finds the perfect position. "If you respect it so much, why call a meeting?"

"As I said, my brother would like to marry your niece."

Giovanni parts his lips, ready to speak, but my grandfather holds up his hand to interrupt. The atmosphere in the room shifts, quieting to a tense hush as all eyes turn toward the two men locked in a silent battle of wills. "Five years ago, I was at a similar table with your father, Dante. He and I brokered what should have been an advantageous marriage between his son and my daughter. Unfortunately, my daughter passed away. Instead of coming to me and asking if there was anything he could do to benefit my family, Niccolo stole my granddaughter and went his own way."

My grandfather paints an interesting picture of how the events after my mother's death played out. I don't remember Niccolo stealing me away. I remember my uncle offered to take me back to Kansas City, and I made the decision to stay where I had a community of friends.

Dante seems to remember it the same way as I do and speaks in his brother's defense. "If I'm not mistaken, it was *Christine's* choice to remain in Manhattan. She was in high school at the time, and it was agreed upon that disrupting her education would be detrimental at that phase in her life."

"It's funny you use the word *'detrimental'*," Giovanni reenters the conversation. "That's precisely how I'd describe how her reputation is affecting the family."

"What reputation?" Niccolo snarls. "She's done nothing."

Giovanni's anger boils over as he slams his fists down on the sturdy wooden table, causing it to shudder and creak in protest. "She's done *you*, Terlizzi. That's the problem. Now, no man of substance wants her."

A playful smirk dances on Niccolo's lips as he leans in closer, chest pressed against the table. "Are you saying Rocco Castiglione isn't a man of substance?" His eyes glint mischievously as he speaks, his voice low and velvety.

Tension settles in the room, putting everyone on edge. We all know what he's alluding to—Rocco's very public image as a wife killer. Giovanni might have told me to my face that he'd rather see me dead than with Niccolo, but that's because there weren't any witnesses. With Niccolo's brothers around and the Lucatello family here to witness the interaction, Giovanni doesn't repeat his earlier outburst.

"Marriage to Rocco Castiglione is a fine outcome for a woman of Christine's reputation," he says between gritted teeth.

I didn't think I had much of a reputation, but I guess I was wrong. I feel like I've kept my private life pretty quiet, but not according to my uncle.

"Disregarding her *alleged* reputation," Dante dismisses the notion with a wave, "we would like to buy out the marriage contract to Rocco Castiglione."

Once again, Leonardo cuts off Giovanni before he can speak. "The marriage contract between Rocco and Christine has already been signed and sealed by Saverio Castiglione. He has already announced certain *rewards* for this gracious gift of marrying my granddaughter to his most fearsome enforcer. Can you match those benefits?"

"Does this thing of ours have a 401k now?" Niccolo glares. "A retirement plan? An arrangement where you get to live out the rest of your days in Boca Raton? Just come right out and tell us what you want."

"So that's a no." Leonardo settles into his seat, sinking back as he crosses his hands over the broadest part of his stomach.

Niccolo abruptly begins to stand up, but Dante and I swiftly place a hand on his shoulder, halting him in his tracks. He pauses and then slowly sits back down, muttering curses in Italian under his breath.

"$25,000," Dante offers. "And we'll pay it today."

Giovanni snorts at the number, unimpressed. "That's a pathetic offer, and you know it."

"What I *know* is that your dealings with the Castiglione family depend upon Rocco and Christine getting married, which isn't happening until June. So, if something were to happen to either of them, it would be a shame you didn't get your coveted spot. Wouldn't it, Leonardo?" Dante has been dancing around the edges since the meeting began, but now he's taking the gloves off.

To their credit, no one on the Lucatello side of the table even flinches. I think Giovanni pales slightly, but he defers response to his father. I don't think he expected Dante to know about Leonardo's temporary role within the family, a role that will escalate to a permanent position once I'm officially Mrs. Rocco Castiglione.

Leonardo recovers quickly enough, and he gives Dante a nod of respect. "As to your offer," he returns, "we get the $25,000 whether or not she makes it down the aisle?"

"Correct." Dante shoots a look at Luciano, who pulls a briefcase out from under the table. "You can walk away with it today. All you have to do is say the word."

I'm holding my breath, crossing my fingers, and praying my grandfather agrees. I can't marry a wife killer. I won't survive if I'm forced to stay at home and bear Rocco's children for the rest of my life. I'll die if I'm required to be submissive and obedient.

"You're a good replacement for your father," Leonardo begins. "You drive a hard bargain. I expect that one day, you'll be less of a pup and more of a wolf, but you're just starting out. You don't have the experience my sons do. You don't have their killer instinct. But I expect you'll learn it. One day, you're going to be a formidable adversary."

With a controlled and deliberate movement, Luciano gradually lowers the sleek, black briefcase back to the floor. The air around us seems to shift, and I can sense the tension mounting. As my eyes scan the faces of those gathered around the table, it becomes clear that the tides of power are shifting.

Niccolo's normally confident demeanor fades, his face paling with worry, while Marco's features betray a hint of amusement.

"But you overplay your hand. What you're offering is an insult; I expect you're aware of that. It's a lowball offer meant to warn me, but I'm not afraid of you, Terlizzi. You are not yet a formidable opponent. So take your $25,000 and your warning, and shove them up your ass."

I'm as good as dead. I'm going to have to marry Rocco. I know Nic says he has another plan, but how will he ever get it past my grandfather?

Chapter 46
Niccolo

I lean in close to Christine, whispering soothing words in her ear. "It's okay," I reassure her, my voice barely audible. "It's going to be okay."

Dante, irritated, glances at us from the front seat. "What's wrong with her?"

In truth, I have no idea. When Leonardo rejected the money, something inside of Christine snapped. Since then, she has been staring off into the distance, lost in her own thoughts. Even as I guided her from the restaurant to the car, her gaze remained fixed ahead, devoid of expression.

"Shock, maybe." I speculate. Taking her hand, I gently bring it to my lips, pressing kisses to her knuckles and fingertips. "What's wrong, Christine? Tell me how I can help you."

Luciano interrupts our conversation, announcing, "Sally's free. He claims he's best friends with the guys who were keeping an eye on him."

I can hear Dante roll his eyes; that's how sarcastic the air in the car becomes. Though I smile at the two of them, I give my full attention to Christine. "We anticipated this, *dolcezza*. We knew all along that your uncle would refuse our offer. This is not the end."

Something I say breaks through the wall she's built up. Slowly, Christine turns her head to meet my gaze. There is a deep sense of longing in her eyes, a hollowness that threatens to shatter me into a million pieces. "Someone is going to die," she whispers, her voice barely audible. "They will kill one of us."

I wrap my arms around Christine and pull her into me. She's stopped by the seatbelt, but I don't care. I unbuckle mine and scoot closer until her head is on my chest. "No one is going to die," I respond in a soothing tone.

But something about her prediction makes me uneasy. I fight the uncomfortable feeling growing in my chest for the rest of the drive to Dante's; I pretend not to notice it when I put Christine to bed in one of the spare rooms. But the minute the door closes behind me, the weight of her words weighs me down.

"Is she okay?" Dante's voice startles me, causing me to jump nearly a foot in the air.

"What the hell are you doing out here?" I hiss at him, realizing he has been lurking in the hallway without my knowledge.

"It's my house," he deadpans as if that's enough of an explanation.

I shush him, gesturing for him to follow me down the hall. "For starters, don't ever scare me like that again. What if I was carrying a gun? I would have shot you."

Dante snorts, slapping my back. "That's cute, Lolo. Keep thinking you'll shoot me in my own home."

We make our way downstairs, where Luciano waits in the living room with Salvatore. They speak in muffled whispers as we descend the staircase, but when they see the two of us, they suspiciously stop talking.

"What?" I ask, glaring at them. "What's wrong?"

"Nothing," Luc replies. "What's wrong with you?"

I narrow my eyes at the pair, distrusting Salvatore and Luciano with every fiber of my being. "You two were whispering about something. What was it?"

"Let it go, Nic," counsels Dante. "It's just speculation."

He knows? He wasn't even down here when they were talking. "Someone better tell me what's happening right now." I refuse to be kept in the dark. There is too much to contemplate, too much happening, for me to remain oblivious about the events unfolding within my own family.

My stepdaughter is upstairs having a mental breakdown, and we have to start planning the wedding that will save her life. Classes resume in a few days, and I have yet to make any preparations for the new semester. I'm exhausted, beat down, and there is no stopping the reality train from barreling down the tracks.

"I think she's right," Luciano finally confesses after a pause.

Confusion creases my forehead. "Christine?" She's the only *'she'* that comes to mind. "Right about what?"

Tension weaves through the room like silent, odorless gas, leaving devastation in its wake. My three brothers exchange weary glances as if arguing over who has to break the news to me.

Dante, always willing to seize any opportunity to assert his dominance, offers to shoulder the responsibility. "I think her uncles might attempt to kill you."

I need a stiff drink and a sunny beach. Stat. I can't handle this. I know I was brought up in the same household as the three men in front of me, none of whom even bat an eyelash at the talk of murder, but I can't handle it. My life was always supposed to be easy. I wasn't supposed to have to deal with shit like this. Picking a career outside of the Terlizzi family's reach was supposed to protect me.

"You'll be fine," Luciano interjects, breezily dismissing my concerns. "You'll be on campus for the next few months. They can't kill you on campus."

With my jaw agape, I blink uncomprehendingly at him. "I come home every night, Luc. Are we assuming that if they can't get me on campus, they won't attempt to kill me in my own home?"

A lengthy silence engulfs the room. Eventually, Luciano purses his lips and throws himself onto the couch, propping his feet on the coffee table. "You know, you might be onto something. I take back what I said. You probably *won't* be fine."

"This is why I don't like you." I give my little brother the fiercest glare I can muster. "What the fuck is wrong with you?"

"Mom says I'm perfect just the way I am," Lucky grins.

He's got huge little brother energy. One of these days, it's going to get him popped in the mouth. "Don't talk to me."

A wave of laughter rolls through the room, dispersing some of the tension. It doesn't make me feel better about my impending murder attempt, but it's enough to pierce the nervous energy and get us talking.

Chapter 47
Christine
4.5 Weeks Ago • January 10th

Classes started a few days ago, and Kaye's schedule is still packed from dawn until dusk. I asked her if she wanted to slow down since she is pregnant, but she told me this is the best time to put her foot on the gas.

"In the fall semester, I really will have to slow down because we'll have a baby, but I'm not going to let a baby bump or some morning sickness keep me from achieving my dreams."

It's an inspiring little speech that convinces me to add four more hours to my week. I wanted to double it, but Nic convinced me not to.

"We need to plan a wedding," he reminded me. "And you need to tell your best friend because she needs to be fitted for her bridesmaids dress."

Ignoring him seemed like the easier path to take, so that's what I did. I'd tell Kaye about my impending nuptials eventually—maybe the morning of the dress fitting.

The wedding is in a month—the weekend before Valentine's Day. I asked to push it closer to spring, but Niccolo insisted that we do it sooner rather than later.

It seems like just yesterday it was Christmas. Nic and I were eating ham and potatoes on the couch, watching Jim Carrey's The Grinch. Everything seemed like it would take care of itself, and I didn't have a care in the world.

Now, the bitterly cold January wind whips me in the face, taunting me with its icy clutches. Each gust stings my cheeks and numbs my nose, making it hard to catch my breath. I dart from Seaver Center to the McCade Library, trying to cram homework in between classes.

My watch buzzes when there are ten minutes left before Niccolo's class, and I pack my bag and bundle up to face the harsh winter wind again. It's supposed to be 30 degrees outside, but the Kansas wind chill has gotten it down to 15. Exposed skin can get frostbitten in weather like this, and I make a mad dash for Brewer Hall.

The once lively and bustling campus grounds lay deserted today. The usual gathering spots are eerily still, devoid of chatter and laughter. Everybody is afraid of the cold, and they hole up in the library or their dorm room to hang out and study. It's the perfect weather for curling up by the fire with a cup of cocoa.

Instead, I'm walking from one class to another. I momentarily consider cutting through the Student Union building for warmth, but it'll add an extra five minutes to my walk, so I decide to go around the building.

As I round the corner, my heart jumps into my throat as I come face to face with a pair of looming figures. Clothed entirely in black, they blend into the shadows of the building behind them. It takes me a second to get my bearings after I spin around, but I recognize one of the men standing before me.

"Gio?" I look up at my uncle. "What are you doing here?" The nagging voice in my head says to turn around and run, but I ignore it because my uncle would never hurt me.

"Chrissy," he smiles, "am I glad to see you."

A sharp and sudden surge of fear grips my chest, causing my heart to race and my thoughts to scatter like frightened birds. Did they hurt Nic? Is he safe? Will I arrive at his classroom to find him lying in a pool of his own blood on the cold tile floor? The possibilities swirl in my mind, each more terrifying than the last.

"I wanted to introduce you to your fiancé. Chrissy, this is Rocco," he gracefully steps to the side, gesturing towards the well-dressed gentleman standing behind him. "Rocco, this is your future wife. Isn't she pretty?"

The enforcer is just as fearsome in person as he is in the pictures I've seen of him. His face bears thick scars from past battles, a testament to his strength and brutality. But it's his eyes that truly strike terror into my heart. They hold a crazed look, like a predator ready to pounce on its prey. The intensity of his gaze makes me want to run for cover. This man is not someone to be trifled with, and I can't help but feel small and insignificant in his presence.

As he extends his hand to shake mine, my courage falters. I am paralyzed by fear, unable to move or speak as his outstretched hand lingers between us.

"Don't be disrespectful," Giovanni chides. "Shake his hand, Christine."

My palms grow clammy at the thought, but I force myself to reach up and place my hand in his.

Rocco's grip is like a vice. He clasps my trembling hand and holds it tight, his rough, weathered palm sending a shiver straight through me. His grip tightens briefly, the only warning before the interaction turns sour.

His eyes roam over my body, studying my curves with cold detachment. The weight of his gaze is heavy with insidious intent, and before I can pull away, I'm met with a twisted smile that reveals his yellowed, uneven teeth. "Treat this as a lesson," he announces. Then, without warning, his fist shoots out at lightning speed and crashes into my cheekbone.

Pain explodes through my entire body as I stagger backward, the coppery taste of blood filling my mouth. My uncle speaks, but I can't make out his words over the buzzing in my ears as I try to understand what just happened. The world spins around me, stars dancing before my eyes.

Rocco lunges forward with the grace and ferocity of a wild animal, his movements swift and precise. His next blow connects with my rib, and the bones cracking under his force make a sickening sound. Rocco's eyes glint with primal intensity as he continues his assault, each hit calculated and ruthless. The scent of his blood and sweat fills my nostrils. I instinctively try to recoil, but I am no match for his brutal strength.

Agony grips me as I gasp for air that refuses to enter my lungs. Each breath is a sharp intake of searing pain as I fall to the ground. I try to summon the strength to crawl away, but Rocco is on top of me, his thighs pinning me in the dirt as he rains blow after blow into my stomach. His fists are like hammers, relentless and unyielding as they pummel my defenseless body.

Through blurry, tear-filled eyes, I see Rocco towering over me, his eyes gleaming with sadistic satisfaction. I can feel his hot breath on my face and hear the faint sound of his deep chuckles. He looks down at me with a cruel smirk, relishing in my vulnerability as if it were a delicacy. He revels in every whimper that he pulls from my lips with his well-placed fists. He enjoys my pain.

His knuckles are stained with crimson, evidence of his violence, and still, his thirst for dominance remains. He grazes my jaw with a blow, then my temple. The pain lasts for an eternity, and all I can do is endure and hope that it will end soon.

But just as darkness threatens to swallow me whole, my uncle's voice cuts through the silence. "Shit. Someone's coming."

A figure materializes from the periphery of my shattered vision—a stranger silhouetted in murky grey. He's tall and imposing, no match for Rocco, but a witness to the savagery, and my savior.

"Leave her alone," he growls, the man's voice resonating with chilling authority as he approaches.

Rocco's face contorts with rage and frustration as he forces himself to his feet. He stumbles back, momentarily unsure of himself. But it only takes a moment for my uncle to command the scene.

Giovanni grabs Rocco by the arm and pulls him away from my mangled body. As the stranger yells at them to stop, I watch them begin to sprint.

My head is spinning, a sensation that sends sharp pains radiating through my limbs. Through the haze of my blurry vision, I see a figure crouching beside me, his concerned face coming into focus. It takes a moment, but I realize that I recognize him. "Jackson," I choke out his name. *Carrie's little boy toy.* He is as handsome as I remember, while I have never looked worse.

"Shh. It's okay." With one hand under my legs and the other behind my head, Jackson effortlessly lifts me off the ground. My legs dangle loosely in front of me as I am cradled against his chest, feeling safe and secure in his arms—a distinct difference from how I felt moments before.

The echoes of soothing words are the last sounds I hear before succumbing to unconsciousness. "I've got you," he whispers, his voice a gentle lullaby in the chaos. "I've got you, Christine."

Chapter 48
Christine

I open my eyes, wincing as the harsh fluorescent lights pierce my groggy state. Blinking several times, I try to clear the fog that clouds my vision.

Where am I?

The rhythmic beeping of machines echoes through the sterile room, blending with the soft whispers of nurses and the distant hum of medical equipment. Each chirp and blip is a steady rhythm, stretching endlessly through the clinical and detached room. Methodical, monotonous, surreal.

I'm in the hospital.

I feel like I was run over by a truck. My body feels like it's encased in lead, heavy and unresponsive. I try to move, but a surge of agony shoots through my limbs, effectively immobilizing me.

I am hurt. How did I get hurt?

I force myself to take small, shallow breaths as panic threatens to consume me. Closing my eyes, I focus on the sound of my own ragged breathing, trying to calm the pounding of my heart that echoes in my ears.

I am okay.

Somewhere just beyond the door to my room, I hear arguing. The urgency in their voices fuels the adrenaline coursing through my veins.

My uncle. Rocco. Jackson?

Fleeting remnants of memory flood my mind in disjointed waves, like a tide that never fully recedes. My fingers twitch involuntarily, trembling with a mixture of fear and uncertainty.

I force myself to sit up despite the pain, wincing from the aches of protest. As I scan the room with bleary eyes, I take in the unfeeling white walls adorned with impersonal artwork. The scent of antiseptic lingers in the air. The room is a degree cooler than I'd like, causing goosebumps to form on my arms.

A nurse, her pale pink scrubs crisp and clean, bustles through the door with an air of efficiency. Her face is etched with lines of compassion, but they do little to ease my trepidation. My heart races as she approaches my bedside. "You're awake," she announces with a gentle smile. "You gave us quite a scare. How are you feeling?"

Little tubes and wires protrude from my body, leading to the machines that make up the symphony of my nightmare. "What happened?"

With a sense of purpose, the nurse strides over to my bed and snatches the clipboard from its perch at the end. "Your vitals look good." She makes the rounds to each of the computer screens behind me. My health is displayed in numbers and lines, none of which make sense to me.

Before she can answer, the door creaks open, revealing my unlikely savior. "Morning, sunshine," Jackson greets with a smile.

"Your boyfriend here saved your life." The nurse points at him with her pen. "If he hadn't found you when he did, those thugs might have killed you."

Thugs. Rocco. Giovanni. Might have killed me.

Gently, Jackson's hand settles on my forearm in a comforting gesture. "Can you give us a minute?" His voice is smooth as honey, but his words carry a hint of command as he politely requests the nurse to leave.

"Of course," she replies. "I'll go let the doctor know you're awake. He should be in shortly."

As the nurse leaves the room, Jackson removes his hand. "Sorry," he apologizes with a wince, "but I had to lie. When we got here, the doctor asked about your family, and you started freaking out. They had to give you a sedative because you were yanking out your IVs. I called Carrie, and she said you have a stepfather in Manhattan and some family up in Kansas City, but I figured it was safer to lie and say I didn't have their info. At least until you woke up and could tell me what happened."

The last time I saw Jackson, he was blowing me off at the Pennington estate. I had forgotten that he worked on campus; I had forgotten that he existed at all. "You saved me," I frown.

Jackson nods. "Of course I did. I was headed to lunch when I saw you go behind the student union building. I guess I was nosy," he blushes, cheeks filling with a light shade of pink. "I followed you. I figured if you caught me, I could apologize for my behavior a few weeks ago at Thanksgiving. But I rounded the corner of the union and saw those two guys beating you up. One was just watching, but the other looked like he was going to kill you. When I yelled at them, they ran away."

"Rocco wouldn't have killed me." I don't think so, anyway. He needs me to marry him, but I don't have to *walk* down the aisle to do it. If I'm in a wheelchair and someone is pushing me, I'm sure that counts, too.

"You knew those guys?" Jackson looks at one of the machines next to me, his eyes narrowed in concentration. "Why did they do that to you?"

I open my mouth to reply, but it turns out I don't have anything to say. I don't know why Giovanni and Rocco cornered me on campus, I only know that they did. I assume they were there to issue a warning to Nic and me.

"Thanks for not getting my family involved," I change the subject.

"You seemed really upset when the doctor brought them up."

I don't remember that. The last thing I can recall is Jackson's voice cutting through the onslaught of blows raining down on me. The rest is a blur.

Luckily, the doctor knocks on the door and makes his entrance. He's an older man with salt and pepper sprouting from his beard and a kindness in his hazel eyes that reminds me of warm hugs on a cold day. "Miss Lucatello," he greets, "I'm Dr. Stone, Head of Emergency Medicine. I was on-call when this young man brought you in last night. Do you remember me?"

I shake my head no.

"That's okay." His smile is compassionate and sympathetic. "You had a mild concussion and three fractured ribs. There was some internal bleeding, but we isolated the source and embolized the blood vessels. You had to have a blood transfusion and antibiotics, and you're on pain meds for now, but you're through the worst of it. You have a lot of superficial injuries, several facial lacerations, muscle strains, and some torn ligaments, but I don't think any of them will need surgery. Considering what you looked like when you showed up with Mr. Reid, this is all positive news."

What universe is this clown living in? In what world are three fractured ribs, multiple facial lacerations, and torn ligaments positive news?

The doctor pauses for a minute before breaking more news. "Now that you're awake, I should tell you that I'll be reaching out to Dante Terlizzi to update him about your condition."

A frown blossoms on my face. "Wh-what?" I turn to Jackson to pin him with a glare. "I thought you said you didn't tell them about my family."

Dr. Stone clears his throat. "He didn't, Miss Lucatello. However, Niccolo Terlizzi is named as your emergency contact. I am very familiar with the Terlizzi family… if you know what I mean." He pauses to give me a knowing look. "And I made a personal call to Dante after you were out of critical condition."

I shouldn't be surprised. Why else would the Head of the ER be interested in my case? I'm sure the hospital gets drifters like me coming through their doors every day. I'm not special; I am just related to important people.

"While we are happy to respect your wishes and allow your boyfriend to stay, I feel like it's my duty to inform you that I will be sharing progress updates with Dante."

That means Niccolo is going to know what happened if he

doesn't already. I'm surprised he hasn't busted down the door to see me.

"We'll need to monitor you for a couple of days, Miss Lucatello. In that time, if you'd like us to reach out to any of your family members, we're happy to do so. Do you have any questions for me?"

I guess he already answered when I'm getting out of here. "No," I reply sulkily.

It's only a matter of time until Niccolo shows up. He won't care if I've specified no family allowed. I reckon he'll fight every doctor and nurse that stands in his way to get to me.

"Can I tell Kaye now?" Jackson asks in a stage whisper. "She's called you twelve times."

I look over at Jackson to see him waving my phone in the air. "Oh, god," I groan. She's going to lose her shit when she finds out what my uncle did.

"If you think that's bad, wait until you see how many times your stepfather called."

Chapter 49
Niccolo

"I'm going to find her and kill her," I growl, my voice dripping with a blend of anger and desperation. The living room serves as my battleground, my restless pacing back and forth from one end to another amplifying my frustration with every step.

Dante's been here for hours. I called him after class was over to let him know that Christine hadn't shown up. At first, he said he wasn't my stepdaughter's babysitter, and he didn't care about her whereabouts. But as every phone call went unanswered, when even Kaye had no idea where she was, Dante was willing to admit that something was wrong. He showed up after dinner and has been steadily plying me with drinks ever since.

"You won't kill her," Dante interjects calmly, his voice a steady balm to my raging storm. "Especially if her being gone is through no fault of her own."

I ignore him. "And after I kill her, I'm going to chain her to her bed and never let her leave again."

Dante chuckles, amusement dancing in his eyes as he gets up to pour me another Scotch. "Careful, brother. You're starting to sound more and more like me every day."

With a wrinkle of my nose, I take the glass from his hands and sip. The familiar burn of the amber liquid provides a temporary respite from the chaos swirling within me. "What if she's hurt, D?" I finally vocalize the fear gnawing at my insides.

"She's not hurt," he announces with a suppressed yawn. "Her phone died or something. She's probably in the library."

I pause in my pacing to give him a pointed look. "It's 11:00 pm. The library is closed." Besides, my class was at 2:00. There's no way her phone's been dead for nine hours. "Also, Kaye said she'd let me know the second Christine returns."

Dante looks like he doesn't think much of my relying on one college girl to inform me about another's whereabouts. "Our greatest concern should be if her uncles had anything to do with this. But considering she was on campus all day, someone would've noticed if the two of them were forcibly dragging a screaming redhead into their car."

His words may lack comfort, but the logic behind them is sound. If someone had been kidnapped from campus, we would have heard about it by now. "So you're saying she's fine."

"I'm *saying* if Giovanni taking her to Kansas City is our *primary* concern, we're probably in the clear."

A moment later, Dante reaches into his pocket, pulling out his phone. I didn't hear it go off, but apparently, he did. "Let me take this call."

I swear at him under my breath when he walks out of the room as though he's unbothered by this whole situation. The bastard has never been worried about anything a day in his life; that's what makes him a good leader. I worry too much. Salvatore parties too much. Luciano doesn't care enough. Father would never have expected the three of us to run the business as long as Dante was around.

In my older brother's absence, I consider what I want for my child one day. Christine doesn't want kids yet, but I can't imagine marrying her next month and not starting our family as soon as possible. I want a brood of Terlizzi children, half a dozen at least, running around the house and keeping us busy.

I want to teach my sons how to fish, how to throw a football, how to respect a woman. I want to teach my daughters how to protect themselves, how to play the piano, how to say no to a man that doesn't treat them like a queen.

I don't want my kids to grow up the same way that me and my brothers did. I want them to see that their mother and father love each other. I want them to know that they could come to us with anything. I want them to believe that anything is possible if they're willing to work hard enough.

I will respect if Dante and Adalina have kids one day and choose to bring them up in the traditional Family lifestyle, but I don't want that for my kids. I never even wanted this for myself.

Dante's return jolts me out of my reverie. "Hey, there's news," he declares, a tinge of uncertainty coloring his words. "Well, maybe it's not entirely *good* news, but it's better than nothing."

Maybe it's the Scotch that's muddling my head, but I don't think Dante makes a lot of sense right now. "How about you tell me what the news is, and I'll determine if it's good or bad?"

"See, you're going to think this is bad news, but it's really not." There's a look of apprehension on his face that wasn't there before. Dante uncharacteristically walks over to the portable bar and pours himself a drink.

I narrow my eyes at him. I've been around my brother long enough to know when he's keeping something from me. "What aren't you telling me, Dante?"

He sips on the amber liquid, his nose scrunching with distaste. "This stuff is terrible. I should've gotten you something better for Christmas."

"Dante," I snap my fingers, demanding his attention. "Who was on the phone?"

He tosses back the rest of his Scotch, slamming the glass on the bar when he finishes. "You're going to want to freak out, but I suggest that you don't, okay? There's a lot of factors in play and too much at stake to lose your—"

"Just spit it out," I cut him off.

"Christine is in the hospital, but don't worry, she's alright!" He hurriedly adds. "Just a few broken ribs, lots of swelling and bruising, the usual for when someone is attacked."

His admission takes me right back to July 4th, when the police called and told me that Christine was in an accident. They said she'd be fine. They comforted me with facts about her health. They told me she was on her way to the hospital, and I could see her anytime. But their cold, unfeeling delivery only served to make me feel worse.

"I have to see her," I mumble.

Thankfully, Dante moves quicker than my whiskey-laden mind, stepping in front of me and gripping my shoulders firmly. "No,

Nic. Silas said when he brought up her family during intake, she started having a panic attack. They had to sedate her, and she hasn't woken up yet. When they asked her boyfriend about contacting her family, he said he didn't have anyone's info, and he'd wait until she woke up first to make any decisions."

The unfamiliar name sends my anger spiraling. "Who the *fuck* is Silas?"

"Silas Stone," Dante states calmly. "He's the Head of Emergency Medicine at the hospital, and he's on the Family payroll. He saw your name on Christine's intake paperwork as her emergency contact. He called me because he was worried after her reaction when she arrived."

I was threatening to kill her and lock her up when all along she'd been at the hospital. I'm a terrible human being. I'm the worst man in the world. I deserve every bad thing that's happening to me. "You said her boyfriend was with her. Who is with her, Dante?" I demand, dark clouds of jealousy thundering inside me.

His face morphs into a wince. "I don't know, honestly. Silas said the intake paperwork was filled out by a man named Jackson Reid."

The name doesn't ring any bells. But the good news is that it means he probably isn't related to her uncles.

"I know that the two of you have become really close lately," Dante begins, carefully picking and choosing his words. "But could it be that she was seeing someone else?"

"No," I declare with unwavering conviction. If Christine had been seeing another man, I would have known, and I would have eliminated him before he had the chance to touch her. "We need to go to the hospital. I need answers. I have to—"

But my brother cuts me off with a shake of his head. "Right now, she isn't accepting visitors. Silas said when she wakes up, he'll see if he can get her to change her mind. But for now, all we can do is wait."

"Wait?" The word echoes off my tongue with uncertainty. "I can't *wait*, Dante. I feel like I'm going crazy. Every fiber of my being is screaming at me to rip you limb from limb until you can't stop me from going to the hospital. I want to hurt you. I want to hurt you to make myself feel better."

In an uncharacteristic move, Dante takes a step back and spreads his arms out. "Then do it," he declares. "If hitting me would make you feel better, then hit me. I'll let you hit me until I can't take it anymore."

His acceptance dulls the painful throbbing of fear and anger in my chest. "Why would you let me do that?"

"Because right now, we don't have all the facts. All we know is Christine arrived at the hospital badly beaten, accompanied by a man we've never heard of. We don't know what we'd be walking into if we went to the hospital right now. So if staying here and waiting makes your skin crawl, take it out on me. I can handle it. Whatever you need, little brother, you just tell me, and I'll make it happen."

Dante's speech stops me in my tracks. I don't think I've given him his due. For years now, I've hated him because everyone likes him so much. I thought because I didn't like him, he was probably kissing everyone else's ass to make them like him. I never considered that everyone liked him because he's a stand-up guy.

"Let's find out who this Jackson guy is," I decide, determination morphing my expression.

He lowers his arms, but the look on his face never changes—sincerity mixed with genuine concern. "If that's what you want, Nic."

I nod my head slowly, feeling the itchy feeling in my chest begin to fade. "Reid, you said?"

"Jackson Reid," Dante confirms. "You want to start making phone calls?"

Chapter 50
Christine
3 Weeks Ago • January 20th

"When we were kids dreaming of our future weddings, I never anticipated security guards standing watch," Kaye grumbles, casting an anxious glance at the two men in black stationed at the entrance of the bridal shop. "And I definitely didn't imagine the bride looking like she went three rounds with Mike Tyson."

I'm healing rather quickly, except for the ribs. Every time I laugh too hard, a searing pain radiates through my entire body. It's a truly unique experience, and I hope I never have to experience it again.

"Bonus. Every shade of white seems to go with faded bruises," I observe with a lopsided smile. "Just look how well the soft purples and yellows go with this cream dress."

Kaye does not look impressed. Her eyes travel the length of my body with a sour expression on her features. "You know, when I suggested a few weeks ago that you should tell your uncle you didn't want an arranged marriage, I didn't mean you should have chosen to marry Nic instead."

"Pretty judgmental considering you're wearing your *stepbrother's* engagement ring around your neck, and you're pregnant with his child." I retort, glancing at her belly. Lately, she's been putting on more weight. Perhaps not to the untrained eye, but I've known her since kindergarten, and I can tell that she's pregnant. Anyone else would just assume she's put on the freshman fifteen.

Kaye sweeps her hand across her stomach with a small smile playing on her lips. "Okay, yeah, fair enough. But I love Xave."

"You've *grown* to love Xave," I correct her. "A few months ago, you would have run him over with your car if given the chance."

"And wouldn't you have done the same to Niccolo?" she challenges.

Yes. No. Maybe so. "I wouldn't have run him over," I decide with a frown. "I might have hit him with the car door, but I wouldn't have run him over."

Kaye doesn't respond. Instead, she dismisses the dress I have on with a wave, changing the subject. "You've never been a mermaid-style kind of girl. Try another one."

With only three weeks remaining until the wedding, I have to pick a dress today. Niccolo said that he would make sure any alterations were completed in time, but I have to make a choice if I want someone to start working on it.

"Sorry, I'm late!" Sienna rushes through the front door. "Those guys outside had my name down as *Sierra*, and I swear to God they ran a full background check instead of just poking their head inside and asking if I belonged here." She drops her bag down on a chair and sizes me up. "Cute dress."

"No. Terrible dress," Kaye glares. "If she has to hightail it out of the church because she realizes that marrying her stepfather is a mistake, she needs less restrictive material around her knees."

Sienna waves off Kaye's concern with a dismissive hand gesture. "All we need in the event of a runaway bride is a waiting car. If we scoop her up and toss her in the backseat, she doesn't have to run anywhere."

The two of them eagerly chat about the best way to whisk me away from the mistake they think I'm making while I reenter the dressing room to try on another gown.

My best friend reminds Sienna that if we run from this wedding, we'll be on the run for the rest of our lives. "So we'll probably have to pack a bag or two in advance. You know, Xavier is going to be upset if I go on the lamb with you, but I think if we make him the getaway driver, he'll get over it."

Xavier and I have a begrudging relationship with one another built solely on our mutual love and respect for Kaye. I'm sure he'd love to be the getaway driver at my wedding because he'd see it as another way to curry favor with the mother of his child.

"You think we'll *all* have to disappear?" Sienna asks, her voice tinged with a frown. "Because we have mid-terms two weeks after the wedding. If we aren't going to be here, I'm not going to study."

I poke my head out from behind the curtain concealing the dressing room. "I'm not running away from my wedding. I love Niccolo."

"Pretty sure the first time we talked about him, you said he had a stupid, ugly face," Sienna recalls.

I let the curtain fall shut, glaring at the wall instead of Sienna. "I've changed my mind. People are allowed to change their minds."

In a stage whisper, Kaye adds, "Kind of like how I changed my mind about Xavier when we fell in love, except she's marrying Nic for safety."

This is what I get for all the half-truths. If Kaye and Sienna could understand what I'm running from, they wouldn't be so nonchalant about it. But it's my fault for not confiding in them that the man who assaulted me is also the man I'm supposed to marry in June. I didn't want them to freak out, and Nic thought we could spare them some concern if we fibbed. Now look at the mess we've gotten ourselves into.

I throw back the curtain and stand before them, partially clothed in a wedding dress that I haven't pulled up past my waist. "Listen because I'm only going to say this once. My relationship with Niccolo is not conventional. We've blurred a lot of lines together, lines that society frowns upon. And yes, I'm marrying him to get out of another marriage, but it would have happened eventually. Nic understands me on a level so much deeper than anyone else ever has. And whether we get married next month or five years from now, nothing will change. I love him. Our journey might have been a little messy, but who has the perfect love story? Really? Tell me one couple that didn't have to go through struggles."

Silence falls upon the room. For a long minute, we stand there staring at one another, tension mounting with each passing second until finally, Sienna breaks the quiet with a whisper. "That's a really nice bra. It makes your boobs look great. Where did you get it?"

We dissolve into fits of giggles, the gravity of the moment shattered by our laughter. I pull up the dress, covering myself while shaking my head at the two of them. "I should've picked more serious bridesmaids."

Kaye and Sienna walk over to assist with fastening the dress's closures, their hands moving with tender grace. "But where would be the fun in that?" Kaye remarks.

I wince as the dress cinches tight against my ribs, a reminder of why we're doing this.

In the beginning, I thought Niccolo came up with the idea of getting married so he could claim ownership over me. Getting married would mean that no other man could have me. I'd have a ring on my finger and an MRS that warned off the boys.

But my uncle deliberately allowed a man with a notorious mean streak to beat me until I blacked out. My future fiancé took great pleasure in delivering every blow in an effort to teach me a so-called lesson.

If I have to marry into this lifestyle, I'd rather marry into it for love.

Love with a man that respects me.

Love with a man that would do anything for me.

Love with a man that would never put his hands on me the way Rocco Castiglione did.

Chapter 51
Niccolo

My mantra has become: Never let Christine out of my sight.

My brothers insist that it's impractical to watch her every second of the day. But I know better. For the right price, you can do anything.

I have carefully selected security guards who are constantly on high alert, their eyes trained on Christine's every move.

Sometimes she's aware of their presence, like now as she embarks on wedding dress shopping with her bridesmaids. The guards stand outside in their crisp black suits and earpieces, reporting back to me every ten minutes.

But occasionally, the guards seamlessly blend into the sea of students at Blackmore, remaining unrecognizable while she is oblivious to their presence. They go to class with her and make sure she is safe at all times—and she is none the wiser.

After finding out she was in the hospital, every second felt like an eternity as I waited for her call. I thought that I would go crazy and rampage through the city before she called. Silas Stone got back to Dante with news that she was awake. She called me a few minutes later.

I wasn't mad at her for what happened. How could I be?

According to Christine, her uncle and Rocco ambushed her on campus. She had been going about her usual routine, nothing out of the ordinary, when she decided to take a shortcut behind a building that she usually didn't take. And that's where they appeared, blocking her path with sinister grins and menacing intentions.

I almost had to take Dante up on his offer to beat the shit out of him when I hung up with Christine. I was so upset by what her uncle had allowed Rocco to do to her that I was murderous. I knew it was retaliation for going against him. I knew it was a response to the Terlizzi family putting out an announcement that we would marry in February. I knew it was a message.

Yet, I found myself relegated to the sidelines, my anger festering helplessly. It didn't matter if it was a message, a warning, or a lesson—as Rocco so graciously called it. I couldn't do anything.

But as it turned out, Christine's savior, Jackson Reid, is connected to Kaye's mom. I offered him a reward for saving Christine's life, but he graciously refused, deeming it a fair repayment for insulting her on Thanksgiving. I didn't know what he meant by that, but I let it go because whatever happened at Thanksgiving couldn't possibly have been as bad as what would have happened if he hadn't stood up to Giovanni and Rocco.

Christine tells me that she's getting better day by day, but every time I catch a glimpse of the dark bruises that mar her beautiful face, I get angry all over again.

When Giovanni backhanded Christine for disrespecting him, I let him get away with it. I warned him not to touch her again; I told him what would happen if he put his hands on her again. He may not have been the savage beast that beat Christine, but he gave the order. And he'll pay for it.

In the silent moments in between classes…

In the early morning hours before my alarm pierces the silence…

In the late nights when I delve into the depths of poorly written psychology papers…

I am consumed by thoughts of revenge.

Dante says that marrying and protecting Christine is all I need to do, but no one has ever hurt the woman he loves. He doesn't understand the primal need inside me to make Giovanni pay.

Like a predator stalking its prey, I will find out his weakness. I'll study his routines and habits to find out when and where he's most vulnerable. Then I will meticulously plan my retribution.

Giovanni Lucatello will soon find out that all of his money and connections offer no sanctuary from my wrath. I will bring him to his knees and revel in the cries of his suffering.

No one hurts Christine and gets away with it. Not now. Not ever.

Chapter 52
Niccolo
1.5 Weeks Ago • February 1st

Ten days. The wedding is in ten days.

Ten days until I stand at the end of the aisle, heart pounding as I wait for my beautiful bride.

Ten days until I place a ring on Christine's finger and lock her down forever.

Ten days until the bounty on my head raises exponentially.

"Hey, Lover boy," Dante snaps his fingers at me, bringing me back to the present. "Are we planning our revenge or daydreaming? Get over here."

I move away from the window, cheeks dressed in a hue of embarrassment. "Sorry. I was just thinking about how much my life is going to change in ten days."

Dante shoots me an exasperated look. "It's going to change even more in eleven days when you're dead if you don't get the fuck over here and help us figure out the plan."

I walk over to the kitchen table to find it littered with pizza boxes and empty beer cans; it's like a frat party threw up in here. "The plan is simple. The morning after the wedding, Sal and Luc will grab Giovanni. While my wife is having a nice brunch with her bridesmaids, we'll be beating the shit out of her uncle. By the time we clean up and make it back home, he'll have bled out in an alley, and all our problems will be behind us. What else is there to figure out?"

"Contingencies." Dante's expression remains stern. "What if Sal and Luc can't find Giovanni? Or worse, what if one of them gets injured? Or there's an unexpected security sweep at the location where we're planning to take Giovanni?" He leans back in the chair, his body language rippling with unspoken tension. "What if he takes a shot at you, and you show up the day after your wedding with a black eye?"

Dante thinks he's so smart because he plans for every eventuality; there isn't a spontaneous bone in his body.

"If I get a black eye, it'll be the least of our concerns," I retort, trying to alleviate the tension.

My brother snarls, "Then why don't I give you one right now?"

"Touchy, touchy," I click my tongue at him playfully. "What crawled up your ass and died?"

Dante stands up so fast that he flings the chair into the wall. "*You*, actually," he says with a glare. "You were all *'let me be part of the family'* and *'I'll do whatever it takes for Christine'*. To the point that you might be bringing the wrath of the entire Castiglione family down on our heads. All because you want to fuck your stepdaughter. I knew there'd be some reconfiguring after Father died, but I didn't think it would end with us breaking off from the Midwest faction."

I don't think I understood half of what he just said. "What Midwest faction?"

He roars like an injured beast. "The fucking Castiglione family, you dumb fuck. You think we're strong enough to withstand a war? All because you want to protect your stepdaughter?"

Salvatore gets to his feet, anxiously laughing. "Dante, leave him alone. This isn't his fault. He's just doing—"

"Shut up," Dante snaps at Salvatore before turning his attention back to me. "Do you understand the predicament we're in? I'm arranging troops like I'm a god damn war General."

I curl my hands into fists, urging myself to remain calm. Dante and I need to find common ground amidst our frustrations; fighting only weakens us. "I never intended for it to escalate like this, and you know that," I say, meeting his gaze head-on.

He takes a menacing step towards me, his ire palpable. "Forget your good intentions, Nic. You have no idea the pressure I'm under right now. I'm trying to resolve your issues with the Lucatellos, predict the actions of the Castiglione family when we defy Saverio, and my wife is—" Dante pauses mid-sentence, his anger biting off his words before they fully form.

"What about your wife?" Luciano chimes in. "Is everything all right with Adalina?"

Dante is strung tighter than a bow. The look in his eyes makes me unsure if he wants to confide in me or kill me. "She's pregnant," he admits with a begrudging half-smile.

The room erupts with congratulatory sentiments from our younger brothers. Salvatore starts rummaging through my fridge, looking for champagne, while Luciano starts making bets on the baby's gender. But Dante and I continue staring at one another, locked in a stalemate of our making.

"You're afraid," I accuse. "The Dante Terlizzi I know would have taken on a hundred armies for his family. But now you're afraid."

His jaw ticks, biceps rippling as he clenches his fists. "Watch yourself, Nic. I don't care if your wedding *is* next Saturday. I'll knock you the fuck out right now."

But I press my luck. "You're having your first child, and that's why you're afraid. You don't want to do anything that might get you killed before the kid's birth. You're going to be a *father*, Dante," I place emphasis on his new responsibilities. "There's nothing wrong with wanting to take a lesser role if it means protecting the ones you love."

"You would know all about changing roles for the ones you love, wouldn't you?" Dante's eyes flicker with a mix of emotions.

"I do, actually. I took up a mantle I wanted no part of because the person I care about, the woman I want to spend the rest of my life with, is in danger. I'm doing things and hearing things I *never* wanted to be a part of. I stepped the fuck up because that's what I have to do." I don't realize I'm shouting until I hear my voice echo back to me from other rooms. "If you want to do the opposite and take a step back because that's the safest route for you and Adalina, then do it. But I understand better than anyone how you feel about making a choice that contradicts who you are."

Salvatore returns with his keys out. "I'm going to run to the liquor store so we can celebrate properly. You guys need anything? Beer? A *'Get Along'* shirt?"

His joke breaks the spell between us. Dante smiles despite himself and reaches forward with an open hand to take mine. "There's a lot of pressure on me right now. Forgive me, brother."

I take his hand, and he pulls me into a hug. "Forgive me for making your burden heavier. What do we need to figure out about next Sunday?"

Family has its unique way of weathering storms—the ability to disagree fiercely one moment and stand united, ready to die for each other, the next. Family means being there for each other through the good times and the bad—without judgment, without conditions.

I've never quite felt like I completely fit in with my brothers, but I've always known that if I needed them, they'd be there for me. No questions asked.

Chapter 53
Christine
Present Day • Morning of the Wedding

Butterflies would be a blessing right now. I feel like there are elephants stampeding through my stomach.

"*Technically*," Kaye begins as gently as she can, "you're underage, and no one will buy you liquor. I asked one of Niccolo's brothers, and he laughed at me."

I don't know which one it was, but I hope someone knocks him out. "Go back out there and tell him I just need one drink to settle my nerves. Or a Valium. Whatever he's got. I'm not picky."

With a quick, graceful movement, Sienna springs up from her spot on the couch, her hands clapping together to redirect our attention. "No, babe, you don't need either of those things. You're marrying the man you love today. You're going to be okay. You have nothing to worry about." She pauses in the middle of her monologue to ask, "But for funsies, can you tell us why you're feeling this way? Maybe talking about it will ease your nerves."

Any other day, I might keep my thoughts to myself to protect them, but it's my wedding day. If I don't share what's going through my head, I might explode.

"I had a dream last night that my uncle showed up at the wedding and shot everyone. I'm worried that one of these days, he's going to walk on campus and kill Niccolo in his classroom. I'm afraid that Rocco is going to show up at my dorm room when I'm alone and kidnap me. I'm worried that my uncle will follow through with killing me because he said he'd rather I be dead than happy with Niccolo. I don't know what people are going to think about my relationship with Nic, and I'm scared they're going to judge us when they find out that he used to be my stepfather. And I think I'm most terrified that this entire crazy plan of Nic's is *actually* going to work out, and all this worrying is for nothing." As I finish and catch my breath, I feel my heart pounding.

Kaye and Sienna stare at me for a long minute, both of them trying and failing to hide their shock. After a long moment, my best friend turns on her heel and leaves the room. We can hear snippets of her conversation with the man outside, and I think she's talking to Salvatore.

When she returns, Kaye is red in the face and holding her swelling stomach. "He said he'd get mimosas," she announces proudly.

My eyebrows shoot up, impressed by the way Kaye stood up to Niccolo's brother. "What?"

"I thought it was cold feet or something," she explains with an apologetic wince. "But what you're worried about are *real* problems."

"Scary problems," Sienna adds in a dramatic whisper.

Kaye nods her head in agreement. "So if you're thinking about all that and the only thing you need to settle your nerves is a little liquid courage, then I'll make it happen. I'll make anything happen for you today, Chris."

Their comforting words help, maybe more than the mimosas will. My heart rate slows, and I don't feel like I'm teetering on the edge of a panic attack anymore.

I walk over to the couch in the bridal suite and flop down. "I don't think I could do this without the two of you."

Sienna and Kaye rush to the nearest chairs, taking their responsibilities as bridesmaids seriously. "You don't have to do anything without me," Kaye assures me.

"You've had a pretty good life without me in it," Sienna adds, "but your life is going to be even better now that I'm here. Just think about it: me yelling at some cousin of yours because he looks at you judgmentally for marrying your stepfather. No one is messing with you today, chica. Not on our watch."

A few months ago, I didn't even like Sienna. Her confidence and unfiltered honesty intimidated me. But now, she's someone I rely on for emotional support. She's my best friend, second only to Kaye. "I love Niccolo, I really do. I've thought about marrying him, but I didn't think it would happen until I was finished with my Bachelor's degree, at least. This," I pause, struggling to find the words. "I didn't expect any of this to happen."

Kaye reaches out to take my hand, entwining her fingers with mine. "In life, you are never going to expect the moments that change your life. They're going to happen to you whether you're ready for them or not. Life is lived forward, but we only understand it in reverse. One of these days, this is all going to make sense. I promise."

There's a question on the tip of my tongue, a dozen of them. How can she promise that this will make sense? How can she be so calm about it? How can she act like there isn't life or death waiting on the other side of this madness?

But I don't ask any of my questions. Because maybe she's right. Maybe I need to live through today and a thousand days just like it before it all makes sense.

Chapter 54
Niccolo

"Last chance," Dante reminds me as we line up outside the church doors and wait for the music to begin. "If you want to back out, tell me now. I'll get Lucky to cause a diversion."

Since Christine only wanted two bridesmaids, I had to make the difficult decision of picking between my brothers. When I didn't pick Luciano, he wasn't hurt. Instead, he got it into his head that he should officiate the wedding instead. He made a big deal out of getting ordained online in less than ten minutes; Mother did not approve.

If anyone can cause a diversion so I could run out of here without being noticed, it would be Luciano.

"I'm good. I'm ready for this," I tell him. This isn't the first time I've gotten married, but it's the first time I'm marrying someone of my choosing. If Giovanni came through the doors right now and offered me a million dollars to walk away from Christine, I wouldn't even look at him twice.

Dante turns to fuss over my tie, his hands shaking with secondhand nervousness. For what feels like the hundredth time in the past hour, he straightens the knot and tucks in a stray strand of fabric. Every time he makes eye contact with me, he looks like he might burst into tears. It's a side of Dante that I've never seen before—raw, vulnerable, and emotionally charged.

"I'm proud of you, Nicci," he begins.

We're going to miss our cue. The music is going to start playing, and we'll need to walk through the doors to the waiting audience, and we'll miss it. Then Lucky will think I ran away, and he'll start freestyle rapping. I have to divert this conversation before it causes a scene.

"This isn't my first wedding," I remind him with a tight smile. It isn't even my first wedding to someone in the Lucatello family.

"I know." Dante continues to fuss over my tie. "But this is the first time you're marrying someone you love. It is an extraordinary feeling, isn't it? Life changing, some say. When I married Ada…" his voice trails off, breaking into a whisper as his throat constricts with emotion.

I place a gentle hand on his arm, urging him to continue his story. He doesn't talk about his wife much, even though he says they're deliriously happy. "What happened when you married Adalina?"

He runs his thumb across the knot of my silk tie before raising his gaze to meet mine. "Marrying Adalina was the single most beautiful moment of my life. I'll never forget the way she looked in her dress or how I felt walking back down the aisle with her hand in mine."

Their marriage, which happened a year ago, was a touching affair. I stood next to Dante as his best man and watched him recite his vows to her in Italian—a declaration of love so deep and intense that I felt like I was intruding.

"I hope you, Sal, and Luc find what I have. When you see Christine walking down the aisle, I hope you realize how much you'd be willing to sacrifice for her. And most of all, I hope you're happy, little brother." Dante's hands drop to his sides as the sketch of a smile blooms on his lips.

Despite all the teasing and jokes my brothers and I make about Dante's contentious relationship with his wife, we don't know what happens behind closed doors. Maybe they're tender to one another; maybe they're happier than we know.

"Christine is everything to me, Dante. She is the sun and the moon, the stars that guide my path. She's the only person that could have made me turn my entire life upside down." My love for her has changed me, and she never asked for any of it.

Dante brushes invisible particles of dust off my shoulder before playfully tapping my cheek, his affection for me evident in the gesture. "I don't pretend to understand your relationship, Nic, but if she is the one you want to be with, then so be it. I don't have to understand it; no one does. It's your marriage, and the only person that needs to understand it is you."

The swell of music from inside the church breaks the spell.

Salvatore, who had been standing off to the side, unnoticed, throughout this entire conversation, now steps forward and claps a firm hand on both my and Dante's shoulders. "Well, kiddos, it's time to go on a walk. Unless you're talking about running away. In which case, I wish someone would have told me so I could have brought my running shoes."

I chuckle and sweep away my brother's grip. "I'll never run from Christine; I'll only ever run *to* her."

"Well, if you don't start running down that aisle, people will start thinking that you skipped out on your bride," Salvatore reminds me.

Dante gestures me forward. "What's the over-under on whether or not *she* runs out on *him*?" My face turns sheet white until my big brother bursts into laughter. "I'm kidding, Lolo. That girl loves you. Now go get married; it's time to begin the rest of your life."

Chapter 55
Christine

The wedding happens in the blink of an eye. One minute, I'm getting dressed with Kaye and Sienna; the next, we're lining up to walk down the aisle.

"Last chance," Sienna whispers loudly, "we can still run away if we need to."

But my nerves have long since settled. Once I pulled on the wedding dress, a simple white strapless gown, I realized there was nowhere else I'd rather be.

I walk through the doors of the church, and everyone stands, turning to stare at me with all the love and affection of newfound family and friends. But the only person I see is Niccolo.

He waits on the altar, his face breaking into a smile when he sees me. And I realize in that moment that whatever comes next, it's all worth it.

We recite the usual vows and promise to love one another for as long as we both shall live, and then Niccolo places the ring on my finger, and it's over. The ceremony takes no more than twenty minutes from start to finish, including a prayer of safety composed entirely in Italian by his mother. It's quick but meaningful. We bound ourselves with oaths, promising each other the rest of our lives.

The line of well-wishers consists of Terlizzi men hugging me and welcoming me to the family. Of cousins kissing my cheeks and telling me how excited they are for us. Of my best friends laughing and crying as they send us to the hotel in a bulletproof SUV.

"My love," Niccolo whispers in my ear as we step into the hotel's ballroom where the reception is being held, "this is all for you."

The room erupts with cheers when they see us. For a minute, I almost forget that this hastily arranged marriage was to save me from another. While we're sitting down to eat, I pretend I'm not bothered by the fact that I'm the only Lucatello in the room. When Niccolo spins me around the dance floor, I barely notice my aching ribs—a wedding present from my uncle and former betrothed.

The scent of wine hangs thick in the air, blending with the pounding beat of the music that brings couples to the dance floor. As our wedding guests party and mingle, their laughter and voices fill every corner of the room. And I never feel alone, not even for a second. When I excuse myself to go to the bathroom, Kaye and Sienna are there to help me hold my dress.

"How are you doing?" Kaye asks as we wash our hands.

Despite all my fears and concerns, I'm fine. The mimosas from earlier in the day did their job, calming my nerves and leaving behind a pleasant warmth in my stomach that helped to carry me through the wedding. But a nagging sensation in my chest puts me on edge.

"Is it weird that this day has been almost perfect?" I check my makeup in the mirror, half expecting to see mascara trailing down my face or a hair out of place. "Given the reason we had to get married so quickly, isn't it weird that nothing bad has happened?"

Sienna hops up on the bathroom counter, her legs swinging back and forth as she waits for us to finish. "Isn't that a *good* thing?"

"It just makes me nervous," I reply with a frown. I feel like I'm waiting for the other shoe to drop; something always goes wrong at a wedding. The photographer gets stuck in traffic, or the mother of the groom wears white to the wedding. Something bad *always* happens, and then the wedding goes on. But nothing has gone wrong yet, and it makes me wary.

"What if the bad thing is the SUV blowing up when we leave or someone setting our house on fire when we're sleeping tonight?"

"Jesus," Sienna whispers under her breath. "Morbid much?"

It brings a smile to my face despite the nerves beginning to rear their ugly head again. "Sorry," I apologize. "I would feel better if someone vomited on the dance floor or something."

Kaye offers to be the sacrifice, her face appearing a little green in the dimly lit bathroom. "I'm feeling queasy anyway. Did you guys *have* to have a seafood option?" She complains with a smile.

We make our way back to the reception, shaking hands and accepting hugs along the way. I didn't realize Niccolo's family was so large. I meet what feels like a dozen aunts and uncles and a hundred cousins. Not to mention Nic's friends among the Blackmore University staff and people close to the Terlizzi family who have been invited out of respect. There are over 300 guests, and they're all happy to see us.

"You mind if I go dance with Xave?" Kaye asks. "I keep seeing the same busty Italian girl over there trying to climb into his lap."

I look at her baby bump and raise an eyebrow. "You think he cares about one of Niccolo's cousins when you're carrying his child? He only has eyes for you, Kaye. Go on," I gesture with my head. "Go enjoy time with your man."

I quickly spot my husband in the bustling crowd. Niccolo and his siblings stand around a table together, throwing back celebratory shots. As I walk over, Lucia spots me and comes running up, squealing. She wraps her arms around my neck and excitedly says, "I'm finally going to have a sister!"

"Hey!" Dante glares. "What about Adalina?"

She releases me and squares her shoulders, meeting her brother's intense gaze with one of her own. Kudos to Lucia for having the courage to stand up to him because Dante Terlizzi scares the shit out of me. "I can't be friends with a ghost, Dante. Maybe if Adalina showed up to a family event, we could—" but she stops mid-sentence when the brunette beauty appears, as if summoned because her name was spoken too many times.

"Lucia, a pleasure." Adalina walks up, slipping into Dante's arms like they were made just for her. Her gaze flickers toward me, and a curious smile curls around her lips. "Welcome to the family, Christine." She pauses for a moment before chuckling, "*Again*, anyway. Wife is a more fitting title than *stepdaughter*, don't you think?"

Dante's arm tightens around his wife's waist, his jaw tightening as his lips form a hard line. "Ada," he chastises, "stop."

She turns to look at him with all the poison of a rattlesnake ready to strike. "You finally let me out of my cage, darling. Let me have a little fun."

If his hands dig into her skin any harder, he's going to leave bruises. "Excuse us for a minute." Dante looks like a man trying to smile through getting stabbed. He whisks his wife away, leaving us standing there in awkward silence as we watch them retreat.

Maybe this was the bad thing that has been gnawing at me all day. I mean, Adalina being bitchy wasn't on my bingo card of things that could have ruined the day, but I'll accept it.

Luciano clears his throat, garnering the attention of everyone in the Terlizzi inner circle. "I don't want to rain on anyone's parade, but I imagine you *didn't* send your uncle a wedding invitation, right?"

I snort because I can't help myself, shoulders shaking slightly as I try to stifle my amusement. "I'm sure he's aware it's happening. That was the whole point, right? But no, I didn't invite him."

"Alright. So I have some bad news." Luciano uses his chin to gesture to the entrance of the banquet hall. "I think we've got wedding crashers."

Our heads turn in unison as Giovanni and Marco stroll into the room, dressed to impress in their finest attire. Gio's hair has been freshly cut and dyed, adding to his polished appearance. Their presence commands attention, drawing all eyes towards them.

"Congratulations, Chrissy!" Giovanni announces, his face erupting with a wide, beaming grin. With a confident stride, he weaves through the parting crowd with a bottle in hand. The glass glints in the light as he shakes it, the liquid inside preparing for an explosion. "My niece just got married! It's time to party everyone!" He removes the cork with a satisfying pop, sending a spray of bubbles and liquid into the air.

My heart sinks as I realize Adalina wasn't the worst thing to happen on my wedding day. It is my uncle arriving uninvited and wreaking havoc by showering our guests in champagne.

The celebratory atmosphere quickly turns chaotic as Giovanni tosses the bottle, and glass shatters across the dance floor.

Chapter 56
Niccolo

I should have seen this coming; the Lucatellos have been quiet for weeks now. Ever since Rocco put Christine in the hospital, I've been waiting for a second attack, but it never came.

I was beginning to think we were out of danger because we said our vows and made a promise to one another, but I was wrong.

I wrap my arm around my wife's waist and pull her close. "Don't worry," I reassure her, "it's going to be okay."

But terror sparks in Christine's eyes as she flashes back to the last time she saw Giovanni. In a desperate attempt to ground herself, she reaches out and tightly grasps my hand, her fingers trembling as her nails dig into my skin. "You have to make them leave, Nic," she whispers, her voice full of fright.

Salvatore cracks his knuckles. "Let me be the one, Nicci. It's your wedding. You don't want to get blood on your suit."

"No!" Christine hesitates. "I don't want you to hurt them."

I keep my eyes trained on my bride, not daring to look at Giovanni and Marco. "Do you trust me, *dolcezza*?"

Out of the corner of my eye, I see Giovanni pouting on the dance floor. "No one wants to party?" He tosses the champagne bottle into the air, and it lands on the ground behind him with a sickening display of glass shards. "I think my invite got lost in the mail, Chrissy."

She leans in closer to me, almost hiding behind my frame. "Yes," she whispers. "I trust you, Niccolo."

That's all I need to hear. I bring her hand to my lips and place the gentlest of kisses on the back of it. "Lucia, take care of her."

My sister reaches out to grab Christine's other hand. "Let's go freshen up," she announces with a smile. "They'll have it all taken care of by the time we return."

Hotel employees arrive to clean up the mess, and our Event Coordinator tries to politely explain to Giovanni that his behavior is grounds for removal. Marco bullies his way between the two of them as if silently demanding an explanation. Guests are in an uproar, shouting at the staff and the uninvited guests for ruining the party.

I wait until Lucia has dragged Christine to the bathroom before I take action. Salvatore, Luciano, and I step forward to mitigate the fight brewing between the Lucatello brothers and the Event Coordinator. She's a tiny, docile little thing, and they're ganging up on her.

"Enough, Gio." I am as cordial as I can be, but there's venom coursing through my veins. "If you want to talk, we can go outside. These people are not responsible for—"

"*All* of you are responsible," Giovanni cuts me off. "Responsible for upending an arranged marriage you had *no business* dallying in."

We planned for a fight. Dante and I knew that no matter what happened between the Terlizzis and the Castigliones as a result of this marriage, Giovanni would come for me.

Our hope was to strike first in the quiet hours of dawn when the dust had settled, and I had formally claimed Christine as my wife. But these are the unpredictable events Dante wanted to prepare for.

"We can discuss it outside," I suggest again, more forceful this time. "This is between you and me, not you and any of my guests." I turn to the brother on my left, hissing at Luciano to find Dante.

Giovanni's laugh echoes off the walls of the reception hall. "You scared of me, Nic? Afraid I'm going to rip you limb from limb in front of all your family and friends?" He takes a menacing step closer, his eyes narrowing in the process. "Because I am."

"This has been a delight," Salvatore booms, interrupting us with a boisterous laugh. "Marco, buddy, why don't we chat?" When he steps forward and slams his fist right into the larger man's chest, the wedding party goes nuts. Women scream, babies cry, and men start rolling up their sleeves for a fight. Giovanni walked into a lion's den when he decided to show up here; he'll be lucky to make it out alive.

Thankfully, Luciano returns with Dante a few moments later. The four of us are enough to bully the Lucatellos out of the banquet hall and into the parking lot. The Hotel Manager follows behind, threatening to call the police if we ever step foot in the hotel again.

"You think marrying Christine was smart?" Giovanni shouts, his voice echoing through the parking lot. "She's going to get you killed. You signed your death certificate today, Terlizzi. As for her," he shoves a finger at the hotel building, gesturing wildly at his niece within, "she'll be crippled before the week is up. You'll be lucky if Rocco doesn't kill her. When he finds out that she married you, he'll make sure she never walks again."

My blood runs cold, amplified by the winter wind whipping around us.

"That little beating a few weeks back was supposed to teach her a lesson. It was supposed to show her what would happen if she ever, *EVER* disobeyed me or her future husband again." He clenches his jaw and twists his neck, a primal growl escaping through tightly gritted teeth. His eyes flash with feral intensity, like a rabid dog ready to pounce. "You Terlizzis are so fucking stupid. Saverio is going to kill you," he says as he points at Dante. "He won't have to kill you since I'll do the job," he glares at me. "Your two brothers," Giovanni sneers, "will probably wind up being ground into chicken feed for the cock fighting rings. So you can internalize and deal with that however you want. You fucked your whole family, Niccolo. Not to mention your little sister."

With a fierce snarl, Luciano lunges forward with all his might, his clenched fist connecting with Giovanni's brow in a sudden burst of violence. The unexpected attack catches us all off guard, even Marco, who stands frozen in shock.

"Don't you dare threaten my sister!" He roars at Giovanni.

The man's eyebrow splits open, and a dribble of blood trickles down the side of his face. Giovanni looks at Luciano with begrudging respect in his eyes. "I'd have done the same thing for my sister when she was alive. But you'll regret that, kid."

"Thank fuck," Dante announces under his breath. He looks past the Lucatello brothers to a van coming our way with its lights off. As it pulls up beside us, the window rolls down, and the Lucatellos duck, afraid the driver has a gun.

Instead, I see Adalina behind the wheel, and she tosses a metal baseball bat out the window at Dante. He catches it with ease, turns, and bashes Marco in the back of the skull.

"Get in the fucking van," he orders Giovanni. "Unless you want to wake up with a knot the size of Texas on the back of *your* head, get in the motherfucking van."

Dante uses the bat to escort Giovanni into the backseat while Luciano and Salvatore pick up Marco.

"He's still breathing," Luc announces as they throw him into the van beside his brother.

"You'll regret this. All of you." Giovanni kneels next to Marco, checking his pulse. A look of fear clouds his features, but it's gone as quickly as it materializes. "We're the second most powerful family in the Midwest. We'll—"

Dante slams the door on Giovanni before he can finish his sentence. "Get in the front seat," he barks at me. "You two, get a car and follow us. We're going to an abandoned building off Poyntz. You know the one," he nods at Sal.

"Are you sure this is a good idea?" I look back at the hotel, thinking about my wife waiting for me inside. She's going to be worried if I don't come back soon.

"We had a plan, and it backfired," Dante replies gruffly. "Now we're taking matters into our own hands. This is why you *always* have a backup plan, Lolo."

I hate to admit it, but he's right. None of us predicted that Giovanni would show up at the wedding reception to wreak havoc—no one except Dante.

Adalina climbs out of the driver's seat and walks around the van. "You owe me," she smiles at her husband.

Dante walks up to her, grabs her face with both hands and places a kiss on her lips that makes all of us shift with unease from the intimacy. "I'll never stop owing you, *cara mia*."

She saunters away, heels clicking against the concrete as she walks back into the hotel.

Dante transforms before our eyes. Gone is the intense emotion Adalina brought out in him, replaced with anger and ferocity. "Let's go."

Chapter 57
Christine

Lucia leads me down the narrow hallway that leads to the restrooms, with Kaye and Sienna trailing close behind. The overhead lights cast a harsh, unflattering glow on my anxious features. While my new sister-in-law checks her hair in the mirror, my heart feels like it's beating in my throat.

"What do I do?" I start panicking. "Do I tell everyone to go home? Do we call the cops?"

Kaye reaches out to stop me as I begin to pace, but I glide past her waiting arms. If I stop moving, I'll scream. "I'm sure the hotel is used to unruly guests," she voices. "They'll get the security guards to escort your uncles out of the building. It'll all be okay, Chris."

"I think we should call the cops," Sienna argues. "I'm sorry, but your uncle is scary. Kaye's lucky she got off the dance floor when she did. What if, when the bottle exploded, you would have been cut by the shards of glass?"

Kaye looks like she's about to disagree, but then shrugs her shoulders in defeat. "Xave was really upset. He's actually standing outside the bathroom right now."

I scrunch my nose in disgust, momentarily caught off guard by the admission. "Gross. Give us some privacy, Xavier!" I yell at the closed door as if he can hear me.

My best friend swats at me, telling me to hush. "Leave him alone, Christine. He's an overprotective soon-to-be baby daddy."

"And prospective fiancé," Sienna points out. "Can't have his baby mama bride-to-be getting killed at her best friend's wedding."

Lucia, who's been relatively quiet throughout this whole conversation, clears her throat with a sharp cough to draw our attention. "Listen. I know what happened out there was scary, but don't get the cops involved. My brothers know what they're doing."

Sienna, who had forgotten Lucia was in the room, jumps a foot in the air and clutches her chest like she's about to have a heart attack. "Oh, my god. I forgot you were here. You know," she shifts the conversation, "you look *just like* the pretty brother that officiated the wedding. Can you introduce me?"

"That's my twin," she deadpans. When Sienna continues to wait expectantly for an answer about the introduction, Lucia turns her attention to me. "You *know* Niccolo," she emphasizes with a pointed look. "You know that if there's a problem, he will take care of it. Luc, Sal, and even good ol' Danny Boy will help when he gets back from wherever he went with Adalina." Lucia calmly adds, "Whatever you do, do *not* get the cops involved. My brothers will handle it."

An eerie silence settles in the room, the only sound being the faint echo of tension bouncing off the walls. Then two sharp knocks upend the stillness, echoing through the bathroom. They're quickly followed by the quiet creak of the door opening.

A head pokes through the gap, cautiously peeking inside before fully entering the room. "Hey," Xavier smiles awkwardly, "just checking on Kaye. Is everything alright? There's some commotion out here. I think everyone's being asked to leave."

With a firm and confident tone, Lucia takes control of the situation. "Let's go upstairs to our rooms," she announces, eyes scanning the group for any sign of hesitation.

"I don't have a room," Sienna interjects. "It was expensive for one night, even with the room block. I can just—"

But my new sister-in-law holds up her hand to cut Sienna off. "I'll get you a room. Consider it a gift from the Terlizzis."

"No offense, lady," Xavier glares at Lucia, "but why should we do what *you* tell us to? Who even are you?"

"Xave!" Kaye hisses.

Lucia pulls on a patient smile, and it's obvious that she works with kids by how she handles Xavier. "Xave, I take it?" Her voice is steady and unwavering. "I understand your skepticism because you don't know me. However, going upstairs to our rooms will give us a chance to regroup and figure out what we're dealing with. It'll also allow my brothers, including Christine's new husband, to take care of the situation. If in an hour or two you want to leave, I won't stop you. But for everyone's safety, especially your *pregnant* girlfriend's, I recommend going back to your room for the night and letting this all blow over."

The sound of her voice is like warm honey, soothing and calming the tense atmosphere in the room. A hush falls over the crowd as her words linger in the air. Her composure speaks volumes, reassuring us that while this outcome was unexpected, it will sort itself out. And she acknowledges Xavier's need for control, giving him the opportunity to leave in a couple of hours if he still wants to.

Xavier's anger wanes, replaced by a flicker of acceptance and reluctant respect. "Fine, but only because I want to protect Kaye and my unborn child."

"You'll be okay?" My best friend asks me, her eyes wavering with uncertainty.

I try to harness Lucia's ability to remain calm under pressure, but there's an air of doubt in my tone that rings regardless. "Of course. I'm sure Nic will be back soon."

Lucia instructs Xavier and Kaye to take Sienna to the front desk and charge another room to her bill. "Whatever room you'd like," she insists, "even the Presidential suite. I don't care. I just want you to be safe."

As they leave the bathroom, I'm left alone with my sister-in-law. The serene expression on her face gradually dissipates, revealing a well of anxiety as deep as my own.

"Everything will be alright, right?" I ask, feeling the frenetic energy in my nerves begin anew.

Lucia doesn't pretend to know the answer; she shrugs and loops her arm through mine. "My brothers have faced worse than your uncles. They'll be fine. But if Nic doesn't come back tonight, don't freak out, okay?"

Just a few hours ago, we stood together in front of all our

family and friends and promised to take care of one another until the day we died.

Could Niccolo's promise be fulfilled so soon?

Will I wake up tomorrow a widow?

Chapter 58
Niccolo

Crimson gushes from Giovanni's fractured knee, staining the bare concrete floor beneath him. In less than a second, his face contorts through a kaleidoscope of emotions—a moment of understanding, followed by the realization that he is in excruciating pain. Agony and suffering twist his features, etching lines of fear into his once calm face. His eyes widen, and a guttural scream rips through the air, echoing off the walls around us. The sound is primal and filled with torment, sending a delightful shiver down my spine.

"Do you know how I felt when I found out Christine was in the hospital?" I don't wait for Giovanni to respond; it's a rhetorical question. "I thought my entire world was shattering around me. I was black with rage. I wanted to kill you."

In a matter of hours, Dante had pieced together the events that led to Christine's hospitalization. We anxiously waited for her to be cleared for visitors, and when the time finally came, we filed into her room in pairs.

Jackson stood mute in the corner while the love of my life lay there, hooked up to an IV and a morphine drip, trying her best to recount what happened. As she struggled to fill in the gaps, Jackson chimed in with whatever information he could offer.

Marco stands in the corner, his chest heaving with anger and frustration. His arms are bound tightly above his head, but he struggles and thrashes against the restraints like a wild animal caught in a trap. His eyes burn with a mixture of pain and fury as I monologue to his beaten brother.

Dante tells Marco to keep it down, but his efforts are futile. The enforcer kicks around like a child stomping their feet to protest being forced to eat peas.

"Let me take care of this," I decide. Bat in hand, I approach Giovanni's bodyguard and tap him on the chest to get his attention. "If you don't stop in the next five seconds, I'm going to break your jaw."

I say a silent prayer that the man keeps fighting. I'm sure God disapproves, but he reluctantly answers. Instead of falling silent in the face of physical violence, Marco rages like a cornered animal, his muscles tensing and his eyes blazing with defiance.

I take slow, methodical breaths and count to five in my head before following through with my promise. "Batter up, Marco." I pull back, aiming at the hinge of his jaw like a baseball. As the metal makes contact with Marco's face, I am slightly off-target. The sharp edge connects with his chin instead, and he crumples with pain.

"Sorry about that," I wince apologetically. "I was never really good at baseball. I hit the catcher in the head once in middle school. The coach was really upset."

Blood dribbles down Marco's chest, the light in his eyes extinguished from the blow. Maybe that'll teach him to be on the wrong side of history.

I turn my attention back to Giovanni, who is attempting to scoot across the floor in the chair, but his mangled knee refuses to cooperate. The muscles in his face are contorted with determination as he desperately tries to find a way to escape the fate that's coming to him. Sweat beads on his forehead, highlighting his fear of what's to come.

"Gio, where ya going, buddy?" It takes me half a dozen strides to reach his chair. I place my hand on the back of it and stop him in his tracks. He's only made it a couple of feet from where he began, but he won't make it any further. "We have more to discuss."

He grits his teeth and stifles a cry, unwilling to let us see his weakness. "Let me go, Terlizzi. You'll regret this if you don't. My father will come for you."

I walk around to the front of the chair, using the tip of the bat to shove him back. "That's what I'm banking on. You think I'm afraid of Leonardo Lucatello? You think I'm afraid of a frail old man?"

"You were when you married Cat," he taunts.

"I have a healthy *respect* for Leonardo. I don't have any respect for you. Especially not after the stunt you pulled with Rocco. Tell me. Did he enjoy beating my wife?" I pull back the bat again, aiming it straight at his chest. The weight of the bat in my hands is both comforting and intimidating, a tool of protection and destruction. "Did he like watching her writhe in pain?"

Giovanni meets my gaze with raw, unadulterated panic in his eyes. And yet, despite his trepidation about what he's about to face, he spits on the floor and puffs out his chest confidently. "He fucking *loved* it. I wish I'd have taken a video."

As I bring the bat down, it cracks his ribs with a sickening blow. Giovanni coughs, and blood sprays from his mouth, painting the concrete in a Rorschach inkblot. "I think I see a butterfly," I announce with a smile. "I wonder what other animals you can create."

My brothers watch from the perimeter as I treat Giovanni like a human piñata. Every swing of the bat brings a new explosion of blood. My wedding suit is ruined. The expensive cuff links will be stained with contrasting memories from this night: marrying the love of my life and nearly ending the life of her uncle.

Giovanni loses consciousness at some point. His face is unrecognizable, a mosaic of black and blue bruises from the bat. Blood pools and spatters in the ten-foot radius around him. His body slumps over, limp and lifeless, as if death is already beginning to creep in.

I drop the weapon, and the metal echoes through the room as I crouch down to get on Gio's level. I grab him by the chin and force him to meet my gaze, his lids fluttering open despite the swelling. I can barely make out the white of his eyes from the broken blood vessels. "You think you're so tough, don't you? But the only reason you get to live today is because of *Dante's* goodwill. If it were up to me, you'd be dead."

He doesn't say anything but instead wheezes, struggling to catch his breath with broken ribs threatening to puncture his lungs. The stench of sweat and urine fills the space between us.

He's bloodied and broken, and I should feel a sense of satisfaction, but instead, I feel hollow and numb inside.

"But since I can't kill you, I want you to watch me beat your brother into a bloody pulp. If you fall asleep, Giovanni, trust me when I say you won't like what you see when you wake up."

I walk over to the hanging sack of skin and bones that once resembled Marco Lucatello and unleash the rest of my anger with my fists. Every time I make contact with his body, he releases a crescendo of pain and suffering in the form of grunts and groans. With each hit, I can feel myself letting go of some of the rage that has been building up inside me for so long. But it's not enough. It will never be enough. Not until Christine is safe.

"Dante," I nod at my brother, breathless from exertion.

My older brother knows me so well that I don't even need to speak my desires aloud. He takes a step forward, confidently replacing me and unleashing a flurry of blows into Marco's already bruised and bloodied body. My eyes wander lazily, the fight going out of me with each passing second.

Adrenaline forced my hand. Revenge made me do this. And now that I've sought the blood price for what these mongrels did to Christine, I'm too exhausted to go on.

"Nic!" Someone yells.

It's the last thing I hear before I pass out.

Chapter 59
Niccolo

My consciousness returns a few moments later, and I wake to find Dante on the ground beside me, slapping my face. "Wake the fuck up, Nic. God damn it. Luc, help him!"

I turn my head in the direction Dante is pointing and see Salvatore trying to lift Marco off the floor. "Someone cut him down," I frown.

My older brother breathes a sigh of relief. "Good. You're awake. Help me get Giovanni into the van."

My head feels dull and sluggish as I struggle to push myself off the ground. Dante extends a hand towards me to help but quickly abandons the gesture in favor of helping Salvatore.

I notice that the heavy metal bat I was using earlier has disappeared. The chair Giovanni was tied to is spattered with his blood but left in the center of the abandoned building. "Should we take this?" I frown.

Dante smacks my arm. "Grab his feet, Niccolo." His tone is patient, but he looks at me with a sense of urgency. His eyes plead with me to understand the importance of what he's saying, urging me not to waste time.

Though my head feels like it's full of scrambled eggs, I force myself to put one foot in front of the other. While Salvatore and Luciano struggle to get Marco out of the building and into the van, Dante and I whiz past the two of them and toss Giovanni in first. My hands are covered in blood, my knuckles are bruised, and they're swelling. I look down at my shoes to see red droplets dried onto the leather. Even the once-pristine white fabric of my wedding undershirt is stained with Lucatello blood.

"You're in shock." Dante places his hands on my shoulders. "This is the first time you've done something like this, so that's normal. Let Luc take you home, and Sally and I will drop these two off at the hospital."

I start shaking my head in disagreement. "I need to see this through." I have to be there when we throw them out of the van at the hospital. I need to make sure when I go back to Christine, I can tell her that her uncles are alive.

Dante huffs in frustration as he walks over to help Salvatore and Luciano. "Nic, you did your part, and you did a great job, but let me handle the rest. I *promise* I will take care of it."

My brother, with his broad shoulders and determined gaze, has always been our protector. I wonder if he knows how much it means to all of us that he's stood by our side no matter what.

But shock or no shock, we're in this position because of me. I need to get my shit together and follow through with my responsibilities. "I can handle it, Dante. This is my mess. Let me help clean it up."

He doesn't have time to argue. The two men in the back of the van are a liability that needs to be taken care of immediately. "Fine. You can drive," he gruffly replies.

I slide into the worn driver's seat, my hand automatically reaching for the keys in the ignition. I'm relieved that the van wasn't taken while we were inside. Manhattan isn't exactly riddled with crime, but when a car is sitting outside with the keys in it, you're asking for it to be stolen. But luck seems to be on our side tonight.

The back doors of the van shut a second before Dante jumps into the passenger seat. "Alright. Let's go."

St. Francis Hospital is a seven-minute drive from the abandoned building we were in. The neon lights from the Emergency sign beckon us into the parking lot, but Dante directs me past the entrance and to the staff-only door in the back.

"I told Silas I'd leave the bodies here. He said it was the best-case scenario because someone is always coming out for a smoke break. Which means we need to hurry up."

I pull the van up next to the hospital, its tall brick walls looming over us like a fortress. A single door made of thick, heavy metal leads into the back of the building and has a small window that peers into a dimly lit hallway.

I glance around nervously, but there's no sign of anyone coming, so Dante and I climb out of the van and carefully begin unloading the bodies from the back. The air is chilly and breezy, carrying the distinct scent of antiseptic and illness. We move quickly, our footsteps echoing against the quiet exterior of the hospital.

"God, he's so heavy," Dante groans as we dismount Marco. "I'm surprised we were able to get the jump on him." When Marco groans, we pause our actions for a minute before moving on to his brother.

With a grunt of effort, we manage to hoist Giovanni's limp body on top of Marco's. His mouth hangs open, his lips forming silent words as if he's desperately trying to communicate with us. But his eyes are crusted shut with blood, making it clear that he is in no condition to speak or see what is happening around him.

"Do you think he's going to die?"

Dante takes a look at Gio's bruised and beaten body and shrugs. "Frankly, I don't know. He's breathing, and that's a good sign, but he probably has internal bleeding and a punctured lung, minimum."

"Christine had internal bleeding." *Does it make me a sociopath if I don't feel guilty? Or a psychopath if I wish I could do it again?*

My brother gestures for me to get back in the van before we're caught out here with two half-dead Lucatellos. He waits until we're a safe distance away from the hospital before asking if I'm okay.

I grind my teeth against one another, feeling my jaw tick with indescribable rage. I'm not sure if there's a right answer to Dante's question; I'm not even sure how I feel. "I don't know," I finally reply after what feels like an eternity. "After you took over, I felt all the anger go out of me. But looking at Gio again just now, remembering that that piece of shit ordered Rocco Castiglione to beat my wife senseless, made me want to do it all over again. I hate him. I hate his entire family. What kind of sick fuck watches his niece get beaten bloody without trying to save her?"

My voice cracks with desperation, and anger engulfs me. I feel every emotion vividly and painfully in every limb of my body.

"The first time I ever hurt someone as badly as you hurt Giovanni, I was fifteen years old." Dante stares straight ahead, his face a block of granite as he recounts the first person he nearly killed.

"Father asked me to come with him to deal with some guy that owed him money. When the man refused to pay up, Father told me it was my chance to prove myself. He said if I ever hoped to take over the Terlizzi family and be a valuable member within the Castiglione regime, I would beat the man until he was blind." The way he recounts the events is chilling, devoid of emotion or remorse.

I don't know where to go, but I keep my foot on the gas pedal and continue driving.

"I was fine for the most part. I tuned out the little voice in my head saying this was my last chance to turn back and become an honorable man, the kind people write books about and women romanticize. Then I beat on that man until I had nothing left inside me." Dante pauses for half a second. "Father said he was proud of me. He bought me a high-end escort to show his gratitude. Have I ever told you that? Father *paid* for me to lose my virginity as a thank you for almost killing a man whose only crime was borrowing money he couldn't pay back."

When Dante laughs, there is no joy in the sound, only misery. "I went home that night and threw up. I was sick for the next three days. At one point, I thought I'd have to tell Father I couldn't do this anymore. But then I got up on the morning of the fourth day, and everything felt okay again. *I* felt okay."

"Am I going to go through that, too?" I ask. I keep waiting for regret to set in, but all I feel is vindication for my actions.

Dante shrugs his shoulders. "Maybe, maybe not. I only tell you this story to highlight the differences between what *I* did and what *you* did. I was doing Father's bidding. I didn't hurt that man because he deserved it; I hurt him because Father said I had to." He turns to face me, his eyes full of determination and pride. "Your foray into this lifestyle has been because you wanted to protect the people you loved. I think, in some ways, you exemplify the traits of our ancestors. You did this for your family the same way men in the 19th century did for theirs. When the law allowed people to hurt our ancestors and their families, they sought justice the only way they knew how: they formed the mafiosi to combat the *in*justice."

I never would have joined the family if it wasn't for Christine. If her life hadn't been in danger, I would have been content with my current existence, without any ties or obligations to the Terlizzis. But fate had other plans for me.

"You're a *good man*, Niccolo. However you feel in the morning, know that what you did tonight was justified." His arm stretches across the front seat of the van, his hand coming to rest on my shoulder; the touch grounds me to reality and soothes my frazzled nerves. "You protected the woman you love; nothing is more honorable than that."

Chapter 60
Christine

Lucia escorts me to the honeymoon suite, and I stare at my phone for hours, waiting for it to ring. But Niccolo never calls.

As I stand under the hot, steaming water of the shower, it washes away my carefully applied makeup and rinses the hairspray from my locks. My sister-in-law stands guard, sitting on the couch and waiting for my return. I spend my wedding night playing cards and trying to avoid talking about my absent husband.

When I crawl into bed around midnight, Lucia tucks me in like a child. She can't be much older than me, but her experience teaching elementary students has taught her how to take charge in the middle of chaos.

"I know this isn't how you expected to spend your wedding night, but thank you for trusting me. I don't know what my brothers are doing; they live by their own codes and laws. But I'm sure whatever it is, they are trying to protect you."

I slip into a dreamless sleep, punctuated by an endless opening of doors. I am too exhausted to make sense of it all.

Lucia leaves, then she returns a couple of hours later with Niccolo in tow. I roll over onto my side and curl into a ball because I'm freezing despite the comforter, only to see them standing in the bathroom doorway, arguing in hushed whispers. The little voice in my head screams at me to wake up and investigate, but exhaustion pulls me under.

When I wake the next morning, I find Niccolo sleeping on the tiny little couch in front of the electric fireplace. He's still wearing his wedding clothes. Dark, scuffed shoes peek out from the arm of the couch. His arm is tossed over the edge, the black suit stretching toward his wrist.

My heart stops when I see a spray of crimson on the white shirt underneath the suit jacket. "Nic." My voice sounds hesitant and unsure, and I'm too quiet to wake him up. I reach forward to touch his blanketed form, shaking his ankle gently before calling his name even louder. "Niccolo, wake up."

His eyes shoot open in fear, and he instinctively recoils. It takes him a moment to track his surroundings before he realizes he's safe; he's in our shared hotel room, and nothing bad is going to happen to him.

"Is that blood on your shirt?"

Niccolo sits up on the couch, making a face of unease as he strips off the blanket and tosses it on the floor. "Probably," he groans. "This couch has very poor lumbar support."

But I can't hear him over the sound of fear crashing in my ears. There is blood everywhere, decorating his suit in a macabre pattern. "Whose blood is that?" I manage to squeak out.

He looks down at his chest, and realization dawns on him. "Christine, this isn't what it looks like."

"I-I don't know what it looks like. You didn't come back last night. You left. You left, and you didn't come back," I start stuttering. "What happened? Where did you go? Why are you covered in blood?"

Niccolo jumps off the couch and strips off his suit jacket, tossing it on the ground with the blanket. "We took care of your uncles last night," he admits. "They won't bother you anymore."

Are they dead? Is that why he looks like this? "Your knuckles," I breathe, trying to make sense of it all. "What happened to your hands?"

"Nothing is wrong," he says gently. "It's just some bruising from using my fists to beat the shit out of Marco. I'll be fine."

Nobody wanted my uncles at the wedding last night, but I didn't want them dead, either. "Tell me what happened. I need to know."

He offers me a seat on the couch. Though flecks of blood stain the sofa, I reluctantly sit beside him. "For starters, Giovanni and Marco are alive. They're at St. Francis receiving life-sustaining care. They are *alive*, Christine."

Relief floods through me knowing they're okay, but a tinge of disappointment prickles in my chest. "So this was just another setback," I voice.

"No," Niccolo cuts me off. "This was *not* a setback. This will ensure your safety. We were going to do this today," he manages with an awkward smile. "I wanted to have my wedding night with you before getting my hands dirty, but we didn't anticipate Giovanni and Marco showing up to the reception. I mean, maybe Dante anticipated it, but I didn't."

I wish they wouldn't have come; their appearance ruined the rest of the night. "What did you do to them?"

He reaches up to rub the back of his neck anxiously. "You can't be mad," he prefaces. "We didn't kill them. Remember that."

I'm not mad; I'm nervous.

"I beat Giovanni with a bat, and then Dante and I took turns using Marco as a punching bag. But again," he adds as he sees my face begin to contort with shock, "neither of them is dead. They're both alive and well at the hospital. Well, not *well*, per se," Niccolo shrugs, "but not in the ICU."

I can't believe Nic. I don't understand why he'd do this. "How is this supposed to help us?" When Grandfather finds out, he's going to want revenge. He'll have Niccolo killed, and I'll be a widow by next week. I haven't even had sex with my husband yet, and I already have to say my goodbyes.

Niccolo reaches forward to take my hand in his, bringing it up to his lips to kiss away the tension in my muscles. All I can focus on is the black and blue of his knuckles, swollen from his ministrations.

"Leonardo will hear about what happened this morning. Dante is sending emissaries to your grandfather with a peace offering. If Leonardo agrees to take no revenge, Dante will give him the $25,000 he originally promised for you and sign an agreement that says the Terlizzi family won't go after Giovanni and Marco again."

"This is insane; this plan is madness. He'll never agree. You nearly killed his heirs. *Both* of them," I emphasize. "He'll never forgive you."

"I don't need him to forgive me," Niccolo's tone hardens. "I need him to promise he won't seek revenge against you or the family. Because you're one of us now, Christine. And I swear to God, if he hurts you or sends someone to hurt the Terlizzis, I will end the entire Lucatello line."

His words chill me to the bone; this is a side of Niccolo I've never seen before. He's always been sweet and tender with me. Even when he was fucking me up against the shower wall, it was with all the sweetness of a lover.

This murderous man, the one willing to kill if that's what it takes to keep me safe, is someone I've never met before.

"I love you, Christine. Yesterday, when you said for better or worse—this is it, this is the *worse*. Everything from here on out can only get better. I had to do this for us, *dolcezza*; you have to understand that."

He gets off the couch, falling on his knees in front of me. "How we got here doesn't matter. What we went through is in the past. All that matters from here on out is you and me, forever, for the rest of our lives."

In this moment, I can see past the violence and chaos. I understand why he fought for me. I appreciate that he risked his life for us. All the fear and doubt that threatens to consume my mind dissipates like mist in the sunlight.

I lean forward to press my lips to his, telling myself that if it could have happened any other way, it would have.

Niccolo had to meet and marry my mother…

My mother had to get cancer and pass away…

I had to spend three years as his stepdaughter…

He had to follow his shameful desires for me…

We had to be together at the university…

Giovanni had to arrange my marriage to another man…

I had to be beaten by my new fiancé…

Niccolo and I had to get married quickly…

He had to bludgeon my uncle with a baseball bat…

Otherwise, we wouldn't be here right now.

His rough, calloused hands cradle my face, leaning into the kiss like a lifeline.

Our story couldn't have happened any other way. And looking back, I wouldn't have wanted it to.

Every touch we share, every moment we get to be together, is a reminder of the journey we had to take to get here. We fought a thousand fights to wind up in each other's arms, and it turns out Kaye was right: it all makes sense looking back, even when it didn't make sense while it was happening.

Epilogue
Christine • 1 Week Later

I pull my hair into a tight bun at the top of my head. The anticipation and nerves make my hands tremble as I rest them back in my lap, trying to steady myself. "And you're sure this is safe?"

"If it weren't, I wouldn't let you be here," Niccolo insists. "But Dr. Stone said that Giovanni is still too weak to do much of anything, let alone hurt you."

I remember Dr. Stone from my stay at the hospital. He seemed like a very nice guy up until he told me that he was reporting my injuries to Dante. "I shouldn't be nervous, right? He can't hurt me. I should feel safe." I say the words to Niccolo, but I'm speaking them to myself.

My husband's warm hand reaches out, brushing against the sleeve of my shirt before finding its place on my arm. His touch brings a sense of reassurance that immediately calms my anxieties. "It's okay to be nervous about this. The last few times you saw your uncle were traumatizing. He brought Rocco to your school, and you wound up in the hospital. Then he showed up at your wedding reception and upended the party. Being nervous about seeing someone like that is perfectly normal."

I repeat his words in my head. *Perfectly normal. Perfectly normal. Perfectly normal.*

"I'll be by your side no matter what, and we can leave any time. We don't even have to go in if you don't want to," he assures me. "This is up to you. Whatever you want to do, we'll do it."

My gaze lingers on the imposing visitor's entrance of St. Francis Hospital, my mind already playing out the next few minutes in vivid detail.

I can see myself walking through the doors with Niccolo by my side, signing in at the visitor's station as Christine Terlizzi. They'll ask my relation to the patient and I'll tell them I'm his niece, newly married.

They'll send us to the fifth floor, where my uncle is being held, and I'll check in at another desk. The nurse on duty will lead us to his room, quietly telling us on the walk that he hasn't had any visitors.

I will ignore his broken body lying motionless on the bed and tell him that it's over, that Grandfather agreed to the terms Dante set forth. I'll tell Giovanni that he can never put his hands on me or Niccolo ever again, or else he'll pay with his life.

"Let's go home," I decide.

I don't need to witness Giovanni lose his mind if I follow through with my plan. Dr. Stone has been updating us on his progress since he was admitted to the hospital a week ago, but the news has been far from reassuring. Though my uncle shows slight improvements each day, one arm and both legs remain encased in traction, rendering him immobile. A thin wire holds his jaw shut, preventing any form of communication. He's hooked up to a dozen machines that keep track of every breath he takes and every beat of his heart. Though he can't talk, I know that underneath the surface, he is going insane.

Niccolo twists the key in the ignition with a satisfying click. The car springs to life, music filtering through the speakers as the heater blows hot air at us. "Are you sure? You really wanted to see him yesterday."

I wanted to see Giovanni, so I could rub it in his face that his plan didn't work.

I wanted to see the look in his eyes when I told him that despite how much he wanted to control my life, he would never see me again.

And I wanted to thank him for driving me into the arms of the man he hated.

If he hadn't shown up Thanksgiving weekend to announce my newly arranged marriage, I would have tried to flee from Nic. I was ashamed of how I felt about him, and I hated his threats to get me pregnant against my will. If it wasn't for Giovanni, there's a chance that Niccolo and I would be nothing more than former stepfather and former stepdaughter.

But Giovanni's actions forced us into each other's arms. He is responsible for the outcome he so desperately wanted to avoid. And I wanted to see the look on his face when I told him so. It was a matter of pride and revenge, but I don't need it. Not anymore.

"I'm sure." I don't need to cause Giovanni more pain just to prove a point. All I crave now is my husband by my side. His presence brings me the peace and comfort I've needed since this ordeal began.

Niccolo leans over, his warm breath tickling my skin as he presses his lips gently against my cheek. "If you change your mind, even if we're already home, just tell me, and I'll bring you back."

"I need you to take me back to campus, actually," I announce with a wince. "I need to study for mid-terms next week." We might have married a week ago, but weddings don't delay tests.

His warm eyes darken as he narrows them at me. "You can study for mid-terms at the house."

"But Kaye is on campus." I've gotten away with sleeping in our dorm once this week by telling Niccolo I needed to study. He was reluctant at first, but he gave in when I told him I needed to pass my mid-terms if I wanted to continue on my career path.

With a soft hum, Niccolo shifts the car into reverse and slowly eases out of the parking spot. "Tell Kaye to come here," he offers.

"Sienna is also on campus," I remind him sweetly.

His knuckles tighten on the steering wheel. "She can come to our home as well. I like Sienna. She's a good counter to Kaye."

I knew we'd have to have this conversation eventually, and I take a deep breath before launching into my planned argument. "Nic, I love you, but I'm still a student. I still have friends I want to see and study groups I want to participate in because I *still* want to become a Child Psychologist one day. I have goals and things I want to achieve, and I need to be an active participant in my own life to do so. This little love bubble we've been in these last few days has been wonderful, but I need more. I need you alongside every other aspect of my life that I had before everything was blown up by my family. Can you understand that?"

He puts the car in drive and navigates the visitor parking lot, turning onto a busy street as he pulls out of the hospital. We drive in silence through Manhattan as he makes his way to the highway. I start to second guess having this conversation so soon after our wedding, but eventually, Niccolo sighs and agrees.

"I understand. I just want you all to myself, all the time," he adds. "But I have a job, and you have homework, and I *guess* I can let you go for the day. But don't make a habit of this," Niccolo warns, shooting a glare across the car. "If you aren't home a minimum of 3 nights a week, I'll walk into your dorm, throw you over my shoulder, and *make* you come home."

I laugh and roll my eyes at his caveman behavior. "I think I'd like you to do that anyway. It sounds hot."

He shoots a look across the car, his gaze hot with desire. "Don't talk like that when I'm taking you back to school," Niccolo orders. "Or I'll have to pull this car over and fuck you in the backseat."

I drag my tongue across my bottom lip, feeling lust bloom in my stomach. "I bet you won't."

"Don't tease me, little girl." He eases off the gas and begins to pull over. "I'm a simple man with simple desires. And if I want to fuck my wife on the side of the highway, believe me, sweetheart, I will."

About the Author

Cora Kent fell for her first villain before she even knew what romance was. Ever since Scar was denied a happily ever after, she's been on a mission to give all the dark, dangerous anti-heroes the endings they deserve. If the Big Bad Wolf had swept Little Red off her feet, it might have saved the fairy tale—so that's exactly what Cora does in her novels: grants her bad boys redemption through passion, power, and the women who can handle them.

When she's not spinning tales of morally gray heroes and forbidden desires, you'll find her snuggled up with her cat, sipping a margarita, and watching Grey's Anatomy.

Printed in Great Britain
by Amazon